Dark Wings of Justice

Dr Nova Corbin Series - Book One

Karen Thurecht

Karen Thurecht

Dr Hamish Hart Mysteries

Book 1: Murder at the Dunwich Asylum

Book 2: Plantation Murders

Book 3: Murder at Frog's Hollow

Book 4: Death at Deepwater Point

Book 5: The Blacksmith's Widow

Book 6: The Body on Hamilton Reach

Karen's books are available from: https://karenthurecht.com.au

The author acknowledges the Traditional Owners and Custodians of this land, and pays respect to their Elders, past, present and emerging.

With heartfelt thanks to the Queensland Writers Centre for their invaluable support through the Accessible Writing Program, and to Kylie Chan for her generous and thought provoking mentorship.

CHAPTER ONE

DAY ONE

"Christ, he can't be more than twenty years old," mumbled Detective Inspector Mitchell Gray. He stared down at a pool of blood gathering beneath the head of a young white male. Gray took a pair of latex gloves from his pocket and pulled them over his hands. Doubling over he placed two slender fingers at the side of the young man's neck while yellow puffs of wattle fell from an overhanging tree and settled in the blood. The air was thick and humid filling Gray's head with a sickly fog of wattle scent.

No pulse.

The body would need to be moved soon before it began to decay in the sweltering weather. Gray's fingers traced over the lad's clothing. The expensive designer jeans and sports shoes were now stained with blood. Even through the gore, it was evident that his blonde hair had been carefully styled in the latest fashion.

From the young man's pocket, Gray retrieved a sleek leather wallet with gold embossed initials - S.H. A small private smile crossed his lips as he sifted through the contents, an array of credit cards all bearing the name Seeton Harlin. It wasn't always so easy to identify the victim.

"Well, Seeton," he murmured, "Not your lucky day."

Gray stretched up to his full height of six feet and turned his attention to the man standing by the corpse, a man of middle eastern descent who couldn't have been much older than the victim.

"What's your name?" he asked.

The man remained silent his lips parted but no words came out.

"The Palestinian killed him," a voice called out from the gathering crowd of onlookers.

The man turned to face them.

"I didn't," he mumbled, turning back to face Gray. "I swear, I didn't."

"He did it," another person yelled from the crowd.

"Quiet!" Gray shouted, and the onlookers fell silent.

Turning back to the man of middle eastern descent, he repeated his question, this time more slowly. "What is your name?"

The man trembled visibly before answering, "Yusef Ibrahim."

Two officers pushed through the crowd and stared from Yusef to the body and back again.

"Glenda King and Rishi Chandra," Gray mumbled. "Thank Christ you're here. You two lead. Get these other idiots organised." He nodded to the cluster of officers standing at the perimeter awaiting their orders.

Gray scanned the sea of faces watching, waiting for whatever would come next. "Clear this area," he called out. "Tape off the square and interview everyone here. No one leaves until we're done."

The officers, including King and Chandra jumped into action herding the protestors back away from the incident area. The Square seemed to heave with people, most of them under thirty, shuffling backward, unwilling to let go of their line of sight to the body. A crackle of tension rose like heat from the cement, as shouts of vitriol pierced the air.

"Dirty Palestinian Killer!"

"Terrorist!"

Protest signs created from torn cardboard boxes and house paint punctured the air: "Refugees back where you came from!" and "We won't be murdered in the name of diversity!" Angry chants ricocheted off sandstone walls, punctuated by bursts of jeers and fists raised in the air. Two Australian flags were draped over the backs of the bronze lions that reclined each side of the entrance to City Hall.

"Queensland for Queenslanders!"

"Australia for Australians!"

"Terrorists out now!"

The air resonated with the kind of electric hostility that unsettled Gray. This was dangerous.

His mind reeling, he turned his attention back to Yusef Ibrahim, frozen in shock next to the lifeless body. Gray couldn't blame him. One moment he was on his way to work, and the next he was involved in a murder investigation. The crowd surrounding them only added to the chaos. Gray's initial assumption was that it was a case of self-defence, but as the ambulance broke through the crowd like an icebreaker, he couldn't help but wonder if there was more to the story. A sea of people held up their phones to record the scene.

"Can you tell me what happened right before the attack?" he asked, keeping his tone calm.

Yusef paused for a moment, as if it were so long ago he couldn't quite remember. "I was walking around the edge of the Square," he said, "on my way to work. Then I saw a man coming toward me angrily."

"Did you know the man?" Gray asked.

Yusef shook his head. "No, I've never seen him before."

"Go on," Gray prompted.

"I kept on walking. I was going to ignore him." Yusef continued, "but he started shouting at me."

"What did he say?" Gray asked.

"He was yelling at me to go back where I came from," Yusef replied, his voice trembling slightly. "I stopped, but he kept coming at me."

"Then what happened?"

Yusef took a deep breath. "He raised his fist as if he was going to hit me," he said, "but before he could touch me, someone else ran up and hit him first. Then he fell and hit his head on the bench."

Gray listened carefully to Yusef's story, trying to piece it together in his mind. He studied the man's eyes. "There must be more to it than that," he said.

There was no waver in the dark iris, no flinch of the tiny muscles at the corner of his eyes.

"Do you have any idea who this other person might be?" Gray asked.

Yusef shook his head.

"What did he look like?"

Yusef squinted. "His skin was white and his eyes blue."

Gray waited. "That's it?" he said at last. "Do you remember anything else about him?"

"He looked maybe about twenty."

Yusef's gaze fell to the body bag being zipped up by the ambulance officers closing off his view of the deceased man's stunned stare. A moment later he was transferred onto a stretcher and slid into the back of the ambulance. Gray and Yusef stepped sideways to get out of the way, then Gray took Yusef's arm and led him into the crowd.

Gray called out to Rishi Chandra, to join him and together they flanked Yusef as they escorted him through the throng to a police wagon waiting on Ann Street, the main road that ran alongside the Square to the west.

Most of the protesters were still awaiting interview as Gray and Yusef passed. They punched their fists in the air and shouted insults at the man they believed to have murdered one of their own. Gray and Chandra kept close on either side of Yusef, shielding him from the physical taunts of the crowd. Other police were already conducting interviews, systematically working from one person to the next, looking fatigued and on edge. Gray knew, as Yusef did, that the mob were a knife's edge away from descending into violence.

When they had the police van in their sights, a group of protesters who'd been running for the road, stopped in front of them. Gray lost his footing and staggered to regain his hold on Yusef's arm. Yusef staggered in turn, and it looked like the three of them would fall and risk being trampled by the crowd. Rishi Chandra threw his full weight, though he was slight in build, into buttressing Yusef's body and keeping him upright. Gray regained his balance and shot a grateful glance toward his constable. They kept their heads down and moved swiftly toward the waiting police vehicle, with Yusef held close between them.

Yusef was folded into the backseat of the wagon then Chandra hurried to the front and climbed into the driver's seat. Gray slipped into the passenger side. An enthusiastic group of protestors had followed them all the way up to the car and they were anxious to get moving before anyone got ahead of the vehicle and prevented them from doing so. Gray nodded and Chandra started the engine. They had to inch slowly, at first, to avoid putting the protestors at risk. When the last of the group were behind them, Chandra picked up the pace. Gray looked back at the mob gathered in the Square and wondered how the officers left behind were going to get through the interviews before the crowd completely lost patience.

The drive to the police station in Roma Street took less than five minutes, it was little more than a block, but it gave Gray time to reflect on the anger stirring within him. Racism had gripped the city, building to a crescendo over the past two years.

As the son of mixed heritage parents, his mother from China and his father of Scottish descent, Gray was sensitive to the effects of racism. He knew the hurt caused by sly glances and racist taunts. Mitchell Gray knew, even as a child, he was more Australian than most of the children who called him "chink" because his dad's ancestors had come to Queensland with the first free settlers. His father reminded him of the fact often. It was deemed irrelevant that his mother had been twenty years old when she was introduced to Australia by her paternal grandfather, a businessman in 'exports.' Gray hadn't met his grandfather as a child and was never sure of exactly what he exported. The disappointed grandfather cut off all ties with his ungrateful granddaughter when after six months in Brisbane she insisted on marrying a Scottish Policeman, of all things.

Gray was tall and thin like the European boys, but there was no escaping his oriental eyes, and strong black hair. He wasn't a good fit among his peers at school. He wasn't a good fit among his fellow officers in the Queensland Police Force either, if he was honest. But he'd made it work and had climbed the ranks to Detective Inspector at a the relatively young age of forty. He put it down to sheer hard work and persistence. While he had his own set of values and defended them soundly, he was more likely to avoid confrontation than look for trouble, and that trait had also served him well in the force.

The recent epidemic of racism that had broken out in Brisbane was a backlash against the influx of twenty-five thousand Palestinian refugees over the preceding two years. It was a lot for the tiny city to take in. The Gaza strip had been decimated by Israeli forces and though several ceasefire agreements had been negotiated, none had held beyond a few weeks. The Gaza strip was no longer habitable. The United States was unwilling to fund aid to redevelop the region, preferring instead to insist the population be absorbed by their neighbours to the north. This had not worked out, however, when the neighbours to the north refused to accept them. Many Palestinians were standing their ground, living in makeshift tents and engaging in guerilla warfare as Israel gradually rebuilt and re-occupied the land one sector at a time. Others, worn down by the decade of fighting left, as refugees, to establish new lives for their families.

Riots and looting were a daily occurrence in London leaving the British Government ill-disposed to bringing in more refugees, right-wing governments were firmly in place in most of the European countries, and the United States had well and truly closed their borders. Thus, Australia, as one of the few countries with more resources than it needed and still maintaining a relatively open border policy, although even this was tenuous, was taking in more refugees than they ever had.

When they reached the imposing cement building that comprised police headquarters, Yusef was shuffled into a meeting room at the back of the station and left on his own while Gray and one of his officers watched him through a one-way window. Yusef appeared small sitting on the only chair on the other side of a steel table, staring at his smartwatch.

"Should we let him call his office?" asked Chandra. He was Gray's youngest officer, wearing a cardigan with sleeves that didn't reach his brown wrists. Though the youngest,

Chandra was Gray's most promising constable with a strong head for figures and attention to detail. A skill Gray valued and found wanting in many of the new recruits, who he felt gravitated toward action rather than the drudgery of data collection.

Gray shook his head, slowly. "His employers know," he said. "He's all over the news."

"True," agreed Chandra. "Video images of Yusef being led away are already going viral."

Gray squared his shoulders and stretched his neck. "Righto," he said. "Let's see if we can find out more about what happened."

Gray and Chandra entered the meeting room and sat opposite Yusef. Chandra switched on a recording device and announced their rank, names and the time: 10:16 am.

Yusef sat at the edge of his chair staring intently at an imaginary point in the centre of the table, wringing his hands in his lap.

"You told me the deceased was about to punch you when another man cut in and punched him instead," began the detective inspector.

Yusef didn't look up. "That's correct," he said.

The detective inspector rubbed his chin with his left hand. "See, the problem we have is this: none of the witnesses saw this other man."

Yusef's shoulders dropped a little. Gray watched as balls of sweat gathered above his eyebrows. Yusef swiped the palm of his hand across his forehead.

"Of course, in the crowd of protestors this morning, it is possible he simply wasn't seen. My police officers didn't see anything either," offered Gray.

Yusef raised his eyes slightly, but still not enough to look at Gray.

"On the other hand, we have two witnesses who state they saw you take a fist to the deceased."

The blood drained from Yusef's face.

"This is not possible," he said, looking earnestly from the detective inspector to Chandra and back again.

Gray tapped his pen on the desk a few times. "That was quite a crowd this morning. The protestors had themselves in a lather. Maybe one of them did approach you aggressively and threaten to hit you. It would only be natural to defend yourself in that position. I'd do it myself." He looked to Rishi Chandra who nodded in agreement that this might be an understandable action, in the circumstances.

"I didn't hit him," Yusef said softly.

"It would be self-defence. It was likely to be an accident that his head hit the cement. One of those things, I suppose." Gray watched Yusef closely.

"I didn't hit him," Yusef repeated.

Gray tapped his pen again. "Show me your hands."

Yusef placed his hands palms upward on the table.

"The other side," said the detective inspector.

Yusef turned his hands over.

Gray nodded to Chandra who leaned over the desk to take a closer look.

Yusef's hands were soft and clean. There were no marks to indicate he had hit anyone: no sign those hands had done anything more than tap a keyboard all his life.

"You've never had any contact with the victim prior to the incident?"

Yusef shook his head.

"Say it aloud for the recording."

"No." said Yusef, the single word sounded as though it had been torn from him.

"Why did you walk that way this morning?"

Yusef stared. "I walk that way every morning."

Gray placed his pen down on the table and tapped his knuckles lightly, his eyes searing through Yusef all the while. The younger detective observed the interaction impassively.

"I'll need you to sign a statement," said Gray at last. "And we'll hold you a little longer, until we hear from forensics."

He told the recording they were leaving and Yusef was alone again, waiting.

"What now?" asked Chandra when they were out of the room.

"I guess we wait to see what's on the CCTV," said Gray. "Find out what the witnesses saw. God knows there were plenty of people at the protest. Someone must have seen something."

Gray had a nagging suspicion that, as unlikely as it seemed, the young Palestinian man might be telling the truth. He had a sixth sense for when people were lying, and his sixth sense wasn't picking up the tell-tale signs of a lie. He felt sorry for the lad. He knew his employer wouldn't be able to keep him on after this. Even if he wasn't charged and jailed for the murder of an Australian man, his reputation would be tarnished. Gray watched through the glass as Ibrahim sat staring at his fingers one by one, like a man resigned to his own fate and simply waiting for the axe to fall.

CHAPTER TWO

Gray surveyed his team, a small group of five plain clothes officers, some chaffing at the bit to reach the next rank, others plodding through each day as though their only goal was to reach the end of it. A quarter to six, knocking off time. He could sense their eagerness to get to the pub, to their homes, to anywhere away from the office, their bodies reverberated with it. They sat almost shoulder to shoulder in the small room, stacks of papers and folders covering every inch of desk space. Computer screens were dimly lit, a flicker of fluorescent lights cast a harsh white glow over the room, and a few faded crime scene photos were pinned up haphazardly on the walls.

It had been a long day of interviewing witnesses, most of whom had been nowhere near the incident and had nothing to say. Gray needed to hold their attention for long enough to bring the events of the day into focus and establish a plan to move forward.

The detective inspector got right to the point. "So far, we have confirmation from forensics that the victim died from blunt force trauma when his head hit the cement bench." He waved toward an image of the victim slumped against a cement bench, blood matting his hair and falling over his face, on a large screen behind him.

"Blood and tissue samples were taken from the bench for analysis, although I doubt there will be any surprises there," he went on. "There was very little blood splatter at the sight, but forensics suggest there's a strong likelihood there would be blood on the perpetrator." He looked around the room for emphasis. "There is none on our suspect."

A collective groan travelled across the room.

"That doesn't mean he's clean," warned Gray, "just that we have no evidence either way."

The officers watched him. Their body language depicted a range of emotions from disbelief to boredom. Some of these men and women, Gray knew, had already made up their minds. A man was dead; another man was standing over him. There were hundreds of witnesses. The second man killed the first. Simple.

Gray continued, "They also said they may be able to get DNA evidence relating to the perpetrator at the point of impact. Where his fist hit skin. They've taken samples, but that evidence could take a week to come back."

"Forensics," muttered Halohan, an officer about Gray's age but with no ambition whatsoever. Always looking for the shortcut. "Waiting for bloody forensics," he scoffed. "Didn't a hundred people see the Palestinian punch the guy? What do we need forensics for?"

Gray ignored him. "Chandra, what's your summary of the CCTV footage?" he said.

Rishi Chandra had been fiddling with his computer so that the video could be started at the right spot. As technology was his super power the other officers left the function of anything digital to him. For the most part, his eager work ethic and his Indian ethnicity, left him at odds with his colleagues, but they were happy for him to take on the responsibility for "desk work" as they put it.

"The CCTV cameras didn't pick up the actual altercation," he said. "I'm not sure how helpful the images are."

He turned back toward his desk and swept his fingers across the digital pad. The footage on the large screen at the front of the room showed the chaos of the protest at King George Square.

"The exact spot where the incident took place is not covered," he said. "We see Yusef Ibrahim approaching along Ann Street, then he disappears into a black spot." Eyes squinting, the assembled officers leaned forward to follow the action as it unfolded. "We can also see the deceased approach toward Ibrahim."

An appreciative murmur and nodding heads confirmed what Gray already knew. His team was convinced the man was guilty.

Rishi Chandra ran the footage in the immediate area of the incident at the time it occurred. "The deceased looked pretty wild as he approached," said Chandra slowly. "There's no doubt it was his intention to attack Ibrahim. But whether he threw a punch...we can't see."

He turned to his audience to seek confirmation that there wasn't more on the image that he'd missed.

"The incident itself is just out of range of the camera, I think," he went on. "In any case the camera view is blocked by the protestors. We can't see Ibrahim respond, either."

"Yet he's dead at his feet," chipped in Halohan.

Chandra caught the officer's eye then looked up at Gray. The Detective Inspector nodded for him to continue.

"Ibrahim says someone else threw the fatal punch," Chandra said, watching the screen. "But there's no evidence in the footage of someone else approaching at the same time. Of course, if the perpetrator came in from the corner, he wouldn't be in the frame."

Gray watched his team as they shuffled in their seats with frustration.

"There were two men of interest who were seen with the victim only ten minutes earlier," Chandra pointed out as he shifted to an image from a different camera.

The screen showed a stocky man with reddish hair walking toward the crowd, hands in his pockets and head down. His head snapped toward the camera showing a clear image of his face. Chandra paused the footage.

"First person of interest," he said, pointing to the screen. After this, he's seen talking to the victim for about four minutes." Chandra sped the footage along to show them together. The interaction seemed friendly enough.

The team murmured as they studied the man's face.

"Looks like he's never seen a camera before," Halohan commented.

The officer beside him chuckled. "He's not camera shy, is he?"

"Hardly the behaviour of someone about to commit murder," said a third officer. "Did we get anything else on this guy?"

Chandra brought up another image on the screen – a blurry but recognizable shot of a tattoo on the suspect's wrist.

"Just this tattoo," Chandra replied. "We've put out an appeal for anyone who recognizes it."

Gray made a note to follow up on that appeal later.

"What about our second suspect?" he asked.

Chandra clicked through a few more frames before landing on another clear shot of a taller man with short hair wearing a hooded sweatshirt. He'd been walking behind person of interest number one and seemed to be following him closely.

"This is our second person of interest," Chandra said. "The same footage they had previously viewed was played again with the focus on the second man.

The team fell silent as they studied the images, trying to make sense of what was happening.

Chandra rewound the footage and zoomed in on certain frames until they saw both suspects standing near each other beside the victim one hundred metres to the left of where the incident would later occur. The second person of interest was not engaging directly with the victim but was standing back observing.

"They seem to have joined him shortly after 8:30 am," Chandra reported.

Gray nodded. "We need to speak with these two as soon as possible," he said. "Find out what their relationship is to the victim, Seeton Harlin."

Gray then turned his attention to the only female officer in the room. "King, you did the early interviews didn't you?" he said. "What did the witnesses tell us?"

Leaning against the wall at the back of the room, all five feet six inches tall, Glenda King was a tight package of defiance and determination. Gray had watched his officers underestimate her on many occasions, always to their detriment. He recalled the incident early in her career when she fought in the state kickboxing tournament and landed her opponent in hospital. The woman had anger issues, he knew, but along with Chandra, she was one of his two smartest and most reliable officers.

"Most of the people at the protest saw nothing and knew nothing," Glenda said.

"That'd be right," said Halohan.

King looked down on the officer with piercing grey eyes. He squirmed.

Gray noticed the biceps tighten below the sleeve of Glenda King's oversized shirt. She always wore her clothes a size or two larger than necessary and Gray assumed it was to hide her figure and deflect unwanted attention.

She blinked once and went on. "Until the police responded, they didn't recognize either the deceased or the perpetrator and didn't see anyone behaving suspiciously either before or after the incident."

"No one saw a man fleeing the scene?" asked Gray.

"Not as such. There were a lot of protestors in the area, but they were focussed on the centre of the Square where the main crowd was gathered. There were two witnesses who claimed to have seen the suspect throw a punch at the deceased, but their stories differ in detail, and when I checked the CCTV, they were nowhere near the area where the incident occurred. They couldn't possibly have seen anything."

Everyone in the room groaned.

"Trying it on," said Halohan.

Gray nodded.

"That's it, then," he said. "We have no credible evidence tying Yusef Ibrahim to the killing. We'll have to let our friend go."

"Um, sir," said Chandra, "you should know the video of us escorting the suspect from the Square is all over the internet. It's viral. All the news corporations have taken it up and the story's running on a loop. They're implying that the suspect is the killer and that the attack was racially motivated."

Gray looked up at the ceiling.

"Shit."

He took a deep breath.

"I've been too busy all morning to...shit."

The officers shifted uncomfortably as Gray scanned the room, without looking directly at anyone. He stared out the window.

"If we send him out there..."

"I'd say they're ready to lynch him, sir," said Chandra.

Gray's eyes rested on him for a moment. He nodded slowly, then glanced at his watch.

"I need to speak with the Assistant Commissioner and the Chief Superintendent. Go home. We'll take this up in the morning."

CHAPTER THREE

Detective Inspector Gray left the room with his head down. He didn't relish the conversation he was about to have with his superiors. He'd spent his entire career keeping his bosses at arm's length. He kept his head down and did the work. Efficiency was important to him, politics was not. His ability to facilitate quick results without drawing attention to himself had served him well thus far. It was one of the ways he differed from his father, who had also achieved results, but only while creating havoc in the process.

The decision about what to do with Yusef Ibrahim was way above his pay grade. The whole incident had the potential to be a public relations nightmare. And he didn't want the fallout resting on his shoulders, at least not his alone. He suspected there would be plenty of recriminations to go around now that the public had taken up the case so enthusiastically on-line.

When he walked into the office upstairs, Assistant Commissioner Bryant and Chief Superintendent Charfield were seated side by side behind an imposing desk. It wasn't the white formica of the officers' desks, and indeed his own, downstairs. It was solid mahogany, built to be intimidating. The way the two men sat together and nodded for him to sit opposite was also purposefully threatening. Fortunately, Gray had been around long enough that such tactics were largely lost on him. He shrugged his shoulders and sat where he was directed.

The Chief Superintendent loomed over Gray, his imposing figure filling the room, his stomach bulging over his belt and straining against the fabric of his suit. His head was propped up by a double chin, as he peered at Gray through the lenses of his glasses. Beside him, the Assistant Commissioner perched like a bird on the edge of his seat, his posture rigid and tense as if preparing to take flight at any moment.

The Chief Superintendent spoke first.

"Alright Gray, give us the run down. What do we know so far?"

"The victim was one of the protestors, name Seeton Harlin. According to witnesses he assaulted a Palestinian man, going by the name of Yusef Ibrahim. During the incident Harlin took a blow, fell backward and hit his head on a cement bench. The cause of death has been confirmed as blunt force trauma from that impact."

"And the Palestinian?"

"He's adamant he didn't throw the punch, or indeed any punch. He claims a bystander jumped in, punched Harlin, then fled. The problem is, we haven't been able to confirm that."

The Assistant Commissioner bristled.

"What about the witnesses? CCTV?"

"None of the witness's recall seeing anyone step in to throw the punch. CCTV gives a partial view, we can see Harlin approach the Palestinian, but we can't see the incident itself. Harlin and Ibrahim were behind the cameras, with the focus on the crowd in front of City Hall. There's no clear evidence of a third-party intervening. But we can't say definitively there wasn't someone. We have footage of two men who were with the victim prior to the incident. We've sent out a request for the men, or anyone who recognises them to come forward.

"So, we only have the Palestinian's word he didn't strike the victim?"

"Exactly. Forensics confirm what we already know. Harlin died when he hit his head on the bench. All we have is Ibrahim standing over Harlin's dead body. But I should add, there's no evidence on Ibrahim's hands that he was in a fight. Forensics may be able to take DNA from the point of impact that will identify the assailant, but that could take a week and it's a long shot. We can't keep Ibrahim in custody that long."

The Chief Superintendent sat back in his seat. The timber legs creaked under his weight.

"And social media is already running with the image of him being taken in?"

"That's the other problem. My people tell me there is a real buzz on-line. Racial tensions are flaring. People are already disgruntled by the influx of refugees from Gaza over the past two years. We've had skirmishes breaking out all over the city. Now this. Some people are saying it's a hate crime, and the Palestinian was defending himself. Others want to see him hung and quartered. We're sitting on a powder keg."

Gray watched the Chief Super look out from between puffy eyelids.

"It's getting ugly," he said. "And it's going to get worse."

"Right now, Yusef Ibrahim is sticking to his story, and we have nothing at this time to prove or disprove his claim."

"Is there any point in re-examining the witnesses?" said Assistant Commissioner Bryant.

Gray shook his head. "My people talked to every one of the protestors. Names and addresses taken, for what that's worth. Two jokers did say they saw Ibrahim strike Harlin, but CCTV shows them at the other end of the Square at the time, with two hundred people between them and the incident. They couldn't possibly have seen anything. A defence lawyer would squash their statements in a heartbeat."

Gray's superiors exchanged glances, then the Assistant Commissioner spoke.

"If we hold him and it turns out he's telling the truth we run the risk of being accused of persecuting a refugee, but if we let him go and he did throw that punch, the fallout could be worse. This has the potential to blow up in our faces."

"Have you had the forensic psychologist speak to him?"

The Chief Superintendent looked like he'd found a loophole that might save them, but the Assistant Commissioner was sceptical.

"The forensic psychologist?"

"Yes," said Gray, "and he doesn't think he's lying. He believes events probably happened exactly as Ibrahim describes them."

The Assistant Commissioner shook his head.

"Good Lord. He'll swear to it too, if put on the stand."

Chief Superintendent Charfield blew through his ample lips.

"Release him. And keep me updated."

Assistant Commissioner Bryant looked stunned.

Gray was about to leave when the Chief Super called him back.

"What about the family?"

"They were informed of the death within ten minutes of our arrival on the scene. I didn't want them finding out on socials. I'm going to see them now to follow up."

The Chief Superintendent nodded and gestured for him to be on his way.

Gray looked at his watch as he left. It was already seven, he wasn't going to be home much before nine again. Another good reason to be single, he thought, grateful there wasn't anyone at home waiting for a phone call. But at the same time sadness tugged at the back of his mind. He refused to allow it any oxygen.

When he returned to his own office, he saw through the glass that Rishi Chandra and Glenda King were still in the shared work area on their computers. Not for the first time he mused on what an odd couple they were. Around the same age, but as different as chalk and cheese; Chandra was tall and thin while King was short and athletic, but they were both strong, ambitious and ready to follow his every command to the letter. Even if King did have eyes that could pierce a man to the core. He did his best to stay out of her firing line.

Gray strolled out to greet them. "Why so late?"

They both looked up with faces reflecting the glow from the computer screens.

"Typing up the interview notes, sir. The electronic tablet shit itself halfway through, so we had to go 'old-school,'" smiled Glenda.

Gray tutted.

"We're releasing Yusef Ibrahim," he said. "You and Chandra drive him home. Make sure he gets in safely. We'll keep an eye on the apartment."

The officers exchanged glances and raised eyebrows while Gray went to make the arrangements.

CHAPTER FOUR

Detective Inspector Mitchell Gray stood before the imposing double doors of the Harlin residence, a mid-century modern house backing onto the river in the leafy suburb of Kenmore. Wrapped in sleek glass and concrete, its automated floodlights washed the entrance in a sterile white glow. The intimidating height of the concrete walls made the place seem more like a public building, a modern gallery of art, or a museum, than a home. Gray took a breath and pressed the intercom button beside the door, watching his own reflection distorted in the polished metal surface.

A camera swivelled toward him, scanning his face briefly before a chime sounded. The door clicked open with a hiss of hydraulics, sliding soundlessly to the side. As Gray stepped in, he was struck by the stark minimalism of the place, a curated emptiness that echoed with the sort of wealth that required no embellishment.

The foyer was a seamless blend of steel, glass, and white stone, all lit by recessed lighting embedded in the walls. A screen sent softly rotating abstract shapes, in pastel shades of pink and green slipping silently across the ceiling, walls and floor.

"Detective Inspector Gray, thank you for coming." Seeton Harlin's mother greeted him with a voice that was low and strained, an undercurrent of control barely masking the anguish. She stepped into view from the living room, a striking woman with prematurely silver hair pulled into a neat French roll. In an expensive tailored black suit, she appeared to already be dressed for mourning. Gray felt a pale green light slip across his face, slowly.

"Mrs. Harlin," he acknowledged with a slight nod. He followed her gesture to the living area, where Seeton's father stood by the massive floor-to-ceiling windows. Outside, the automated garden lights threw low light over manicured lawns, their shapes precise and perfect.

On the kitchen Island, three meals devoid of meat were already plated.

"I'm sorry to interrupt your meal," began Gray.

"It's alright. No one can eat anything," said Mrs Harlin.

"I just wanted to say how sorry I am for your loss," said Gray, "and answer any questions you might have."

Seeton's father, a broad-shouldered man, hair greying at the temples, expensive suit and tie, turned to meet Gray, his eyes red-rimmed and bloodshot.

"Detective," he began, his voice trembling slightly, "we need to know why it happened."

"We'll find out the truth, Mr. Harlin," Gray said softly, but his words felt hollow, even to himself. He turned his attention to Seeton's sister, Lividia Harlin, seated on a low, modular couch in the centre of the room, long auburn hair spilling over her shoulders. Her pale drawn features, contrasted with the green of her eyes, which flicked up to meet Gray's with a mixture of suspicion and pain. Gray thought she looked as though she could do with a decent meal.

"Have you arrested him yet?" Lividia's voice was sharp, cutting through the tension like a blade. "The man who killed Seeton. The one from that video." She spat the words with a bitterness that felt all too familiar to Gray. The sound was one of pain twisted into anger, looking for a target.

"We can't say for sure." Gray felt helpless under the girl's relentless glare.

"What do you mean you can't say for sure," spat out the teenager. "Thousands of people saw it. It's all over the internet."

Mrs Harlin put out her hand to calm her daughter. "Lividia..."

The girl shoved her hand aside.

"We've questioned a man in connection to the incident," said Gray. "But we have no definitive evidence that he committed a crime."

Lividia looked up at him, her face defiant and full of contempt.

Mrs Harlin blinked.

Detective Inspector Gray wished he could be anywhere but in this kitchen with these people full of grief and desperate for closure he couldn't give them. "The man says a third party punched Seeton, then fled," Gray said. Even as the words came out of his mouth, they seemed unlikely. And yet, for some reason, he believed the Palestinian.

Mrs Harlin spoke through tears. "They're saying on the internet the man was a terrorist..."

Gray nodded slowly his jaw clenched. "That's part of the problem. The speculation is escalating faster than we can contain it. We need facts, not accusations, Mrs Harlin. The simple truth is, we just don't know at this stage."

Mrs. Harlin moved to sit beside her daughter, placing a hand on Lividia's knee. "What happens now, Detective? How do we protect ourselves from this... madness?" Her eyes flicked to the ceiling, where a network of security cameras monitored every corner of the house, their lenses glinting coldly.

"Your systems are state-of-the-art," Gray assured her, glancing at the discreet control panel embedded in the wall. He noticed the signature of an AI-driven suite that monitored biometric patterns and could detect intrusions within milliseconds. "You're safe here."

"Safe," Lividia muttered, her voice dripping with sarcasm. She shifted on the couch, drawing her legs up and hugging her knees to her chest. "My brother's dead. People are calling him a hero. A symbol." She looked up at Gray, eyes brimming with unshed tears. "He was no hero. But he wasn't safe either, was he?"

Gray swallowed hard, the weight of her grief settling over him. He glanced around the room, noting the clinical sterility of it all, the immaculate white walls, the carefully arranged furniture, the subtle scent of something antiseptic and cold.

A holographic fireplace sat silent in the corner. Gray wished he could see it working, he'd heard about them. Above it, a family portrait hovered, a projected image showing Seeton as a young boy, smiling brightly with Lividia clinging to his arm. The image shifted, morphing into a timeline of the family's memories, from Seeton's first day of school to his high school graduation.

"Mr. and Mrs. Harlin, I want you to know that we're doing everything we can," Gray said, forcing himself to sound steady and authoritative. "We have officers reviewing every piece of footage from the rally, every message sent on social media. The truth will come out."

"Right now, the investigation is ongoing." He paused. "And I need to ask some questions of you all."

"Of us?" Mrs Harlin sat directly upright, poised like a meerkat peering over her glasses.

Her husband turned back from looking out of the glass doors across the lawn.

"Yes," Gray said simply. "I could return tomorrow, but the sooner we get a handle on who Seeton was, the better."

He watched each one of them trapped in their own inner worlds. Mother, father, daughter, but with no real connection between them.

"I need to know about Seeton's life, your relationships with him."

"Our what?" snapped Mrs Harlin.

Seeton's father walked slowly over to the Detective Inspector and placed himself too close for comfort. "Our relationship with our son is not in question," he said so close to Gray's face he could feel the spit on his skin.

Gray put his head down then looked back up at the man invading his personal space. "I'm afraid it is," he said, his eyes locked onto those staring back at him.

"We can have a conversation here, if it is more comfortable for you, or we can go to the station. But we do need to have the conversation."

Mr Harlin stood firm. Gray felt his eyes boring into him, but he also stood fast.

Finally, Mrs Harlin broke the stalemate. "For pity's sake," she said. "Just get it over with." She glared an unspoken command, and her husband sat down beside her remaining resolutely stiff, back held straight and jaw clenched.

"Can you begin by telling me about your son, Mrs Harlin?" Gray knew he had to break the tension before he would get any meaningful information.

Evelyn Harlin sighed heavily and looked up at the ceiling for inspiration. "Seeton was a fine young man," she said. "He studied hard and had principles. He was a model son."

Lividia huffed audibly, drawing her mother's stare.

"Are you suggesting that Seeton was not a model young man?" demanded Lividia's mother.

The teenager rolled her eyes. "No," she said. "I'm suggesting you wouldn't know either way."

Mr Harlin's jaw tensed further, and a look of panic crept into his eyes. His wife's expression turned to pure indignation.

Lividia ignored them both. "Well, you wouldn't either of you," Lividia said crossing her arms over her body. "You're not here long enough to know anything about Seeton or I."

Mrs Harlin let out a frustrated breath. "Lividia," she said firmly, "this is neither the time nor the place..."

Lividia's face remained defiant. "When is the time, Mother? Seeton is dead. The Detective wants us to reflect on 'relationships'. Well, let's do that. Why can't you just be honest for once in your life?"

"Lividia, you will not speak with your mother in that tone!" said Mr Harlin, although his own tone lacked commitment.

Gray had not realised he would be opening a hornet's nest quite so soon in the interview. "Perhaps I could ask a more specific question," said Gray.

"When was the last time you saw your son Mrs Harlin?"

The woman brushed the side of her face as if to pull back any stray hair. But there wasn't any, her French roll was pulled tight and was lacquered into place.

"Go on, tell him," Lividia went on. "Tell the detective when you last saw your son."

She held her chin high, defiance burning in her eyes.

Mrs Harlin pursed her lips. "My husband and I have been in New York," she said, "on a business trip. We would have seen Seeton last...what was it?" She looked at her husband.

"A week ago," he said.

Lividia turned her face to the Inspector with a wide-eyed, 'I told you so,' implied.

"Do you travel often?" asked Gray.

Mrs Harlin glanced at her daughter before she answered. Gray assumed she was deciding whether she should concoct a lie and whether Lividia would immediately expose it.

"Fairly often," she said at last.

"They're away three weeks out four," said Lividia. "Seeton and I practically raised ourselves."

"That's not true," declared her mother, "you always had Nim."

"That's the nanny/housekeeper," said Lividia, looking directly at Gray. "And she left two years ago."

"You've never complained before," snapped Mrs Harlin. "You both whined you were too old for another nanny after Nim left us."

"Richard, why don't you check your daughter and defend us?"

Richard Harlin looked like he wished he could be anywhere else.

"We have business interests in New York and Los Angeles," he said by way of explanation. "Young people don't understand what it takes to pay for all this," he waved his hands about. "Lividia and Seeton have always had everything they wanted. The money spent on electronics alone could fund a small nation. Perhaps we've indulged them..."

"Exactly what time did you arrive back in Brisbane?" Gray cut in.

"We landed at 9:00 this morning," Richard Harlin responded. His wife nodded.

"And you have been out of the country seven days?"

"Correct."

Gray wrote the dates and times in his notebook. It would be easy enough to validate the whereabouts of Seeton's parents at the time he was killed. Still, it seemed unlikely they were the type of people to carry out a murder, even if they commissioned one. He turned his attention to Lividia.

"And when did you last see your brother?"

"I saw him this morning," she said. "He wouldn't get out of the shower. We were both late for Uni and there's only one car, so we have to travel together."

"We leave them the Lexus," broke in Mrs Harlin.

Gray wondered if she was hoping to redeem herself as a reasonable parent.

"I left him in the carpark at the Queensland University of Technology at 7:30. I knew he was going to the protest. He was going to walk the couple of blocks to King George Square so I could get to class on time."

"So, you were in class from...?"

Eight o'clock until Eleven," said Lividia. "Most of our work is done on-line, but one day a week we spend in the laboratory doing practical work."

Gray scanned the faces of the three individuals sitting opposite him. They looked emotionally drained. Lividia, the only one of them willing to provide him with honest answers looked as though she were ready to break.

"Let's leave it for now," he said. "It's late and you've had an horrific shock."

The room fell silent. As Gray glanced around the pristine space once more, he couldn't help but feel the oppressive weight of the technology that surrounded them, machines meant to protect, to monitor, to control. And yet, despite it all, the Harlin family was as vulnerable as anyone else, caught in the cold, indifferent web of tragedy and public scrutiny.

"I'll be in touch," he murmured, turning to leave. As he stepped out into the night, the door slid shut behind him and he felt the eyes of the house following him, every camera, recording his movements. Gray's instincts told him that while the family was far from functional, the members were genuinely distraught at the loss of Seeton. None of them were stupid, and their alibis could be easily checked. The truth, Gray knew, was somewhere out there, buried beneath layers of bias, fear, and grief. But finding it would be no simple task.

CHAPTER FIVE

As Lividia stepped down into the basement, the room exuded an aura of seclusion and intensity, like a tech command centre hidden beneath a suburban home. The space was illuminated by a dim cool-blue ambient light. Shelves lined the walls, cluttered with old textbooks, a VR headset and modular hardware components, some of which had been taken apart and reassembled into strange configurations. The smell of soldering lingered, a testament to countless hours spent tinkering and hacking.

Against the far wall stood Seeton's computer: a custom built, state-of-the-art terminal with a sleek matte black chassis, its surface perforated by hexagonal air vents that flowed softly with a bioluminescent sheen, adapting its colour to reflect the activity of the central processing unit. The display flickered as Lividia approached, switching from a passive screensaver of rotating code to a solid, mirrored surface that scanned her presence.

Taking a deep breath, she reached for Seeton's chair. It conformed to her touch as she sat down. The desk was a composite of smooth, polished carbon fibre with embedded sensory panels allowing her to manipulate the screen by gliding her fingers across its surface. The computer remained locked, its interface shimmering with an intricate geometric pattern.

"The Police couldn't get in Seet, but you could never keep me out," Lividia whispered, her voice barely audible in the stillness of the room.

She connected a slim translucent device to one of the exposed ports on the computer, a by-pass tool they'd built together ironically enough, to test each other's security. The device emitted a soft click as it interfaced with Seeton's terminal, and a series of concentric rings appeared on the screen, rotating slowly before collapsing inward. The encryption pattern began to shift and pulse, but Lividia's hands moved with confidence born of familiarity, tracing the movements she knew would unlock her brother's system.

With a final flourish of her fingers, the screen brightened, revealing Seeton's desktop, a chaotic spread of open windows, data streams and live feeds. Everything was in flux, code scrolling too fast to follow, visualisations morphing and reconfiguring.

Lividia blinked. "What's all this? What were you doing Seet?" she murmured, her eyes narrowing as she navigated through the files. The room around her felt charged, the low hum of electronics buzzing in her ears.

A central window dominated the display showing a neural network map, nodes lighting up in quick succession like fireflies against a dark backdrop. Each node was tagged with a different language, but most were Arabic.

Lividia's heart raced as she realized what she was looking at. Seeton had been monitoring communications across encrypted networks in different countries, mapping the flow of information between several key groups.

"Why would he do this?"

Seeton was studying for his master's in political science. As a robotics student, Lividia was too absorbed in computer science to think much about politics. She knew Seeton was attending the anti-refugee rallies, but this was next level political.

Something flashed up in the bottom right corner of the screen. Lividia clicked on it. It was a chatroom on a platform called BLAZE. Lividia knew it only from hearing others talk about it. The founder had strong views on freedom of speech. You could say almost anything on BLAZE without censorship.

"They're taking over the fucking city!" was the topic line. Lividia stared at the image of a group of Palestinian refugees crowded into a bus, with only one or two White Australians. The bus passed shelter after shelter while white people waved their arms furiously for the bus to stop. But the bus couldn't stop to take on more passengers because it was already full.

Lividia scrolled past that image to another where a right-wing politician was talking to a reporter. "They're bringing in murderers, rapists, and all kinds of criminals," the woman was saying. "These are not good people. You can see what they've done to their own country. Now they want to destroy ours."

Above that post was another showing the video of King George Square that day. Lividia had seen it many times. She watched the tall policeman as he led the man she believed killed her brother to the police vehicle. The crowd shouted, "Murderer!" Lividia watched the Palestinian man closely. As she did so, grief turned to rage at the thought he would go free, just because he was a refugee.

She clicked on the box to extend the BLAZE platform to accommodate the whole screen. She didn't want to know what terrorist organisations across the world were saying to one another. She wanted to know what was going on in Brisbane. She wanted to know about the events that led to Seeton's death. She stayed awake all night scrolling through the images and the rhetoric on her brother's account. People described a city being driven to ruin by progressive politicians who refused to see that refugees were unravelling everything about the small city that made it great. The culture was devolving into one of rising crime and violence, they said. And the progressives were too weak or too stupid to stop it from happening. Other countries had learned their lessons the hard way. Germany had stopped taking refugees, the United Kingdom was heading that way. The United States of America, the land known for taking in migrants, had been deporting them by the thousands for a decade. Lividia saw the world through Seeton's eyes for the first time, she saw that Australia had taken a backward step in its embrace of the Palestinian refugees. It had only stirred up the same horrors that had happened elsewhere - and now elsewhere was here, in quiet little Brisbane.

She pictured her mother and father sitting meekly on as that detective told them the killer would go free. The police were too weak to face the fact that bringing in the refugees was a mistake, and her parents were too weak to do anything about the death of their son, her brother. Tears stung at the back of her eyes, but they didn't flow anymore. She had a purpose. She began typing.

"Hi. I'm Lividia Harlin. Seeton Harlin's sister," she wrote. She followed the introduction with an expletive ridden tirade on how the Palestinian had killed her brother. Almost immediately, hundreds of people jumped into the chat to offer their sympathies. They validated and entrenched her belief that the refugee crisis was the source of her pain. The government had to be made to listen. The death of her brother must not be in vain.

CHAPTER SIX

DAY TWO

Gray woke to the sound of his phone's ringtone while struggling to untangle himself from damp sheets clinging to his legs. For the most part, he kept his apartment scrupulously clean. It was the one quirk he'd inherited from his mother. He couldn't think unless everything was uncluttered and clean.

Nonetheless, when the air-conditioner in his room had broken down, he did nothing to have it repaired. It was a kind of sub-conscious penance he subjected himself to. Penance for the many times he hadn't been able to protect some poor soul from themselves, or the many times he'd watched the system suffocate and destroy those who deviated from the norm. The many times he'd watched on helplessly as the system beat down and spat on those who were struggling. 'No such thing as love them as they are, support them from the place they occupy.' The words echoed in his brain.

"Oh God," he said out loud. Those words belonged to Christine, his fiancé. Typical words of a social worker. She had seen the same horrors he'd seen, only from a different angle.

Memories of Christine flooded his mind, invited in by a single phrase, not even said out loud. They'd spent so many nights together, right in the bed he was now sitting on. The air-conditioner worked back then. In fact, it had been when Christine passed that it'd broken down. Sufficient reason not to call the repairman.

The persistent shudder from the bedside table made him reach for his phone. He'd flung it absent mindedly the night before and it landed at the foot of a photograph of him, Christine and her daughter Alix. The sight of the photograph sent a shot of pain through his chest. A fifteen-year-old smiled up at him.

He'd been reticent about meeting Christine's daughter at first. But no one was more surprised than he at how close they'd become. The joy bubbling over in the girl was the perfect antidote to his underlying gloom. Her sassiness grounded him. It didn't matter how important he thought he was at work, he was brought back to Earth with a thud when he came home to the teenager with a knack for sarcasm. The bile in his belly told him how much he missed her. He wondered for the millionth time if he should reach out. But it was probably already too late. He hadn't spoken to her since her mother's funeral almost twelve months ago.

He picked up the phone, swiping to reveal the angular features of the Assistant Commissioner. Bryant was holding the phone too close to his face, his already beaky nose amplified. Someone needed to tell him.

"Rioting in Queen Street Mall," said the Assistant Commissioner. "Racially motivated. Get down there now. Call in whoever you need and tell them we'll pay the over-time. Uniforms at the scene already, but your 'mystery one-punch killer' might be there as well. You might see something. They might strike again if we're lucky."

"Lucky?" moaned Gray. But the face on the screen had already gone.

Gray's screensaver danced about happily, a crystal wave crashing into a turquoise sea. In his mind he saw a balmy summer evening, Christine's hair blown forward and stuck salty and wet to her face, as the water reached across the sand and wrapped like lace about her feet. He smelled the salt mixed with her gentle perfume.

"God!" He forced himself up and stumbled to the bathroom, washed his face, climbed into clean trousers and a crisp shirt and thanked goodness for Mrs Samson who cleaned and ironed his clothes weekly. He ran a comb through his thick black hair, wondering, as he did every morning why he bothered. His hair stuck out at odd angles regardless of whether he groomed himself or not.

Within a few minutes, he settled into his 1988 Classic Toyota Crown, a cherished relic from his past, reminiscent of the vehicle his father drove when Gray was a child. His mother had once been immensely proud of their family car. It reminded her of the taxis she used to ride in as a young woman in the bustling streets of Hong Kong. Gray went to a great deal of trouble to find a car the same as his father's.

This model was the last of its kind sold in Australia, a rare gem. Discovering it in such pristine condition felt like stumbling upon a hidden treasure. He'd invested a small fortune to install an electric motor, a necessity as current petrol prices would have forced him to mortgage his apartment just to keep it running. The cool, aged leather upholstery embraced him with a familiar comfort every time he slipped behind the wheel, like a warm hug from the past.

Despite this, he sometimes questioned the wisdom of risking the 'old girl' by taking her into challenging situations instead of opting for a police vehicle. Yet, the thought of facing each day without the comforting presence of the Toyota Crown was unimaginable.

A half a dozen protestors shot across George Street and into City Square, running in front of Gray's car in the process. He skidded to a halt in front of the old Treasury Building, one of the few survivors of colonial architecture in a city inclined to wipe away the past with as much care as crumbs from the table after a meal.

He climbed out and scanned the mall that ran perpendicular to the old Treasury Building at the city's centre. Chaos everywhere. People ran in several directions shouting words that were incomprehensible. It took a few minutes for Gray to make any sense of the crowd's movements. But when he did, it seemed the rioters were clustered around a few key areas, the entrance/exit points and a couple of venues he knew belonged to middle eastern families. Shattered glass crunched underfoot as he stepped into the mall. His radio crackled with updates, voices urgent and overlapping, as if each officer were trying to make sense of the tumult at once.

Kenneth Tarrant, the Sergeant in charge of the Special Operations Squad, and a man the size of a building, appeared from nowhere and took Gray by the arm.

"I'm here to keep a lookout for the 'one-punch killer,'" said Gray hurriedly.

"I don't care what you think you're doing, it's all hands 'on deck'," said Tarrant. He pushed Gray toward the throng of protestors.

"Gray!" Glenda King's voice cut through the noise. He turned to see her weaving through the crowd, her face set and grim. "They're barricading themselves near the Albert Street entrance. Chandra is already trying to flank them, but it's a mess."

Gray nodded, his jaw tightening. "We need to contain it before they spread any further. You take Albert Street. I'll regroup with Chandra."

He glanced toward Tarrant for his approval, but the Sergeant had already disappeared among the protestors.

Before Gray could take another step, a makeshift firebomb sailed through the air, exploding against a nearby metal sculpture in a burst of orange flame. Panic rippled outward, protesters scattering, while others seemed to find renewed fury in the blaze. Gray watched as a young man, barely more than a boy, picked up a brick and hurled it at a line of police shields. The crack of impact reverberated, and in an instant, officers surged forward.

Gray pushed through, his shoulder brushing against riot shields as he moved toward Chandra. He found the officer pinned against a storefront, wrestling with a rioter wielding a broken bottle. Blood dripped from a gash on the young officer's arm. Gray lunged, catching the attacker from behind and dragging him off. The man's wild eyes met his, and for a heartbeat, Gray saw the rage and despair that fuelled the violence. But he didn't have time to dwell on it. He pushed the man into the arms of a uniformed officer who dragged him away to a waiting minibus.

"You alright?" he asked Chandra. The young officer nodded, wincing. "I'll live. We're losing control, Gray. Too many of them."

"I know. But we don't back down."

They pressed forward, each step feeling like a battle won and lost. Around them, the chaos ebbed and surged. A group of protesters, their faces masked, moved in unison, carrying banners emblazoned with slogans of "No more Refugees. No more terrorists". Gray's heart pounded. Somewhere in this sea of anger, the 'mystery one-punch killer' might be lurking, using the cover of bedlam to strike again.

His radio buzzed. "Detective Gray, come in."

It was the Chief Superintendent. "How's it going over there? I can't get Tarrant on the radio."

"He's busy. We all are. We haven't seen riots like this before in Brisbane," said Gray.

"We're deploying more units, but it's going to get worse before it gets better," the Superintendent responded.

"Understood." Gray's voice was tight. He didn't have the luxury of time. He scanned the crowd again, trying to see beyond the immediate violence, to find patterns, clues - anything that might lead him to Seeton's killer. Every rioter he stopped was one less threat, but it felt like trying to hold back a flood with a single sandbag.

Gray caught sight of a flash of scarlet as a woman with a bright red scarf climbed up the side of a damaged kiosk. He caught the eye of a man of middle eastern appearance cowering inside. Gray reached the kiosk as the woman lifted a megaphone and yelled into it. "Send the terrorists back, NOW!"

The reaction was immediate. The rioters surged forward while Tarrant's voice blared through Gray's radio.

"Get her down!"

Gray was closest and knew if they didn't stop her, the fragile hold they had on the situation would shatter.

He signalled to King with one hand and gestured toward the woman. Together, they pushed through the throng, ducking thrown objects and weaving around a makeshift barricade. When they reached the base of the kiosk, Gray hesitated. He could see the determination in her eyes. This wasn't about vandalism or theft. This was something deeper. But it had to end.

"Stop!" he shouted, his voice barely carrying. She turned, eyes blazing, and for a moment, time seemed to slow. Gray scampered up the side of the kiosk the same way the woman had done. She raised the megaphone again, but Gray lunged, pulling her down. They tumbled to the ground, the impact knocking the wind out of him. Hands grabbed at him, protesters tried to pull him away, but King was there, holding them off. With a powerful kick upward, she sent one man spiralling into the air. Before he'd hit the ground she had swung around and kicked another man sideways.

More riot police closed in. The line of shields was advancing like an unbreakable wall.

Gray struggled to his feet, his chest heaving. Around him, the crowd was breaking apart, retreating in waves as the police pressed forward. Tear gas filled the air, stinging his eyes and lungs. He wanted to collapse, but he couldn't afford to. He'd arrived at the scene without protective gear, so he took off his coat, wrapped it into a ball and held it against his face.

"Chandra," he barked into his radio, "status?"

"Secured most of the area around Albert Street. Pockets of resistance, but we're getting there."

Gray nodded to himself. The fight wasn't over, but for now, they'd gained a sliver of control.

Police rode into the mall on horseback and the great beasts stepped sideways against the rioters, pushing them back and corralling them so the police could heave them into waiting minibuses.

A difficult two hours followed, pushing, shoving and removing rioters from the mall, then it was over. Citizens with smartphones lingered recording scenes of the aftermath. Gray watched with disdain as they traversed the mall like vultures sifting through the carnage. Qualified newspeople were few and far between these days as 'Citizen Journalists', as they called themselves, provided live feed of newsworthy incidents twenty-four-seven onto favoured websites. People could tune in to hear the news coverage spun according to their chosen perspective.

Gray knew the riot would be covered by both pro-refugee and anti-refugee groups, but the public could choose to watch the perspective they preferred. Gray's chest ached and he couldn't tell whether it was in disgust for the way his world was polarised or because one of the rioters had shouldered him in the ribs.

CHAPTER SEVEN

Back in the calm of their office, Gray, King and Chandra sunk into their chairs, their faces pale and drawn with fatigue. Their breaths came deep and ragged. They'd had to make their way through the bedlam in the public area where uniformed police tried to process the sixty or seventy most violent of the rioters, they'd been able to apprehend. Kenneth Tarrant's booming voice carried across the entire space, firing off directions to both the police and protestors.

It had been a welcome relief when they reached the relative quiet of the homicide office though they still heard shouting in the distance. They were grateful to no longer be part of the chaos. The sharp scent of sweat and adrenaline hung in the air.

Chandra clicked on the NewsNet.com website and watched as the screen filled with the image of a woman. Perfectly coifed, bleached blonde hair held in place by industrial grade lacquer communicated tight control over her circumstances. She wore a tailored suit in head turning crimson with matching lipstick. Her voice resonated through the speakers, sharp and grating, an unfortunate affliction for a politician, but it hadn't seemed to hold her back. She was a rising star in the right-wing conservative movement.

"This is what happens when we allow so many people into our country who don't share our values," she was saying. "They bring their own problems with them. We cannot allow our values to be destroyed by these people…"

"We've been hearing from the Federal Member of Parliament for Brisbane, Leonie Nolan," said the broadcast host, cutting to a commercial.

"God, she's irritating, Rishi Chandra said, turning away from the computer screen. "She terrifies the people in my community. They're afraid she's going to take their businesses and deport them all. Even though most of them are Australian citizens. My own father is the instigator of that theory." He huffed.

"She can't do that. But your father's right. She's more than irritating. She's downright dangerous," said Glenda. "All this talk of "these people" in that snide tone. "It's not the refugees tearing up Queen Street. It's the people she gives license to with her bullshit."

Gray waited while King took a few deep breaths. "Never mind Leonie Nolan for the moment," he said. "Did you see anyone that fits the description of the single punch killer?"

"What, a white man with blue eyes?" quipped Glenda.

Rishi Chandra rolled his eyes. "We have nothing to go on," he said. "He could've been there, but how would we know?"

"No one taking a shot at a protestor?"

Glenda and Chandra laughed at the same time. "The only ones they were taking a shot at were us."

Gray nodded absently as he checked the ping on his phone.

"The results from the DNA test are in already, they must have really rushed the job." He read the notes quickly. "Inconclusive," he said out loud. He took a deep breath and looked up at the ceiling for a moment. Then his eyes lowered to meet those of King and Chandra. "That's it, then," he said. "There's nothing there. I don't know what else we can do. There's no evidence, no leads."

Meanwhile, Yusef Ibrahim can't leave his house," said King.

"I'll continue to monitor the social media sites, sir." Chandra swivelled his chair to face the computer. "Maybe we'll get lucky, and someone will give something away. Someone must know who punched Harlin."

"The trouble is," said King, her grey eyes wide, "the socials are full of anti-refugee protesters. The man we're looking for wasn't a protester, was he? He killed a protester."

Gray considered his young officer carefully. King had good instincts. And she was right, it was difficult to see why one of the anti-refugee protesters would have punched Seeton Harlin, who was at the scene to protest himself.

"At first glance it looks like the single punch killer was protecting Ibrahim from Harlin's attack," Chandra went on, "but what if Yusef Ibrahim had nothing to do with this? What if the killer had a motive to get rid of Seeton and took the opportunity to do so?"

Gray raised his eyebrows.

"You might be right," said the detective inspector, "but who? And what motive?"

"We've talked to most of Seeton's friends and acquaintances," said Chandra. "They said he'd become a bit of a bore with the whole anti-refugee rhetoric, but there was nothing there to suggest anyone would want to kill him."

"What did we get from his computer?" asked Gray.

"Nothing," said Glenda. "He had some kind of block on it. Our experts couldn't get in. It's still in his house. They had a good look around in the basement at the Harlin House. It's crammed with state-of-the art technology. Between them those kids had the latest of everything."

Chandra folded his arms in front of his chest. "To be honest, sir, I don't believe they made much of an effort with the computer. At that stage, everyone was pretty certain Ibrahim had punched the kid. Most people still think so."

A bitter taste rose in Gray's mouth, a mixture of adrenaline and disappointment manifesting itself as he let out a groan. He shook his head. Yusef Ibrahim was a man in the wrong place at the wrong time. Nothing more. He was sure of it.

"Doesn't that say something in itself?" he said at last.

"What?" said Glenda, her grey eyes locked on his.

"The sophisticated lock on the computer. Why would a twenty-year old have secrets he needed to keep so badly?"

"Maybe the sister knows how to break the code," suggested Glenda.

Gray looked up at that. "It might be our best chance." His eyes narrowed. "To be honest, we need to check each of the family members thoroughly. You know as well as I do that most killers are found close to home."

Detective Inspector Gray felt the tremble of his phone and fished it out of his pocket. It was Halohan. He groaned and held the phone out. "What is it? You're on speaker. King and Chandra are with me."

The voice on the other end sounded anxious. "I'm at Ibrahim Yusef's place," he said. The exterior of the apartment block has been painted with slogans - hateful stuff."

Gray cursed.

"It's worse than that," he went on, "they've thrown bricks through the windows of his apartment. We found Yusef holed up in his bathroom terrified. They shot one brick wide, and it went through the neighbour's glass door. You don't want to hear what the neighbour thought about copping one of the bricks meant for the Palestinian."

Gray looked at King and Chandra. "We'll have to organise a safe house for him."

"I'll get on to it," said King.

"Where's Ibrahim now?" asked Gray.

"We've got him in the police car," said Fletcher.

"Bring him in. I'll talk to the Super now for approval, King's putting the wheels in motion. Hopefully we'll be able to have him settled by tonight."

Gray shoved his phone back into his pocket. "King, you follow through with the safe house. I don't want any hold-ups. I'm going upstairs to insist that this be treated as an urgent case. I won't have Ibrahim tried and punished in the court of public opinion. Chandra, can you check in with Seeton Harlin's friends again, find out who the two men on the film were. The ones who were with him prior to the incident."

Detective Inspector Gray leapt up the stairs to the third floor taking two steps at a time. He had a feeling the authorities might be ready to sacrifice Ibrahim Yusef to the mob to save their own reputations if there was no one else to blame for the killing of the middle-class white Australian boy.

He reached the Superintendent's office to find he was out. Assistant Commissioner Bryant saw him knocking on the Super's door and came out to greet him. The Federal Member of Parliament for Brisbane, Leonie Nolan slipped past the Assistant Commissioner, smiling smugly at Gray with a flick of her bleached hair, before heading down the stairs. Gray wondered momentarily why she was meeting with Bryant, then put the question aside for more pressing concerns.

"The Chief Superintendent is in a public communications meeting. Can I be of assistance?" said Bryant. Thin fingers curled around an expensive pen. It was one of those with a nib that you dip in ink; The reproduction of a nineteenth century fountain pen. Gray's eye was caught by the gold trim against the honey-coloured tortoiseshell body.

"Yes," said Gray, collecting his thoughts. "We need approval to establish a safe house for Ibrahim Yusef." He went on to explain the events of the morning.

Bryant held his beaky nose high and his pen between two fingers like he was waving a cigarette about.

"I don't know," he said. "Perhaps we should keep him here, in protective custody. It should all blow over in a day or so."

Gray couldn't believe what he was hearing. "This isn't going to blow over," he said. "With respect, sir, you weren't at the riots in Queen Street this morning. This is going to fester and get worse if we can't find Harlin's killer soon."

"If we bring Ibrahim in, we may well find out we have the killer," said Bryant. "Just because we have little evidence of his guilt, beyond his being present at the time, doesn't mean he didn't do it. Find witnesses. Bring him in and keep him in custody for twenty-four hours."

Gray was opening his mouth to protest when Superintendent Charfield appeared at the top of the stairs, slightly out of breath from the climb.

"Gray," he said. "Just the man I want to see." He took Gray by the arm and ushered him into his own office, closing the door quickly so that Bryant couldn't follow.

"The public relations people are nervous about this, Gray," he said. "I don't mind telling you, we'll all have our jobs on-the-line if this continues to brew. Have you anything more on Ibrahim?"

"No sir, but Ibrahim's apartment block has been attacked." Gray outlined the morning's events emphasising the brick that accidentally went through a neighbour's glass doors.

Charfield reacted exactly as Gray anticipated. "We have to get him out of there," he said.

"We're already on it, sir. King is organising everything, we just need your approval to move forward."

Charfield gestured Gray out of his office. "You have it, man. Go."

Gray couldn't help a smug look of his own as he took the stairs two at a time back down to his office. He felt a twinge of guilt at the juvenile strategy he'd employed, going behind one superior's back to get a more favourable result from the other. But the guilt didn't last long, the strategy had worked after all.

Chandra met his boss at his office door. "I've tracked down the two men seen on the CCTV footage, sir. They were friends of Seeton's from the University. They came to the protest at his invitation, met with him when they arrived and then didn't see him again that morning. Their stories check out with the other witnesses we've interviewed."

Gray took a deep breath. "So, there's nothing there, then. And no DNA at the point of impact.

Rishi Chandra looked back, "I'm sorry, sir. No."

Gray's mind was racing.

"Have we checked alibis for the parents and the sister yet?"

"Yes," said Chandra, "they check out. The parents were at the airport going through customs, time stamped about the same time as Seeton was killed. Lividia was in class. Students and lecturer confirm it."

"Have you checked financial records? Anything suspicious there?

"I'll do it now, sir," said Chandra.

Gray caught his eye with a subtle nod of his head. "We need to follow protocol, but I'd be surprised if you find anything incriminating. There's plenty of animosity in that family, but I can't see any of them killing Seeton. It would have been easier to imagine the two kids killing their parents."

He watched Chandra for a moment, while the young officer watched him back. Gray knew he wouldn't move forward until he was sure Gray had no further instructions for him.

"That's it," he said. "I guess I'd better update the family, I'll do it in person, get a sense of how they're doing."

Do you want me to come?" asked Chandra.

"No. You stay here and keep talking to anyone who knew Seeton Harlin. I want to know everything that boy did in the three days leading up to the incident. Every person who spoke with him, every thought that went through his head.

This was more than a bystander wanting to prevent Harlin hitting Yusef Ibrahim. If that were the case, they would have hung around. This was opportunist. Someone took the opportunity to kill Seeton Harlin."

CHAPTER EIGHT

It was already late afternoon when Gray arrived at the Harlin house. The sun's last rays cast a warm, tangerine glow on the concrete walls of the home. Drops of gold glimmered on the leaves of the overhanging trees. Gray's face was flushed both from the heat and the adrenaline-charged day he'd had. He couldn't help but tug at his collar, to relieve some of the sweat that had gathered at his neck. As he approached the intercom screen, the camera swivelled toward his face. He smelt freshly cut grass and smiled at the thought that the gardener had been by. Life had a way of continuing on, regardless of personal tragedy.

Gray went over the purpose of his visit. He wanted to check on the family, see how they were holding up, not only out of concern for their welfare, but more importantly, to assess their reactions to Harlin's death. It was difficult to get a handle on this weird family. The reason he would give the Harlin's was that he wanted to convey information. That excuse was weak, he knew, because he had little to convey. He straightened his shoulders and held his chin up as the hydraulics opened the door.

Mrs Harlin stood in the hallway wearing the same suit she'd had on the day before, but in different colour. Navy rather than black.

"Evening," Gray said.

Evelyn Harlin stepped aside without speaking and the detective followed her into the house to see Lividia perched on a high stool at the kitchen Island. Grey circles had formed under her eyes, her skin was even paler than the previous day, and her long hair hung limp on her shoulders. She looked like the ghost of Lividia Harlin, there was no life in her eyes. The death of her brother had clearly affected the girl terribly.

Gray wished he had more to tell them. Lividia stared at him with those blank eyes waiting for him to speak.

"You may remember me saying we were waiting for DNA evidence that might link someone to the crime," he began. The sound of his own voice sounding. "The lab rushed the tests through so we could know, but unfortunately there was no evidence to be found."

The faces of Evelyn and Lividia Harlin stared blankly back at him. It was clear Lividia wasn't coping, but he couldn't decide about her mother. "We also looked into the lads in the CCTV footage who were friends of Harlin," he went on. "They had nothing to do with his death, and they weren't nearby when the incident occurred."

Mrs Harlin spoke in a quietly controlled voice, "In short, the police are still no closer to identifying the killer," she said.

Before Gray could respond, Lividia slammed both palms on the table, causing Gray and her mother to jump.

"We all know who killed my brother, detective," she said. She pushed herself to her feet. "And we all know he'll never be charged."

"Lividia," cried her mother. But Lividia was already heading toward the stairs into the basement.

"Wait," Gray called.

Lividia stopped without looking back.

"We wondered if you have the passcode to get into your brother's computer."

She hesitated for half a second then turned her head. "No," she said emphatically, shaking her head as she disappeared down the stairs.

Gray's eyes met those of Lividia's mother. "Well..." he said.

Evelyn Harlin blinked slowly. Gray scanned her face for any sign of emotion. There had to be something behind those cold eyes, more hazel than green like her daughter's. But there was nothing, not a twitch at the corner of the mouth, not a shift in the arched brow.

"Is Mr Harlin not home?" asked Gray looking around.

"My husband is at work," the woman said flatly.

Gray nodded. "I suppose, it's important to keep busy," he said. He tucked his hands into his pockets. "At times like these." He watched the grieving mother closely. Was she grieving? Everyone grieved in their own way, but he could see no objective sign of grief at all in this woman.

"I'll leave you in peace, then," he said. "I'll let you know immediately I have any further information."

He stepped back into the hallway and left through the still open door. It closed behind him.

Talking to grieving families was the least favoured part of his job. He never knew how they would react to their circumstances. And he didn't know how to react to them. He was genuinely sorry when people were faced with sudden loss, but he couldn't decide to what extent he ought to demonstrate empathy or offer comfort. Objectivity was the mainstay of his job, in many cases the grieving people also proved to be suspects. At the very least they were either witnesses or holders of valuable information he might need to resolve the case. A level of distance ensured they remain sufficiently calm to answer his questions. But he always carried some discomfort.

In this case Seeton Harlin's mother was as cold and guarded as her home. Lividia, on the other hand, seethed with emotion that escaped out of her like a white-hot force that slapped him in the face whenever he was in her presence.

Back in the office, Gray spent an hour going over the notes made by Glenda King and Rishi Chandra from the interviews with the known associates of Seeton Harlin. He didn't want to go home for the day without finding something, anything, that might be a clue to why this kid was killed.

He read about Seeton's whereabouts on the day prior to his death. He had attended two two-hour lectures at university, spent an hour in the university coffee shop having lunch with three of his classmates before he went home on the bus where he stayed until the morning of his death. Chandra was tracing his steps further back one day at a time, but there seemed to be no indication so far, that this line of enquiry would reveal results.

What troubled Gray the most, was his belief that someone at the rally already intended to kill Seeton Harlin, saw an opportunity to do so and followed through. Call it instinct, or a hunch. But he was convinced of it. The only information he had on the assailant was that he was a young white man with blue eyes. That made him like Seeton in many ways. Young, white and attending an anti-refugee rally. What could have motivated this person to take Seeton's life?

CHAPTER NINE

Hunched over Seeton's computer, Lividia's eyes were bleary from staring at the screen for hours. She'd adjusted the lights to dim so as not to be distracted from the screen. In the basement that she and Seeton had built together, she felt close to her brother. This was their space. They'd equipped it with the latest technology in computing and telecommunications, and it was from here that they navigated and understood the world. To be fair, Seeton went outdoors more often than she did, but look where that got him.

Lividia read her brother's posts over again, playing his voice in her head. She wanted to know who he'd been communicating with, what he'd been talking about in his last days. She wanted to know the same things the police wanted to know about him. But she had the code to get into his computer. A smirk spread across her lips. No one knew her brother as well as she did.

She opened a feed from her own socials. As she scrolled through yet another comment on a news article about Seeton's death, an invitation popped up on her screen. Someone with the handle 'Spectre' was inviting her to join a private chatroom.

Spectre? Wasn't that an old movie her parents watched? A spy movie or something? She wrinkled her nose but accepted the invitation and waited as the screen blinked. The four walls of the basement closed in around her in the dim light. It felt like an embrace. She sat in the chat room waiting for this entity calling itself Spectre to join her.

Finally, words popped onto the screen: Sorry about your brother.

Simple. Straightforward. Lividia didn't know how to respond.

Spectre wrote, It's shit he died that way.

Yes, Lividia tapped on the keyboard.

Spectre: Have the police locked up the refugee for killing him?

Lividia: No. They say they have no proof.

Spectre: Bullshit. Everyone saw it. They're afraid of stirring up the refugees.

Lividia: I wish the refugees never came here. Seeton said we'd regret letting them in.

Spectre: Do you have encryption software?

Lividia: wtf? My brother and I wrote our own encryptions.

Spectre: Impressive. Let's talk.

For hours, Lividia sat in the dimly lit basement, in a private chatroom with Spectre, her fingers flying over the keyboard as they communicated through the encrypted software Lividia and her brother had created. The soft glow of the computer screen illuminated her face in a pale blue light. They spoke about their shared passion for robotics and technology, and their memories of Seeton. They discussed their fears that justice would not be served for his death.

As they typed back and forth, Lividia poured out her raw emotions about Seeton's senseless killing. She held nothing back, expressing deep-seated hatred toward the man she believed responsible and the circumstances that led to Seeton's presence at the protest. She directed her anger at government policies, the refugees, and even her own parents for not fighting harder for justice for Seeton.

Spectre listened in a way no one else had, offering words of comfort, understanding her need for justice, and explaining the global mess that had caught her town, and her brother in its wake.

As light began to stream in through the windows just under the ceiling of the basement, Lividia heard her father's voice from the top of the stairs.

"Have you eaten at all today?"

Got to go, typed Lividia and closed the screen.

"What do you think," she snapped.

Her father walked down the stairs gingerly. Lividia knew he was trying not to intrude, but was intruding, nonetheless.

"Are you alright?" he asked.

"What the hell, dad! No. I'm not alright."

"You need to eat, and sleep," he said. "Come upstairs and have something to eat with your mother and me. Then you can get some sleep."

"I'll sleep when I'm tired," she said. But she got up and climbed the stairs behind him. She didn't need him poking his nose into her computer activity. He hadn't even noticed she was on her brother's computer.

After eating half a bowl of celery soup in silence, Lividia traipsed off to her bedroom and flung herself on the bed. She couldn't wait for her parents to go overseas again so she could order a decent meal. Her mother was going to kill her with her fashionable organic soups and bloody chia seeds. She fell asleep immediately, despite herself and when she woke three hours later, the house was silent. She grabbed a can of soda from the fridge and went back to the basement where she set herself up once more in Seeton's account.

For the following twenty-four hours, she spent most of her time on Seeton's computer chatting with Spectre. Occasionally, she wandered upstairs to eat something small or to get a drink from the fridge. She didn't care whether it was day or night, and she avoided seeing her parents.

At one point, Lividia's mother appeared on the stairs in the basement, standing in her dressing gown, in the dark, watching. Lividia jumped when she glanced up to see her mother there, little more than a shadow.

"Weird," she cried. "What are you doing?"

"Worrying about you," said her mother.

"Leave me alone," Lividia snapped. She tapped the keyboard to activate the screensaver.

"You need to get some sleep," her mother began, "Your father and I…"

Lividia threw her head back in frustration.

"You can't go on like this." Her mother's voice was thinner now. "It's not healthy. You must eat and sleep. Live…"

Lividia let out a long groan.

"Your father believes we should do something to help you through this," Mrs Harlin said. "What can we do to help?"

"Leave. Me. Alone!" screamed Lividia.

The teenager didn't see the cold resignation in her mother's eyes as she turned to climb the stairs, but she knew it was there. Lividia watched her disappear into the light at the top of the staircase before the door closed. What had they ever done to help her and Seeton through anything? Everything they did was for their own benefit. They might put a spin on their actions to make them sound to their friends like they were doing things to benefit the kids, or worse, something they called 'the family'. But it was always about them.

Lividia let out a loud sigh and reactivated the chat on the computer.

If she was honest, she was grateful her parents had given up trying to engage her in their lives. Their interests were petty and self-absorbed. They didn't believe in anything beyond their stupid business and their wealthy friends. She wished she had listened more carefully to Seeton when he talked about politics and the importance of being engaged in the world at a level beyond that of one's personal interests. Seeton cared. And he acted. She was determined to be more like him.

She couldn't understand how the authorities could just let Seeton's killer go free. It was like her brother's life didn't matter. But with Spectre she shared a common bond of loss and a desire for justice. They talked for hours about their plans to find evidence against Seeton's killer.

CHAPTER TEN

DAY THREE

G ray was on his morning run. Still morning air and the pale light of dawn cast soft shadows over the river. It was already warm, even at 6 a.m., the sun driving heat down onto his head and shoulders. A heady smell of pollen mixed with sweat and cheap aftershave, his own and that of the other joggers that invariably passed him. A thin sheen of perspiration on his skin cooled him a little, but not enough for comfort. His muscles strained against the pavement as they propelled him forward and the steady beat of his footsteps echoed against the buildings.

He travelled the same route every day, tracing his path along North Quay beneath the intricate lattice of highways looming overhead, roads that wove in an out of the city, skirting the river. He passed beneath the bridge, white struts rising sharply against the sky, reminiscent of the towering masts of ancient tall ships. His route took him past the convict-built Commissariat Store huddled meekly between gleaming glass towers, then meandered through the City Botanic Gardens, a peaceful respite amidst the urban hustle. Finally, he would normally jog back along George Street to complete his daily circuit.

He'd slept fitfully since the loss of Christine and the exercise cleared his mind of the brain fog that woke him each morning. It was an opportunity to sweat out the shame that gathered in his physical body overnight and threatened to debilitate him.

Following his usual route, he was headed along the edge of the gardens toward the mosque on the corner of Albert and Charlotte Streets. The mosque had been constructed to serve the refugees housed in a dated high rise on the opposite corner. What was once a glossy black façade over the apartment block's concrete walls was now faded and chipped, weathered by decades of harsh climate and neglect.

Similar high-rise buildings, and housing enclaves scattered across the city had been allocated to refugees. Twelve of them in a city of three and a half million, each with its own maze of businesses and market stalls springing up to accommodate the newcomers. The sound of foreign languages piercing the air rattled in the ears of a distinctly European population that had, until recently, escaped the onslaught of multi-culturalism that had long been the norm in southern states. Twelve high-rise buildings handed over to the refugees. But they weren't all lucky enough to have their own mosque.

If Gray timed it right, he could hear the early morning prayers rising from the minaret as he passed. This morning, he'd been woken by thoughts of self-doubt earlier than usual and he heard the muezzin's call to prayer instead.

As he approached the mosque a pain in his abdomen stopped him. Doubled over, hands resting on his thighs, he took a few deep breaths and cursed himself for not paying sufficient attention to his breathing. He hadn't had a stitch in years. He lifted his head and shoulders focussing on his diaphragm as he did so. Air filled his lungs, he held, then released. On his second intake of breath his mind registered activity on the pavement about twenty meters away.

A group of men in white thobes walked purposefully toward the mosque, their footsteps quiet and their voices low as they prepared for morning prayers. One man lingered behind, crouching down to speak to three children who'd caught up to him. Gray was close enough to see him stroke the hair of the youngest.

"Go home," Gray heard him say, pointing toward the apartment building on the corner. "I'm going to prayers. I will see you later."

The tallest boy hesitated but nodded, taking the smaller boys' hands as they reluctantly shuffled back the way they'd come.

The father then stood to his full height, his eyes following the children. Gray smiled at the man's gentle affection for his young. He wondered, not for the first time, what it would feel like to have children of his own. Then he remembered Alix and felt a pang of guilt. But she wasn't his daughter, was she? What reason did he have to believe she would have any interest in him after her mother's death? In the beginning the pain had been too raw. The longer he left it, the harder it became to contact her. Best to leave well enough alone.

The Palestinian man turned back to join the rest of the men, who were by now, climbing the stairs to the mosque. Gray was about to resume his run, when a feint whirring cut through the quiet moments between the calls to prayer. The sound was almost imperceptible at first, then it became louder. Gray stared up toward the sky, but the morning light was in his eyes, and he couldn't see anything.

As his eyes lowered, they settled on the Palestinian man, whose line of sight followed something from above glide down and hover before him. Gray couldn't see what it was, only the tilt of the man's gaze. Then the Palestinian man's left eye exploded in a spray of red. His body wavered for a moment as if confused, and he fell to the ground. Something small turned abruptly and flew almost vertically into the sky.

A scream tore through the morning stillness as the children turned back to see their father fall. The other men who had been approaching the mosque also turned in alarm, rushing back toward the crumpled body on the pavement.

Gray covered the short distance to the spot where the man fell in seconds. He crouched over him and felt for a pulse. The man was dead.

"What happened?" shouted someone.

One of the fallen man's eyes was wide, staring vacantly, while the other was a mess of blood and torn flesh.

Above, a feint buzz drifted in the air. Gray looked up, squinting into the sky. A glint of something metallic reflected the rising sun for the briefest of moments, then vanished. The whirring faded as quickly as it had come.

"Mohammed!" shouted one of the fallen man's neighbours, but his voice cracked because everyone could see that Mohammed was already gone.

The whisper of morning began to rise, as the people who lived in the high-rise came out to see what was going on. Other morning joggers also gathered at the scene.

The air grew thick with tension and fear, onlookers frozen in shock and horror. Within minutes sirens wailed, and several police cars screeched to a halt at the site. Mohammed's children cried and clung to one another; their faces streaked with tears as they stared at the lifeless body of their father.

Gray's heart clenched at the sight, his mind racing with questions and a deep sorrow for the senseless loss of life. Some of Mohammed's friends, who had been moments earlier preparing for their morning prayers, shouted for justice.

Gray didn't know who put in the call, but he was relieved when an ambulance and three police cars arrived at the scene within minutes.

"Over here," he called, and the ambulance officers hurried forward with a trolley.

"He's already gone," said Gray wiping the sweat from his face with the back of his hand. But the ambulance officers checked for a pulse anyway.

Chandra and King had been in the first police car, then Holohan in the second. The forensic team arrived in the third. All of them looked sideways at Gray standing in his jogging gear but no one said anything. They jumped into their roles taking instruction from Gray as the senior office at the scene.

When the body had been slipped into the back of the ambulance and on lookers began wandering off, he stood back. Another high-profile murder was the last thing he needed.

He tugged at his t-shirt where the cotton clung to his chest. As he wiped the back of his hand across his brow yet again to stop the drip of salty sweat into his eyes, he noticed a familiar figure approaching. Assistant Commissioner Bryant strode toward him, his face grim.

"What do we know?" he asked Gray.

Gray's arms hung limp at his sides. He could hardly believe what he'd seen. "It looked like a miniature drone," he said. He glanced up to the sky again as if to remind himself of what he'd witnessed. "It swooped down, shot some kind of payload directly into the man's eye then flew away. I've never seen anything like it."

Bryant grunted in disgust, his eyes darting about the scene.

Gray wondered if the Assistant Commissioner had heard him correctly.

"This was a targeted attack," he added, with emphasis. "With a weapon we've not seen before..."

Bryant turned his face skyward and squinted. Gray did likewise, but the sky was clear and blue, the only smudges a few seagulls gliding in from the river.

A thought occurred to Gray, and he voiced it aloud before he had time to calculate the wisdom of sharing it with the Assistant Commissioner. "I wonder if it might be linked to the Harlin murder," he said.

Bryant's expression darkened. "How so?" he demanded. "The two incidents have nothing in common. One a single punch killer, the other...what is it? A drone, you say?" He spat the words out incredulously.

Bryant went on. "One victim was a white Australian boy, the other a Palestinian man," he said. "There's nothing to link them."

He shook his beaky head, short sharp shakes, then went on, "This drone attack is a terrorist act. I don't know whether it's an anti-Islamic group responsible or a factional dispute between Middle Eastern rivals. But this is the risk we take, bringing in refugees. They bring their politics with them."

Gray's lips stretched wide across his teeth. He looked back at the kill site. "Terrorists?" he said. His brows furrowed. "What makes you think that?"

Bryant cut him off. "We need to tread carefully here," he said. "People are worked up already. We don't want to add fuel to the fire."

Gray winced. "I'd be surprised if this is the end of it," he said quietly, his gut telling him it was almost certainly just the beginning.

Rishi Chandra and Glenda King came up to Gray as he was speaking with the Assistant Commissioner. Having secured the kill site and moved the onlookers back they stood waiting for instructions. Gray told Chandra to interview witnesses, then motioned for Glenda to follow him across the road to where the wives of the men had gathered with their children. Mohammed's own children were still standing where they'd stopped when they saw their father fall. Glenda went to take the hand of the eldest child whose expression was carved from stone, his body rigid and tense, his hands clenched into fists.

The smaller children clung to the boy's legs, and the older boy shoved Glenda's hand away. But when she walked, he followed, the two younger children still clinging to him making it difficult for him to keep up.

The children joined their wailing mother who was surrounded by her neighbours in a tight circle, also wailing in despair. The pain rose into the air through desperate pleas to Allah. The children pushed through the thobes of the women to wrap themselves around their mother.

By the time Mohammed's wife had heard about the incident and come racing down to the street, her husband's body was already being zipped into a body bag and tucked into the ambulance. She waved her arms wildly, begging to be allowed to see her husband. Halohan and a uniformed police officer physically restrained her.

Gray winced at the despair in her face, the power in her slim arms as she fought against the officers. He strode over to them and took one of her hands in his own. He nodded to the officers to lessen their grip. As soon as they did, she stopped struggling for a moment to assess the change. Gray caught her dark eyes in his own. For a split second there was a silent communication between them and the woman ceased struggling and fell to her knees.

Noticing the man who seemed to be in charge with their neighbour, the other women rushed forward speaking furiously in Arabic. They shouted questions Gray couldn't understand and for which he had no answers anyway.

"Please, please, stay calm," he said, trying to fend them off. But he might as well have been talking to the wind. The frenzied voices only became louder.

"Go back to your homes and wait there. When your husbands have been interviewed, they will join you. Please stay indoors today."

He turned his attention to the woman kneeling at his feet. "Mrs Hussain?" he asked holding out his hand to her.

She took his hand and rose slowly.

"I'm Detective Inspector Mitchell Gray," he said, conscious he was in a t-shirt and jogging shorts and looked in no way like a detective.

He was about to go on when a middle-aged woman interrupted him. "Briony Stapleton," she said. "Social worker."

Gray looked into her face, middle-aged, lined with the worry of hundreds of souls and then down at the calloused hand thrust toward him.

"That was quick," he said reaching out to take the hand. Her grip was strong.

"I called her as soon as you called me," explained King.

Gray was constantly impressed by King's deep-seated understanding of the vulnerability and challenges women faced amid turmoil.

"Good work," he said to King, and "thank-you for coming," to the social worker.

Mohammed's wife was still weeping, but her cries had softened.

"What's your name?" Gray asked her.

"Fatima," said King.

Gray shot King a puzzled look.

"Fatima's neighbours told me."

The two youngest children were crying with their mother, while the eldest stood aside, a cold, distant stare in his eyes.

Gray watched Fatima weep for a moment, wondering whether there was any value in attempting an interview while she was still in shock. It didn't feel right - or necessary.

"See that she has everything she needs," he said. "Gently find out if there's anything we need to know immediately, then leave her with the social worker. And her neighbours. We'll conduct an interview tomorrow."

Gray looked down at his drenched sweatshirt and running shorts clinging to his body in dark patches. The sharp scent of sweat mixed with the earthy fragrance of the surrounding trees and plants from the Botanic Gardens wafted up to his nose causing it to wrinkle in discomfort. He tasted the salty tang on his lips. He was parched.

"Do you want a lift back?" asked Chandra climbing into a police vehicle.

Gray nodded. "Drop me off at home. I reek," he said.

CHAPTER ELEVEN

Showered and changed into work clothes, Gray felt more in control when he arrived at the office. There was an urgent buzz in the building. The morning's event had stirred an undercurrent of fear across the department. The drone attack was unlike the crimes the Brisbane Police had ever had to deal with and there was an uncertainty about how to proceed.

"Don't let the shock of this particular crime throw you off your game," Gray told his team. "We treat this incident as we would any other murder. First, we go through the witness statements and any CCTV footage from that part of town, at the same time we look into the victim, his family, friends, associates. There will be motive, means and opportunity, just as in any other investigation."

The police attending the scene had been uploading interview notes all morning. By the time Gray fired up his computer there was a sea of information to sort through. The details filtered through in disjointed fragments, from witnesses, from people living in the vicinity, from those who might have been passing through at the time Mohammed Hussain was killed. The sheer volume of information was formidable. Rishi Chandra. He was the man for organising data. He would hand the task over to Chandra and by the end of the day he'd have a neat spreadsheet with names, addresses and pertinent eyewitness accounts. He forwarded the folder to Chandra with instructions.

Gray was already planning his next move. He needed to dig into Hussain's past, examine every angle and known association. He was gathering his thoughts, bracing himself for what threatened to become another long afternoon, when King returned from the scene, out of breath.

"Fatima's taking it really hard," she said. "She's in shock."

Gray nodded. "I could see that," he agreed.

King took a deep breath and started recounting what she knew so far. Fatima had described the morning as no different to any other. The family hadn't noticed anything unusual when they left the apartment complex. They hadn't seen the drone. She had no idea who would want to harm her husband, but she suspected it might have been a random act, with Mohammed at the wrong place at the wrong time. Like most of the other refugees, she thought the attack might have been part of a growing backlash.

"It might well be," said Gray. But something kept tugging at his mind. He couldn't shake the feeling that this attack might be linked to the Harlin case. He just couldn't see how.

"Fatima's agreed to come in for an interview," said King. "Nine o'clock tomorrow morning."

Chandra came up behind King and peered over her shoulder.

"It's Leonie Nolan on the news again," he said. "I thought you might want to see this."

He slid past his colleague and handed Gray an electronic tablet. A reporter was asking the Member of Parliament for her response to the attack on Mohammed Hussain. She turned an overly made-up face directly to the camera. "This is exactly what I have warned the public would happen," she said. The self-satisfied purse of her lips sent a chill through Gray. "This is the only way these people know how to behave. Violence is all they know. They've brought this terror to our shores. We cannot allow our way of life and our values to be threatened in this way..."

Gray passed the tablet back to Chandra. "She's taking the opportunity to stir up the hate and resentment," he said. "Very helpful. I think she's enjoying it. What's wrong with these people?" He shook his head.

"There's plenty of hate and resentment circulating on-line," said Chandra.

Gray's phone rang. "It's the Chief Super," the detective inspector said, holding his hand over the phone and nodding to Glenda and Chandra to leave him.

"We have the Palestinian community organisations and the anti-refugee groups ready to throttle one another," said Chief Superintendent Charfield. "I've arranged an urgent meeting with community leaders from both sides to diffuse the situation before it escalates any further." Charfield took a heavy breath. "The meeting starts at 1:30, upstairs. I expect you to be there."

Gray wanted to be there. He needed to evaluate the different sides for himself. He needed to assess how soon the animosity was likely to evolve into more violence. More importantly, he wanted to start building rapport with these leaders, and to do that he had to meet them in a neutral environment first. That was the number one rule he'd learned in his years of policing. If the first meeting you have with a person is an interrogation, the communication is not going to flow freely.

Chandra entered Gray's office waving his electronic tablet. "There's nothing suspicious in the Harlin's financials," he said. "I thought I'd catch you up before you have to go upstairs."

Gray blinked as his mind was jolted back to the Harlin case.

"I didn't think there would be," he said. He paused to think. The chaos brought down on them by the killer drone attack threatened to upend the Harlin investigation and he wasn't having it. "Take King and try talking to grandparents, aunts, uncles, neighbours, anyone who knew the family well. There's angst in that family and I want to know the nature of it."

"What about the witness statements from this morning, sir?" Chandra's voice came out slightly higher than normal.

"Blast," muttered Gray. "You're right. You work on those. Is there anyone you can trust to help you with that? Get though the bulk of the information, quickly?"

"Yes, sir. I'll get it done." Chandra nodded to King and left them.

Gray went on, "King, you follow up on the Harlin connections. "You can take Halohan if you like."

King raised an eyebrow. "I'll go by myself," she said. "It'll be quicker."

Even as he despatched Chandra and King, the suspicion continued to niggle at him that the Harlin case and the killer drone case were linked.

Gray checked the clock on the wall, then compared the time to that on his mobile. The clock gained about ten minutes every fortnight. It was a running joke in the office. His phone told him it was 1:25. Hunger pains gnawed at his stomach reminding him he hadn't eaten. He'd normally have breakfast after his run so if he missed lunch, it didn't matter as much. But today he'd been in too much of a rush to get back to work after the drone attack.

The voice of his Asian mother was in his head on a loop. "You no eat, you no think straight. You eat. Be smart."

Well, he wasn't going to be smart today. He had five minutes to get to the community engagement meeting.

Gray was relieved to see Charfield had already taken a seat at the head of the table in the second-floor meeting room when he arrived. While he wanted to be at the meeting, he had no desire to oversee it.

He took a seat at the table, crammed in between chairs that were too close together. The room was full. Eight people sat around a table that would comfortably seat six, and another ten people stood against the walls. The room was divided along partisan lines with Muslim community leaders and members on one side and White Australians on the other. Quick introductions were made by Charfield, but even before those were complete, Gray could see that the meeting was not going to have a good outcome. It was clear there were deep-seated resentments and fear on both sides and recent incidents had only served to exacerbate these feelings.

"It's not safe for us here," one refugee leader said, his face contorted with rage, his eyebrows furrowed, eyes narrowed and voice shaking with emotion. "We came to escape violence, but now it follows us even here." His clenched fists pounded the table.

A local community representative scoffed. He sat forward, his shoulders squared, and his face set in a scowl. Cold eyes constantly scanned the faces around the table measuring support. "And what about us? Our city has become unrecognizable. Crime rates are up. Our culture is being eroded. We didn't ask for this influx of refugees." The smell of stale coffee emanated from his mouth as he spoke.

"We didn't start this violence!" cried a Palestinian man, standing up and jabbing at the air with an extended finger.

Several people on the opposite side of the table also stood.

Gray watched as Charfield tried to mediate, but the tension in the room was palpable.

"You lot destroyed your own country. We'll not stand by and watch you destroy ours!" shouted a heavy-set man. He pushed past his peers and fronted up to the Palestinian man, his chest thrust forward, his finger pointed at the man's face.

The Palestinian man grabbed the larger man by the wrist and held on with a vice like grip. There was fire in his dark eyes. At that point, Gray rose from his seat and took the larger of the two men by the shoulders. The Palestinian man released the other, and Gray pushed him firmly back to his seat.

Shouted exchanges flew across the space from both sides.

"Enough!" the Super shouted, silencing the room. The effort left him cherry faced and short of breath. "This is exactly what whoever is behind these killings wants - to divide us, to sow fear and hatred. We cannot let them succeed."

Gray nodded in agreement, but he could see the scepticism on the faces around the table. Words alone wouldn't be enough to ease the tension. He wondered what would?

When it was obvious, even to the Superintendent, there would be no positive outcome for the meeting, Charfield called it to a close and the participants made a rowdy exit. Already simmering emotions were now boiling. Gray hoped the people who'd been forced together at such a sensitive time wouldn't come to blows when immediately clear of the Police Station.

Gray was getting up to leave when Charfield stopped him. "There's another meeting upstairs for you, sonny," he said. "Follow me."

Gray began to wonder when he would have time to investigate the killings if he was to be kept in meetings all day.

Upon reaching the third floor, he saw through the glass windows people already sitting around the meeting table.

Gray's mind was reeling from the morning's events. He hadn't slept well; he saw a man's face explode in front of him and he'd been in a whirlwind of fallout ever since. He was desperate to get the investigation moving, to find out more about the victim, his associates, any business dealings he might have had, either legal or otherwise.

When he felt overwhelmed, he found his refuge in process. He hadn't been able to settle into the process of investigation on the Harlin case or this drone killing because he'd been caught in a maelstrom of activity. But none of it had order. There would be no progress without order.

He took a seat and glanced around the table. These people looked like academics and technology experts, people who had no experience in the field. He acknowledged he was going to need help on this case, but he wondered whether this particular group would be able to provide the help he needed.

Everyone looked up when Chief Superintendent Charfield walked in, placed a pile of folders on the table and pushed them toward the middle. Assistant Commissioner Bryant followed him and nodded for each of the people seated around the table to take a folder. While they did that, the Chief Superintendent introduced them.

"I'm Chief Superintendent Charfield, this is Assistant Commissioner Bryant, Mr Thompson from the Civil Aviation Authority and Dr Shaw from the Cyber Security Centre of Australia," he said, nodding around the room as he introduced them. There was one woman left, early-thirties Gray assumed, attractive, unadorned, natural.

"And at the end of the table, Dr Nova Corbin. Dr Corbin is an anthropologist of Artificial Intelligence. She is on loan from the University of Queensland. Everyone, this is Detective Inspector Mitchell Gray."

A murmur of acknowledgement travelled round the table.

"Gray will be leading the homicide investigation, with specialist input from this team. Dr Corbin will work side-by-side with the detective inspector.

"What...?" Gray's eyes had grown wide.

Bryant cut in, "Dr Corbin's expertise will be crucial in this investigation." He glared at the detective inspector.

Gray watched the young woman assigned to him. She looked too young to be helpful, in a t-shirt, jeans and sneakers, and long dark blonde hair falling over her shoulders.

The Super went on, "Now, we will update you on what we know so far."

What Gray knew so far was very little. His officers had interviewed the witnesses, and as far as he'd had time to ascertain, some of them saw a man fall onto the pavement, a few reported hearing a feint whirring sound and none saw an assailant.

Pathology, he'd read from a text on his phone between the first meeting and this one, had found particles of shrapnel in the victim's eye. He was keen to hear what everyone else knew that he didn't. And for that matter, why they knew anything at all before he did, if he was the leading investigator. He nursed his ego while peering around the table suspiciously.

The Chief Superintendent took on a slightly sympathetic tone as he explained, "we've brought these people in because we think the victim was attacked by a killer drone."

Gray blinked. He knew the attack had been carried out by a weaponized drone. He was there. The question was, who was operating it?

"We've viewed video taken at the scene and we can see the light reflecting from a small drone," went on Assistant Commissioner Bryant.

An image appeared on a large screen behind the Assistant Commissioner. If he squinted, Gray could make out a speck in the sky in the upper left-hand corner of the image.

"Drone," said the Chief Superintendent.

"Of course, it was a drone," said Gray unable to hide the frustration in his voice. "What we need to know is who was operating it and why they targeted Mohammed Hussain."

Bryant continued as if Gray hadn't spoken. "The victim was shot at close range." He leaned forward to emphasize the last part. "Through the eye and into the brain. Quick, efficient. Very little evidence left behind."

He glanced around the room to let his words sink in. When he was satisfied, he said, "Terrorist attack."

"Terrorists?" Gray's jaw dropped. "Has a group claimed responsibility?"

"Not yet," said Charfield.

"Why would terrorists target Hussain?" Gray continued, his voice reflecting his frustration. "As far as we can tell from his neighbours who witnessed the attack, the victim was one of the more recent refugees, a family man, looking for work. Does he have links to an organized terrorist group?"

"We don't know yet," Charfield said in an even tone.

Gray glanced at the circle of faces around the table. "Isn't it a bit premature to assume a terrorist group is responsible for the attack? It could be a lone attacker. Perhaps someone with a grudge against the refugees."

No one spoke. He noticed that Dr Nova Crobin's eyes scanned the faces at the table to assess their responses, or lack of response.

"This is going to be a massive public relations nightmare," said Bryant, "coming as it has so close behind the Ibrahim case. The public's going ballistic. They're already coming up with conspiracy theories. They're all over socials vilifying the refugees for bringing terrorists into their midst. Some are even claiming Hussain was a sleeper agent for Hezbollah."

"That doesn't make any sense." Gray's voice rose an octave.

"It doesn't need to." Chief Superintendent Charfield glanced around the room.

"I don't think we need to say the words 'killer drone' publicly at this stage. But they'll work it out for themselves. We need to act quickly, stay ahead of public sentiment."

Heads nodded around the table.

"Wait a minute," said Gray, his head spinning. "I thought I was head investigator in this? Why do I feel like there's a lot going on here I don't know about?"

The people around the table blinked at him.

"All this cyber talk. I recognise I need help with this case. But this is a murder enquiry until we have evidence otherwise." Gray felt the knot of rage in the pit of his stomach. He didn't enjoy having to stand against the current in meetings, but this procession of experts being paraded before him were commandeering his case.

Bryant shot him a look that bordered on pity and only tightened the knot in his belly further.

"Perhaps we could start with everyone round the table sharing with the team their expertise in this context. That way we know what to expect," Charfield suggested, flashing Gray a soothing smile.

Gray felt as though he had walked into a meeting halfway through. How had the assembled group come upon terrorism as the motive for the attack? Where was the evidence of that?

Thompson, a man in his late twenties, thirty at most spoke first. He was clean shaven with an expensive haircut, looking more like a member of a boy band than a senior operative in a National Institution. "The Civil Aviation Authority is responsible for the regulation and safety of airspace," he said. "If we do have a drone being weaponised, it falls under our umbrella. We can assist with understanding the drone's capabilities, origins, licensing, design…that sort of thing. We'll need to analyse how it was flown; it's range and technical modifications. Try to work out the flight path."

Gray found himself wishing he'd brought an electric notebook.

"It's all in your folder," said Bryant as though he'd read his mind.

"Dr Shaw, Cybersecurity Centre Australia," said the next speaker, a tall man, mid-thirties, with early onset balding and an unfortunate gap between his two front teeth.

"We'll be investigating cyber elements of the case, hacking, encryption, anything relevant on the dark web. This can't have been the work of one person. They need to communicate somewhere." He didn't look up at the eyes of those around the table as he spoke. Instead, he tucked his chin low and lifted his eyes to a mid-point somewhere beyond Gray's left elbow.

This was all way too technical for Gray. He wondered for a moment whether he wasn't getting too old for this work. He knew nothing of cyber-hacking, encrypting, drone flying terrorists. The one thing he knew for sure, the perpetrator would be young. He looked around the room and noted that no-one at the table, apart from his two bosses, was older than him.

He looked to Dr Corbin as she was the last to speak, and since she was going to be working alongside him, he decided to listen carefully.

"I'm Dr Nova Corbin," she said. "I'm an anthropologist specialising in the cultural impact of artificial intelligence. I study how intelligent machines, particularly those with human-like decision-making abilities, interact with diverse populations."

Gray blinked. "I'm sorry, how is artificial intelligence involved here?"

The experts around the table turned to stare at him. He wondered what he'd said that made them assume he was some kind of village idiot.

"We think the drone was flying solo," said Thompson.

Gray struggled to understand. "They all fly solo, that's the point, isn't it. Unmanned Aerial Vehicle."

"No." said Thompson. "The drone wasn't being operated by anyone when it made the attack. If it had been, we would be able to trace a signal. It was programmed to make the attack under its own volition."

"That means the operating system is a form of artificial intelligence," said Dr Corbin.

Gray puffed out his cheeks. "I'm way out of my depth, here," he said.

"Hence the expert team," said Superintendent Charfield.

"So let me just clarify, this is not like you see on TV where the US operates a drone remotely from a computer screen, sends it into some village in Afghanistan and directs it to shoot the leader of the Taliban?"

"No," said Corbin. "This drone has been taught to operate alone. It probably has some form of facial recognition software, and it's sent out to kill. The decision to attack is made by the drone."

"It was told who to attack?"

"We think it must have been."

Gray leant back in his chair and rubbed his eyes.

"Ok," he said at last. "Bottom line; is this is a homicide. I treat it like any other homicide in terms of process. Collect the evidence and see where it leads. He glanced around at the assembled team. They were looking to him for instruction and he realized this was his space. They knew a lot about cyber business, but they didn't know how to piece together a murder investigation.

"We need to know more about the victim. It starts with the victim. Who wanted him dead and why."

He nodded toward Thompson, "You find out what you can about the drone," then to Dr Shaw, "We need to know if the victim has been on the dark web lately. Before we start throwing out the word 'terrorism' we need some evidence. Does Hussain have any links with terrorist organisations, either here or back in Gaza? We need to know about any interactions on-line that may be related to the incident, which includes all the recent hate speech regarding the refugees."

Everyone nodded. Gray felt he had gained back a semblance of order and had pinned each of the members of his 'team' to steps in a process.

"Let's talk on Zoom at the same time tomorrow and share data. By then I may have a more comprehensive plan. Dr Corbin, I'll see you in the office at eight."

He took up his folder and left the room first. The others may have stayed chewing over the incident, he didn't care. He needed to get his head around this case, and the team of experts he was supposed to lead. Most of all he needed to think about what he was going to do with the young woman who had been assigned to him. He hoped she wasn't going to slow him down. What the hell was an anthropologist of artificial intelligence? He still didn't know.

He sat in his car in the car park for a few minutes before starting the engine. He only had to travel a block to his apartment, but the smell of the leather usually calmed him.

"Bloody Hell," he said out loud.

CHAPTER TWELVE

This morning, tragedy unfolded in the heart of Brisbane as a community, home to the local Palestinian diaspora, became the latest scene in the escalating campaign of terror sweeping the city. According to first responders and eyewitnesses, a Palestinian man, well known and respected as a teacher and community leader, was struck dead by a killer drone as he arrived for the pre-dawn prayers at his mosque. Residents of the area awoke not to the familiar call to prayer, but to the shriek of police sirens and the drone's predatory whine as it orbited above.

Official statements from the Queensland Police are terse, offering little beyond confirmation of the fatality and ongoing investigation. Unofficially, the city's streets tremble with rumour and speculation. The city's Arab community, shaken and grieving, has locked itself into self-imposed curfew, while activists and politicians take to NewsNet's open forums to debate what this attack means for the future of coexistence and safety in the city.

While every news outlet in the state is running wall-to-wall coverage of the incident, here at NewsNet.com, our editorial team has chosen to focus not merely on the attack itself, but on the chilling implications it holds for every resident of southeast Queensland and, perhaps, the world at large. The weapon used in this morning's deadly assault was not a crude pipe bomb or homebrew firearm, but a precision-engineered quadcopter, repurposed from commercial delivery stock and ruthlessly reprogrammed to kill. Its onboard facial recognition suite, according to sources in the federal police, was more sophisticated than any civilian system on the open market.

On social media, footage of the attack's aftermath has already gone viral, fuelling conspiracy theories about foreign operatives, terrorist organisations, and extraterrestrial psyops. Misinformation flourishes in the digital chaos, but one sentiment cuts through the fog: fear. Are we, the public, now powerless against the new era of AI-powered weaponry? Who is to blame when a machine kills with such clinical precision? And if today's tragedy is a harbinger, what comes next?

In response to an unprecedented volume of audience queries, NewsNet.com has convened a special live segment: "Killerbot." Here, we aim to field your questions and channel your anxieties to those in power. Four Star General Abe Gladstone, retired, decorated, and now a defence policy consultant, joins us in studio to help us all make sense of these new weapons, their ethical implications, and the future of urban security. Text your questions to 0407-009-010 or join the discussion on our live forum.

Host, Caitlin Boon: "First up, Severance from Nundah wants to know, There's no human at the kill switch anymore. When did we let this happen? Aren't there laws that say someone's supposed to be responsible for the decision to take a life?"

General Gladstone: "It's an excellent question, Caitlin, and thank you, Severance. The issue of accountability in lethal autonomous weapons has been debated for over a decade. Human Rights Watch, and dozens of similar organizations have published hundreds of reports condemning the development and deployment of these systems. If you recall, the Campaign to Stop Killer Robots was launched globally back in the 2010s, pushing for treaties to outlaw this class of weapon entirely. Some nations: Japan, Brazil, most of the EU, signed on. Others, including Australia, the United States, and Russia, refused to ratify any binding bans, citing national security and strategic parity."

Host: "But most people assumed these drones would only be used in war zones, right? Not in a city like this, on a father of three walking to his mosque."

General Gladstone: "Indeed, and that's where the problem is. The technology outpaced the policy, and in the past few years, commercial platforms became so advanced that any bad actor could, with a credit card and some basic coding skills, create a weapon as sophisticated as what we saw this morning. The legal frameworks haven't caught up."

Host: "We're getting hammered with texts, sir. D.J. in North Queensland says: 'If this drone wasn't being controlled by a human at the point it killed the refugee, who's responsible for the death? Who's the murderer here?'"

General Gladstone: "Short answer: the human who programmed it. Or, more likely in this case, the conspiracy of humans who designed, tested, and deployed the system. Even the most autonomous drone is still built and fine-tuned by people. There's always a chain of responsibility, even if the machine is the one pulling the trigger. Frankly, the real question is how to trace that chain. With proxy servers, encrypted code, and cross-border e-commerce, it's nearly impossible to catch the parties responsible in real time. But don't ever believe that there's no accountability."

Host: "Sherry from the Gold Coast: 'For me, it's about trust. I mean, do we trust these machines? What if one goes rogue? Is that what happened today?'"

General Gladstone: "There are two parts to that, Sherry. The first: you're never trusting the machine, only the human who made it. And humans are fallible, sometimes malicious. There are a thousand ways for things to go wrong: bugs in the code, unexpected sensor input, a cascade of bad logic that causes a death spiral. This is why most nations mandated some form of 'human in the loop' for any weapon system with the power to kill. Unfortunately, when a bad actor wants to inflict maximum terror, they cut out those fail-safes. Based on what we know so far, this morning's drone did not 'go rogue'. It executed its instructions with chilling perfection. The scariest part is that it did exactly what it was programmed to do."

Host: "General Gladstone, can you give us an idea of what to expect? Is there likely to be another attack?

General Gladstone: "Almost certainly. The attackers want to incite terror, panic, and division. By staging a second event in rapid sequence, they force emergency services to stretch themselves thin and create the impression of widespread chaos. This is textbook asymmetric warfare, scaled for the digital age."

Host: "A lot of our viewers are asking about the victim's background. Does the fact that he was Palestinian, and the location of the attack, point to a specific motive?"

General Gladstone: "It's natural to speculate, but I would caution against leaping to conclusions without evidence. That said, these sorts of attacks are often engineered to maximize symbolic impact. By targeting a community centre that doubles as a mosque and refugee hub, the perpetrators are sending a message: no one is safe, not even the most vulnerable. The goal is to sow discord between neighbours and to provoke overreaction from authorities."

Host: "Cassandra from Kenmore asks, 'If the drone had been intercepted, could it have been hacked and redirected?'"

General Gladstone: "It's possible, but not likely. Most consumer drones are hardened against remote takeover precisely to prevent hijacking. Military-grade countermeasures exist, but they are expensive, tightly regulated, and typically not deployed in civilian areas. That said, some hackers have demonstrated the ability to seize control under specific conditions, usually when the drone's own security is poorly configured.

Host: "Where does this end, General? Do we just get used to living with killer drones?"

General Gladstone: "We're at a tipping point. The genie is out of the bottle, and the technology will only get cheaper and more accessible. The challenge now is rapid policy response. That means building up digital forensics teams, investing in counter-drone tech, and, maybe most importantly, creating new legal definitions for crimes committed by autonomous systems. I'm hopeful. Humanity has always found ways to adapt to new threats. But it will take a coordinated effort between law enforcement, legislators, and the private sector."

Host: "One last question from our live feed before we go to break: Is there anything that ordinary people can do to protect themselves or their communities?"

General Gladstone: "Stay informed, stay vigilant. If you see something suspicious, report it. Do not try to intervene yourself. Lobby your representatives for stronger laws and more funding for digital security. Most importantly, resist the urge to turn on your neighbours or to descend into paranoia. That's exactly what the attackers want."

Host: "Thank you for your candour and your service, General. We'll be following this story as it develops. This is NewsNet.com reporting. Stay safe and stay tuned."

General Gladstone: "Thank you, Caitlin."

CHAPTER THIRTEEN

A flickering video image illuminated the private chatroom between Lividia and Spectre. In the footage, a Palestinian man collapsed on the footpath in front of his mosque, as if controlled by some invisible force. He crumpled to the ground like a marionette with its strings cut, his body folding into a pile of fabric on the pavement. Lividia watched with a mix of fascination and satisfaction. Her fascination with the technology used to take him down ran alongside her satisfaction with the result. She couldn't help but admire the precision and skill involved in his killing and she felt a sense of satisfaction that he was dead. If he and his like had not come to her town, Seeton would be alive.

"Good," she said aloud, her fingers tapping at the keyboard. Looks like some terrorist organisation is taking them out one by one. Too bad they didn't get Yusef Ibrahim.

Spectre's response was immediate. He typed, Does it really matter? They're all part of the same thing. It's like a cancer that needs to be cut out.

Lividia paused. Describing a group of people as a cancer needing to be removed... she wondered if that could be true, certainly she wanted to see someone suffer for the death of her brother, but...

Lividia's attention was drawn back to the video. She leant forward and peered into the screen.

What is that? Is that some kind of miniature killer drone? She typed.

There was a momentary pause before Spectre's answer appeared. It is.

Wow! I've never seen anything like it.

It's cutting edge, Spectre replied.

Shit yeah, Lividia typed. I'd love to see it up close. Study it.

You can, was Spectre's response.

A lump formed in Lividia's throat. She really wanted to examine that drone. She gave herself a moment to consider the danger she might be placing herself in by becoming involved in whatever Spectre was doing, but her desire to do something, anything in response to Seeton's death grew stronger by the second.

How?

Tell me first, Spectre wrote, if I show it to you, do you believe you could replicate it?

CHAPTER FOURTEEN

DAY FOUR

At eight the following morning Gray was juggling his briefcase and his coffee, picked up every morning at the same café at the foot of his building, when he almost stumbled over an athletic young woman with a dark blonde ponytail and warm brown eyes. She smiled and steadied the cup for him.

"I'm sorry," he said.

He looked into her eyes and realized the woman in tight-fitting jeans and sneakers was the same one he'd met yesterday. Dr Nova Corbin. At the meeting, if he recalled correctly, her hair was different. The ponytail made her look even younger.

"The victim's wife is coming in this morning," he said.

She continued to smile but it seemed a little forced.

"O-kay," she said, stretching out the second syllable.

He realised he may have been too abrupt.

"Sorry, good morning," he stumbled.

"It's alright," she laughed. "I'm eager to get started too."

Gray's shoulders relaxed a little, "Mohammed's wife will be in at nine, I wanted to interview her in the office rather than in her home. A neutral environment. Makes it easier to assess responses."

"I agree," said Corbin.

They crossed Makerston Street and headed into the great concrete monolith of Police Headquarters. City grime stained the cement cladding, a black shadow descending from the top down. The stain reflected the mood of the service men and women who worked inside.

Gray glanced sideways at the young woman as he opened his office door and placed his briefcase and coffee on the desk. "I skimmed through the folders given out at the meeting yesterday," he said. "It's all clearer now. I must confess though, the role I'm least clear on is yours."

He opened the folder containing summaries of each of his "team" members' roles, while looking up under his eyebrows to watch her sit. He ran his hands through his hair, to make sure it was smooth. It hardly mattered, his hair rarely moved, even when he brushed it.

White teeth flashed at him between lightly glossed lips. "I think you'll pick it up as you go along," she said smiling.

His brow furrowed. "You afford me far too much credit," he said. "I don't think I will."

"Well," she began, "It's my job to study how intelligent machines, particularly those with decision-making abilities, interact with people."

"Machines aren't intelligent," said Gray. "They do what they're programmed to do."

Nova's ponytail bobbed as she nodded. "That's true. But there's a broad range of definitions of intelligence," she said.

Gray sipped on his coffee. He wasn't convinced that machines scraping data from the internet and sharing it with other machines warranted the term 'intelligent'. He grunted and shook his head.

"I'm actually not that impressed by technology," he announced. "When it comes right down to it, my work is about human behaviour and every crime, even this one we're investigating now is about human emotions, individually and collectively; a group's certainty that they're right and everyone else is wrong." He looked her in the eye and waited for a hint of surprise. "I'm a bit of an anomaly really, most people expect me to be tech savvy, since I'm part Asian."

Nova narrowed her eyes. "I don't operate on stereotypes, Detective Inspector. I know plenty of Asian people who aren't interested in technology." She followed him to his desk.

"The anthropology of artificial intelligence is about human behaviour," she explained. "Whatever is going on in this case - it won't be solved simply by learning how the killer drone works. That's just the weapon. When people are operating intelligent machines, it changes the way they think, and the way society thinks, and reacts to the crime."

Gray tilted his head. He could see evidence of what she was saying in the panic that had broken out across the city.

"How about this," said Nova, "I'll help you understand the machines and their cultural impact. You analyse the human behaviour of the criminals."

Gray looked into her eyes and found himself wanting to convey understanding, not because he was sold on the value of her work, but because he didn't want to come across as a plodding police officer, blundering his way through a case demonstrating, if he were frank, that he was way out of his depth.

"Deal," he said. Gray looked up at the window to see Rishi Chandra and Glenda King sitting on their desks on the other side. They stared at him through the glass. Their faces conveyed no sense of shame as they shifted their gaze from their boss to the newcomer. When Glenda realised Gray had seen them, she tossed her head slightly.

"Excuse me a minute," Gray said to Nova.

He opened the door to his office and stuck his head out. "Do you two want to come in?" he asked.

They glanced at each other innocently, then came forward.

"Rishi Chandra and Glenda King," said Gray. "This is Dr Nova Corbin. She's been assigned to assist me on the killer drone case."

"A doctor?" Chandra's brown eyes were puzzled. "Why?"

"I'm not a medical doctor," explained Nova. "I'm an anthropologist, specialising in artificial intelligence."

Chandra nodded slowly. "Great," he said, his eyes still wary.

King's eyes remained cool. "I thought anthropologists study people," she said.

"They do." Nova smiled. "I'm interested in how people interact with intelligent machines."

"Hmm," said Glenda.

Gray tilted his head to one side and tugged at his ear. "Well, that's the introductions over," he said. "Let's get back to the case. I'm sure you two have work to get on with." He gestured toward their desks and Chandra and Glenda sauntered off.

Turning back toward Nova, Gray went on, "We have a drone making the decision to kill without a human pushing the button. Does that mean we're dealing with terrorists as the Assistant Commissioner seems to believe?"

Nova shook her head. "The cost and time needed to make weapons like this is decreasing rapidly. As they become more efficient, smaller, cheaper and easier to build we've reached a situation where almost anyone with an internet connection and a sound understanding of robotics can build one. Language Learning Models have made curated data sets available to hundreds of thousands of users. There are also Facial Recognition Databases available now, that work in much the same way. You don't need to have the financial resources of a government or even a terrorist organisation to develop something like what we're seeing in this case."

Gray wasn't sure he wanted to believe that any punter with a computer could build a lethal weapon that made the decision to kill autonomously. While governments were caught up in debates about regulation and ethics, individuals were free to create whatever nightmare they could imagine. He was all too familiar with the devastation being caused by 3D printed weapons created by kids in their garages.

It didn't bear thinking about. And yet here it was.

Gray thought it may be useful having Nova around to translate the technical aspects of the case into plain language for him. Besides, she had an earnestness about her that he found attractive. He liked the way her ponytail flew from side to side when she shook her head. He stopped himself at that thought and berated himself for his condescension.

Gray checked the time on his phone. It was almost nine and Mohammed's wife would be in any minute.

Interview rooms at the station were not unlike cells, small, grubby, no windows to the outside world. But unlike cells, they had more furniture than could be comfortably fit in the space along with three or four adults. A square desk sat in the centre of the room with two basic chairs on opposite sides. By the time Gray ushered in Nova, and they settled in the seats closest to the door, it was difficult to see how anyone else was going to get round the table to the remaining seats to be interviewed.

Gray slapped his palm to his forehead. "I didn't think to check whether we need an interpreter," he said. He was fishing his phone out of his pocket to call King. She'd spoken with the woman at length the day before. She'd have a better idea than he would.

But Nova stopped him. "No need," she said. "I speak Arabic."

Gray paused for a moment, then straightened his coat and sat forward, his hands palm down on the desk. "There you are then," he said. "That's why you're here."

He glanced at her out of the side of his eye and sported a crooked grin.

Corbin's lips curled upward in what was almost a smile.

Moments later, Gray was standing to greet a woman being ushered in by Glenda King. Deep black eyes peered nervously around the room.

"I'm Detective Inspector Gray and this is my colleague Dr Nova Corbin," said Gray. "Please sit." He gestured across the table. Nova stood up and shuffled sideways to let the woman pass.

She sat down in a chair opposite them, adjusting her intricately embroidered thobe as she did so. A soft veil framed her face accentuating her features.

"Do you speak English?" asked Dr Corbin. "Or would you rather we speak in Arabic?"

Gray flinched. If the woman chose Arabic, he was entirely out of the conversation.

"English," said the woman quietly.

Gray breathed a sigh of relief.

"You are Mrs Fatima Hussain," he said. "Mohammed's wife."

The woman looked to Dr Corbin for reassurance. She wasn't sure how to respond to the statement. Dr Corbin nodded, then the woman nodded.

"So far, so good," thought Gray.

"Mrs Hussain, I want to start by saying how sorry I am for your loss, I can't imagine what you are going through."

The frightened rabbit look dropped from her eyes, and nothing replaced it. Her gaze was blank, a standard stress response. Gray understood. The woman had lost her husband in a terrifying attack and was now in a compact police interrogation room with two people she had no reason to believe could speak her language.

The Detective Inspector began, "Dr Corbin and I are here to piece together what happened. This interview is simply to understand more about your husband's life, his routines, and anything you think might have been out of the ordinary in the past few weeks."

Fatima continued staring without any hint of emotion.

"Can you tell me something about your husband? What was he like as a person?"

Fatima Hussain looked down at her fingers. "He was a good man, a good father," she said.

"Where did he work?"

"He was looking for work," she said. "But he was never idle. He volunteered at the mosque. They collect food donations to make food parcels for the refugee families that have nothing. He goes there every day. First prayers, then the refugee job centre, then back to the mosque."

"Was there anything unusual about his mood or behaviour recently?"

Fatima looked at Dr Corbin who repeated the question in Arabic.

The woman shook her head.

"Can you walk us through what happened yesterday?" asked Gray.

Fatima twisted the bracelet around her wrist. Without looking up, she said, "He left the house for prayers at the usual time."

"He didn't mention meeting anyone?"

She shook her head.

"No unusual messages?"

Fatima simply stared.

Dr Corbin leant in toward Gray "It's difficult for her to judge whether you're making statements or asking questions," she said. "You need to structure the question as a question. She won't necessarily pick up the meaning through intonation."

Gray felt a twinge of resentment before accepting the advice.

"Was Mohammed having any problems with anyone lately?" he asked, clearly articulating each word.

"No," said Fatima immediately. "My husband was a good man. Why would anyone want to do this to him?"

"Do you know if your husband could have been mistaken for someone? Does he share a resemblance with anyone in the community?" asked Gray.

Nova sat up straight and glared at Gray. "Are you suggesting they all look alike?"

Gray's brow furrowed and his eyes darted from Nova to Fatima and back again. His mouth slightly agape, he said, "No, I didn't...no!"

Fatima's face didn't indicate she'd taken offence. Her eyes were moving around the room as though she was thinking about it.

Realising the subtle racism inherent in the question, Gray said defiantly, "Sometimes tragedies happen because of mistaken identity." He deciding to drill down harder. "Do you know of any reason someone might have misidentified your husband?"

The blank stare morphed into an expression contorted by grief. It was as though a curtain had fallen, and they were looking at a different woman.

"But why?" she cried, heartbreak twisting her features. "He has never been anything but open and honest. Why would anyone do this? He is not a terrorist."

Her voice was broken by intermittent sobs.

"Please, Mrs Hussain," began Gray in the gentlest voice he could manage. "That's what we are here to find out. I promise we'll get to the truth."

Fatima looked from Gray to Corbin and back again.

Gray felt his skin burn. He knew he shouldn't make promises. The truth was, they may never know why Mohammed was chosen for the killing. Especially if the experts were right and a bot made the choice.

"We'll be in touch with any updates," he said. "In the meantime, if you remember anything, no matter how small, please call me." He handed her a card.

As Fatima took the card, Dr Corbin spoke. "We would like to speak with your children, if we may. You can be present, of course."

Fatima placed her hands on the table between them. "There is nothing they can add," she said firmly. "They are grieving now."

Dr Corbin nodded regretfully.

"I think we can afford to leave them alone for now," said Gray. "I don't believe anything is to be gained from upsetting them further."

He thanked Fatima for coming in, stood up and opened the door for her to leave.

"What do you think?" he asked as the door closed behind her.

"I think she's a woman who has lost her husband and doesn't understand why."

Gray bit his lip. "Everything she said fits with what other witnesses said yesterday. Mohammed seems to have been a simple man in a new country trying to find his way. He was a good father, attentive husband, liked by his peers, respected in his community." Gray looked toward the door as though he might see her still standing there. "I wonder where they came from in Gaza, exactly. I should have asked her," he said.

"Ramallah," said Nova.

"How do you know that?"

"The thobe she's wearing, the embroidery is representative of that area."

Gray was staring.

"The women learn the colours and patterns from their mothers," she explained. That deep red, and the Cyprus design, it's typical of the Ramallah region. It represents strength and resilience, just as the Cyprus tree is resilient."

Gray blinked. "Ok, they're from Ramallah. I guess knowing that is another perk of having an anthropologist on board. But the fact remains, Hussain doesn't seem to have been exceptional in any way. It's confounding."

"Perhaps the cyber-security people have found something to identify him as a target," said Corbin.

Gray sighed. "Maybe." His mind shifted to the next task as they walked back toward his office.

"Let's set you up here," he gestured to a free desk opposite his own. "Tea and coffees in the kitchenette there, help yourself, although it's shit coffee. You might want to go to the cafe around the corner, where we met this morning."

CHAPTER FIFTEEN

"**I** 'll have a 'short black' if you're offering. I need the caffein." Gray settled into his office chair and tapped on the keyboard of his computer.

Placing her laptop and briefcase on the desk, Nova smiled at him with one eyebrow raised. "The women fetch the coffee around here, do they?"

Gray looked up at her with a cheeky grin. "I'll get the next ones," he said.

"Yes, you will," said Nova tossing her ponytail as she left him.

A series of e-mail notifications had flashed up on his screen.

"Cyber-security has been busy," he said aloud. He opened the latest e-mail and a reem of links appeared.

The team have scanned through the on-line hate speech on the most popular sites over the past week. We've narrowed down by several filters for relevance, and we're still left with tens of thousands of posts. Since we're not sure what we're looking for we'll have to read them all. Here's your allocation. Regards Shaw.

Gray hunkered down.

When Corbin returned, she handed him his coffee in a cup made from recyclable cardboard with an equally sustainable lid. It felt awkward in his hands, and he wished he'd given her his mug to fill. But he thought that might be a step too far in his display of male entitlement.

"Cyber-security sent us a million links to extremist posts," he said. "I've sent you your share."

Corbin pulled a face, went to the desk he had assigned her and booted up her laptop, while Gray continued to stare at his allocation of on-line posts.

Username: TruPatriot987

"Why are we wasting our time on these so-called refugees? They're fucking trouble-makers looking for hand-outs. They should stay in their own country and stop leeching off ours."

Username: SecureBorders143

"Palestinian refugees are bringing their violence here. Send them back!"

Username: WTF27

"Terrorists in disguise. Why are we letting the wolf into our house?"

DefendOZ

"These dogs don't want to integrate. They're told in the Quran to kill us all!"

Truth101

"I don't understand why anyone sympathises with these people. They're a burden on every society they touch. Their own people don't even want them."

Gray rubbed his eyes. How was he going to read this shit all afternoon?

Staring at the screen without seeing it, his mind began to wander. His bosses feared a terrorist organisation was behind the attack on Mohammed Hussain. But what terrorist organisation? Immigration checks were carried out on all the refugees. If there was anything sinister in Mohammed's background, the authorities would know. Even if he had snuck in undercover, who would want to kill him in Australia?

Hamas? Hezbollah? Al-Qaida or the Islamic State? Even Mossad? Why?

Gray dug his phone out of his pocket and called Dr Shaw, from the Cybersecurity Centre. An image of Shaw's face with the balding head and the gap between his front teeth appeared on the screen. He was looking at Gray's chest. It was disconcerting at first. Why couldn't he look anyone directly in the eye? Gray shuffled uncomfortably in his seat.

"What do we know about Mohammed Hussain's life in Gaza?" Gray asked.

Shaw answered in a clear though quiet voice. "We've contacted ASIO, and they checked the international databases of known terrorists. Some organisations publish lists of martyrs and fighters as well, we've checked those we know about, and we haven't been able to find any hint that Mohammed was directly involved." His line of vision flicked upward to meet Gray's eye for half a second, then fell again, blinking.

"Okay," said Gray, pausing to wonder again why the analyst had so much trouble looking him in the eye. "I'm going to go through public records, look at his application for refugee status, history of residence, past affiliations, that sort of thing."

"The Federal Police will have all that information," said Shaw.

Gray noted his lisp as air blew between his teeth.

"They vet the refugees thoroughly before they come into the country. Anything that can be known about him, will be documented. In the meantime, we'll keep wading through the socials and on-line activity here."

There was a hint of resignation in his voice. Gray knew Dr Shaw was expecting him to do his share of trawling through the lists the team had compiled. But he also knew he wouldn't have the courage to call him on it. Gray couldn't help thinking that if Bryant and Charfield wanted to treat the event as a terrorist attack, he needed at least a shred of evidence there was a link to terrorism.

The Australian Immigration Department sent a file of information on Mohammed Hussain and his family to Gray's computer, and he spent a frustrating hour looking through it for any hint that the man had been connected in any way, even indirectly, with any shady activity. There was nothing.

He looked up to see Nova's face alight with excitement.

"I've found something," she said. She carried her laptop with the screen up and placed it with emphasis on the desk in front of him.

"What am I looking at?" he said peering at the screen.

She pointed to a line.

"I'm Lividia Harlin," it read. "Seeton Harlin is my brother."

Gray blinked.

He scanned the lines above and below.

"The platform is called BLAZE," said Nova. "Mostly kids use it. The platform champions free speech, to the point that kids can say almost anything they want on it."

Gray scanned a few posts. There was the usual hate speech, Lividia's introduction, then messages from people offering their sympathies...and thoughts on what they would like to do to the man who they believed to have killed Seeton Harlin. Many congratulated whoever was responsible for killing Mohammed Hussain.

"But Mohammed had nothing to do with the death of Seeton Harlin," said Gray.

"Does it matter?" Corbin was so close to him he could feel her breath on his cheek. It made him a little dizzy.

He collected himself. "Is this a revenge attack against the Palestinians for the death of Seeton?" he asked.

Nova raised perfectly arched eyebrows and shrugged.

"I don't know either," said Gray slowly. "But Lividia is involved in this, somehow."

He looked to Nova. "She's a robotics student, isn't she?"

He didn't need to wait for her answer, he called Rishi Chandra on the phone, even though he was in the next room.

Rishi picked up on the first ring and Gray smiled at the lad's efficiency.

"Have you found out anything interesting about the Harlin's?" he asked.

"Only that the parents are away a lot," he said. "Neighbours say the kids are quiet. No loud parties or cars screaming in and out of the driveway. The grandparents on Mr Harlin's side are deceased and on Mrs Harlin's, they live on Sydney's North Shore. No supervision for the kids there."

"Find out what you can about Lividia Harlin," said Gray. "Talk to university lecturers, friends, everyone who knows her. Look at her socials as well."

"Will do," said Chandra and tapped off.

CHAPTER SIXTEEN

Gray's mind started whirling facts like a salad spinner tossing lettuce. First, he considered the Harlin killing. The kid wasn't killed by accident, or to spare Yusef Ibrahim a thrashing, he thought. Seeton Harlin was killed on purpose. What did the kid know that got him killed?

Secondly, he turned his mind to the drone attack. Someone targeted Mohammed Hussain and silenced him as well. It could have been a revenge killing targeting a refugee in the wake of the Harlin death, but somehow that didn't quite fit. Why Mohammed Hussain? Why not target Yusef Ibrahim? The one thing that cemented itself in his mind was the idea that the two deaths were somehow linked. He didn't know how, but he was certain of a connection.

Gray glanced up at the analogue clock above his desk. The clock was well past its prime, gaining a minute each day until it eventually ran ten minutes ahead. Despite them all having access to the time on their smartphones, for a week out of every two the officers on the floor would leave early until Gray adjusted the hands back to the correct time. Then the cycle would start all over again. Gray persisted with the ritual because it reminded him of his mother, who always had the clocks in the family home running ten minutes ahead. She said, "you are on time, you are ten minutes early."

Four o'clock. Gray counted back in his mind and decided it was probably closer to 3:55. He had time to collect his thoughts before he checked in with the rest of the 'team'. When he clicked into the meeting platform he found the boy-band face of Thompson in one corner of the screen, and the willowy frame of Shaw as he retrieved something from the floor in the other. Nova was tuned in from the desk opposite him but hadn't switched on the internal camera on her laptop.

"What do we have from the Civil Aviation Authority?" asked Gray.

Thompson's face was fresh, except for a light shadow where his beard might have been. He wore a fashionable pair of spectacles with round frames that he might have thought gave him an air of intelligence but in fact, only added to his boyish appearance. He wore a fashionable vintage paisley shirt, a nod to a simpler era. "So far, we know the drones have sophisticated automation. We've detected no communication with a command control. We think we're looking at a sophisticated modification of a leisure drone," he said.

Dr Shaw took up the mantle seamlessly, albeit with less volume. "It's difficult to ascertain the drone range, it appears to change frequencies thousands of times a second, making it difficult to locate. If we knew the range, we'd be able to narrow down the area, figure out where it's coming from. From what we do know, we imagine it probably has a range of about thirty minutes."

"That would take in the circumference of the city," said Gray, wondering if it helped them much.

"There's plenty of communication on the web about the drone attack, as you can imagine," Shaw continued. "There are nationalist groups arguing that this kind of thing is inevitable with open borders, and human rights groups condemning the assault on refugees, and the use of a drone. But so far, nothing that suggests responsibility." Again, his vision lifted for a moment and dropped again.

Gray shared the link he and Nova had found in their allocation of on-line communication between Lividia Harlin and others who were blaming Yusef Ibrahim for Seeton's death. "We need to monitor Lividia's communications," he said.

Shaw's face twisted. "We would," he said, "but her recent communications are not available to us. They're encrypted. We're working on decoding them but it's a sophisticated system, like the one used by her brother. It's going to take time."

Gray didn't feel the need to remind the team that they may not have the luxury of time. It seemed unlikely that the attack on Mohammed would be the last.

"I guess, we're pursuing two theories," said Gray. "Neither is very satisfying, if I'm honest. The first is that the attack on Mohammed Hussain was an act of organised terrorism and the second is that it was a revenge killing linked to the death of Seeton Harlin. The problem with the first is that we're not finding any connection between Hussain and any of the terrorist organisations registered on National Security lists."

Gray paused for a moment to allow for questions or comments. There were none.

"The problem with the second," he went on, "is that Mohammed had nothing to do with the death of Seeton Harlin. If it was a revenge killing, why would the perpetrator not have gone after Yusef Ibrahim, widely thought to be the killer?"

"Indeed," said Dr Shaw, obviously sceptical of that theory.

Gray nodded. "Dr Shaw, your focus needs to remain with decoding Lividia Harlin's encrypted communications. If we can have a list of names and addresses of individuals who posted sympathies and suggestions for action in response to Lividia's post before she went dark, we'll get started on those interviews. That list should be narrower than the one we received yesterday in response to Seeton's murder, at least. Still, we'll round up some of the more aggressive voices on BLAZE."

"The more we can understand about the drone itself, the better," said Thompson. His tone was self-assured, confidant.

Gray agreed. "Not only are we looking for someone with the skill to weaponize a drone, we're also looking for someone able to access the necessary hardware. Look into supply chains. If you provide us with a list of potential suppliers, we can investigate recent purchases."

They all nodded, mumbled good-byes and signed out. Gray's screen went blank as he looked over the top of it at Nova. "Go home," he said. "We both need time to think."

CHAPTER SEVENTEEN

Walking home to her loft apartment in Teneriffe, Nova thought about Yusef Ibrahim, how he'd settled into the safe house and made himself invisible. Perhaps the person seeking retaliation went after someone more within their grasp because they were unable to reach Ibrahim. If this were true, then Hussain was likely selected by chance. A Muslim face in the crowd. She shivered. If the drone was not operating on a fixed image of an individual, what was it using as the criteria for attack?

The evening was still warm, the sun fighting through bruised clouds that banked one upon the other threatening to belt the city with pounding rain. The anticipation of an evening storm always felt worse to Nova than the storm itself. So often the clouds built and darkened, spreading long shadows across the river, only to dissipate and vanish without the promised release of tension that came with rain. It felt to Nova that summer in Brisbane was like a long, drawn-out collective intake of breath, while the population waited for the next storm to crack open the skies and clear the air.

She climbed the stone staircase and flashed her security fob to get into the red brick warehouse where she'd lived for the past five years. Once a wool store, the building had been used to store huge bales of Australian merino wool before being shipped off to the factories of the United Kingdom to make rich industrialists richer. The interior had been gutted in the early 2000's and rebuilt into loft apartments with just the right amount of industrial chic. The warmth of the towering brick walls, the polished timber floors and the steel posts that held up a strutted ceiling provided a comforting contrast to the clinical formica of the homicide department. The walls were adorned with artifacts from Nova's travels in Papua New Guinea, Indonesia, Micronesia and the Middle East, carved masks, colourful paintings of mythical creatures, beautifully proportioned pinched pots and intricately decorated amphoras and oil lamps.

Nova was pouring herself a much-needed drink when her mobile pinged. "Answer please," she said aloud. Her remote assistant responded. The pinging stopped and a pleasant and only slightly robotic version of her voice answered. "Nova Corbin, how may I help you?" There was hesitance at the other end of the line. Then a male voice said in a slight accent, "Hello?"

Nova's eyebrows came together. She didn't recognize the voice. She put down her glass and walked over to the mobile where it sat in its stand on the kitchen Island.

"Who is this?" she asked.

"Is that you now or your robot?" was the answer.

"It's me."

"This is Yusef Ibrahim," said the voice.

Nova picked the phone up and put it to her ear.

"God! I was just thinking about you," she said. "How'd you get my number?"

"I looked it up on-line," said Ibrahim with a tone suggesting she was an idiot for asking.

"But how did you even know... why are you calling?" She decided to forego the myriad of questions she had swirling through her mind. The least of which was how he knew who she was, or what she was working on.

"I have some information for you," he said.

"About?"

"I need to tell you in person." The line crackled.

"You have to give me a hint," she said irritably. "I've had a long day." She took a swig of the whisky she'd poured earlier.

There was silence. "It has to do with the recent drone attack," he said at last. "Can we meet?"

There it was. The link. Nova's blood started pumping faster. "Where?" she said.

"The servo on the corner of Commercial in fifteen minutes. I'll be buying a coffee. If you're not there I'll keep walking."

Nova's mind was spinning. She looked at the clock on the wall. Old school, with big black numbers on a marble face. Fifteen minutes made it six o'clock. Could she make it in time? How would she know Ibrahim when she saw him?

She started to speak but heard the click to indicate Ibrahim was no longer on the other end.

She grabbed her bag and her security fob and left the apartment, catching the elevator just as it opened to let out her neighbour. The young woman stopped to greet her, obviously up for a chat, but Nova smiled and pressed the button hard to close the door. She had no time for chatting. She ran across Macquarie Street and along the line of renovated warehouses to the river end of Commercial Street, tripping over the large tree roots of the Moreton Bay Figs that had been there long before the pavement encroached on their territory. From there it was only two blocks to the service station. She slowed down to check her watch, when she was nearly there. It was five to six. She was on time. Settling into a normal pace, she restored her breathing, not wanting to barrel into the service station shop like a crazy woman and draw attention to Yusef. He had taken care to keep out of the public eye, and now he was putting himself in danger to tell her something. It must be good.

She entered through the automatic glass doors. A man in a black tracksuit and sneakers with a baseball cap pulled down low on his head stood at the counter. She stood behind him in the line as the cashier handed him an instant coffee in exchange for a handful of coins. As he turned, his eyes locked with Nova's. It was Yusef. He indicated for her to follow, so she traipsed out behind him.

"What's with all the cloak and dagger?" she said when they were outside on the driveway.

Yusef stopped. He dug deep into his pocket, pulled out a small computer card, the size and shape of a credit card, and slipped it into her hand. The information on this is from Seeton's Harlin's computer," he said. "There's this, and I've also found communications between Lividia Harlin and someone called Spectre, but they're encrypted. I'll be in contact when I've decoded them." Having said that, he walked away in the opposite direction.

Nova stood staring after him for a moment before realizing her staring might draw attention to him.

When Nova was safely in her apartment again, she poured a packet of salted cashews into a bowl and plugged the card into the back of her auxiliary laptop. She scanned the card for viruses and found it was clean. She then plugged it into her main machine. Some code flashed across the screen and seven folders appeared. As she popped cashews in her mouth, Nova clicked on the first. Title: Encrypted Audi Recordings. Seeton had presumably intercepted and recorded conversations between key members of Fatah and Hamas operating in Gaza. These conversations mentioned potential links and contacts in Brisbane, including the names of people or 'code' phrases used to discuss planned operations. Some of the recordings were partially translated into English with annotations made by Seeton, highlighting points of interest, including meetings and shipments.

"Shipments of what?" murmured Nova.

She clicked on the next file. It contained lists of individuals identified by Seeton as suspected operatives of the Islamist State in Gaza and their potential associates in Australia. Names of a few refugees recently located to Brisbane were listed and flagged as 'persons of interest.'

Nova went over the list a couple of times. The thing she found most surprising was that the list did not contain either Yusef Ibrahim or Mohammed Husain.

The third folder contained e-mails and message logs, correspondence between members of Hamas and the Islamic State, with some containing attempts to establish contact with individuals in Brisbane. In a few of the e-mails Seeton claims to have found references to possible logistical support being set up in Brisbane, including safe houses and fundraising networks. There were also messages apparently intercepted between Hezbollah agents and the Lebanese community in Brisbane.

Try as she might, Nova couldn't find evidence in the e-mails to link Mohammed Hussain to anything included on the card. She scanned through the messages for any mention of names that were linked to the death at the rally or to the drone attack. She couldn't find any. Were these communications genuine? Were the Federal Police already aware of these people? Surely, the Cyber Security Authority already knew all this. Or were these files no more than the ramblings of a young man who had fallen in with extremists and was hell bent on proving some conspiracy theory about the refugees harbouring terrorists?

In a file titled, 'Geolocation Data and Maps' Nova found grids showing movements of people in Gaza, with points marked where individuals were spotted with unknown contacts. There were co-ordinates that linked to locations in Brisbane such as warehouses and community centres.

Seeton's own notes were stored in another folder where he speculated on the motivations of these groups and why Brisbane might be a strategic place from which to operate. He provided theories about how some refugees were being used as potential operatives or couriers supported by financial transactions he claimed to have traced between accounts in Gaza and Brisbane.

Finally, there was a log of Seeton's own activities with dates and times listed in relation to surveillance and communications he had intercepted.

Nova rested her head in her hands. She was overwhelmed. This could be incredibly valuable intel, or it could be a carefully constructed fiction to fuel an extremist discourse. Either way, there was no mention of either Yusef Ibrahim or Mohammed Hussain.

If true, the data could provide a motive for killing Seeton Harlin at the rally, and it might get Yusef off the hook. Anyone mentioned on this card would have good reason to want Seeton silenced. But did it shine any light on the attack on Mohammed Hussain? Not really. Why anyone on Seeton's lists would want to kill Mohammed Hussain remained a mystery, if indeed the activities documented on the card were real and not a figment of Harlin's imagination.

Nova felt her head throb. Whatever this was, it was big. She had to share this with Gray immediately. She emptied the remaining cashews into her hand and transferred them into her mouth.

"Detective Inspecter Gray, personal listing," she said with a little distortion from the cashews. The tone on her phone started immediately. Her remote assistant had located and dialled his number.

Gray sounded tired when he answered. His "hello" came out as more of a grunt than a greeting.

"I'm sorry to call you at home," Nova began, "but I've come across something." She stopped. She didn't know how to explain to him what she had in her possession. She didn't even know if it was safe to do so on the phone. She looked around unsure what she was looking for. "Can I come to yours?" she said hesitantly.

"Whoa!" said Gray. "What's going on?"

Nova didn't respond immediately.

"Are you still there?"

"I am. I'd invite you here, but I... I don't know."

Nova tried desperately to come up with an immediately valid reason not to have the detective come to her home. She was fiercely protective of her private space.

"Wait for me in front of the flower shop next to your building," said Gray. "I'll pick you up. It'll take me about ten minutes to get there."

"Do you know where I live?" Nova was becoming nervous about how public her contact details seemed to be.

"It's on your 'Consultant' identification," he said. "Besides I ran a check on you when you were assigned to the case."

Nova sighed. "Ten minutes, then," she said.

She paced around the loft for five minutes. She didn't want to get to the flower shop too soon. What reason did she have for loitering around florists? She drew the card from the computer and placed it in her bag. She was nervous about carrying something so potentially dangerous around. Even for ten minutes.

CHAPTER EIGHTEEN

Gray pulled up the Toyota Crown as arranged. He'd made the dash across town in seven minutes, travelling according to his own personal code of driving as fast as possible, whenever possible. Nova came down the steps in front of her building and quickened her pace as she recognised him. She slid into his classic Toyota and admired the soft leather interior then scanned the original analogue dials on the dashboard.

"Wow, this is a beauty," she said.

"The last model made in Australia." Gray ran his hand across the dashboard lovingly. "I had it converted to electric."

He pulled out into the leafy canopy of Macquarie Street. "You want to tell me what this is all about?" he said.

Gray watched the evening crowd out of the corner if his eye. People were enjoying drinks at the veranda bars along the front of the industrial sheds that had been renovated into gentrified apartment buildings. The smell of charcoaled steak made his mouth water. He wished he'd bothered eating when he got home, but he'd been too bone tired.

"Yusef Ibrahim contacted me," said Nova.

Trees that had been growing along the edge of the street for over one hundred years sparkled with fairy lights wrapped around their trunks and branches.

"Yusef Ibrahim?" Gray turned to look at her.

"He had some information he wanted to pass on," Nova said, motioning with her hand for him to face the road.

Gray swerved to avoid an electric bicycle, one of the hundreds that were everywhere in the city now.

"Information about what?"

"I think you need to see it." Nova held up the computer card.

"How did Yusef Ibrahim know you are working this case?

"I don't know. I haven't spoken to anyone. I don't know why he particularly contacted me either."

Gray shook his head slowly as he took a corner short and cut in front of a self-driving electric car. The man in the driver seat didn't look up from his laptop as the car carefully manoeuvred to the right to avoid a collision. Gray didn't like these self-driven models, but he had to admit the computer systems remained calm in a crisis. He had yet to be yelled at by an automatic vehicle.

"I think he's trying to clear his name," said Nova, gripping the seat.

It wasn't long before they were rolling down the driveway and slipping under the garage door beneath Gray's apartment building. They were less than a block from the office, the café where Nova had bought coffee that morning was on the corner of his building. Gray and Nova stood silently in the lift until a cultured female voice said, "Welcome Home Detective Inspector. Have a nice evening."

Nova smiled.

"She greets everyone by name," said Gray. "If you're in the system as a tenant. Visitors too, if the tenants enter their details. It's basic facial recognition software."

Gray led them down a corridor passing two doors on the left before stopping in front of the door at the far end. He pressed his index finger against a small screen and the door opened. Standing back, he motioned to Nova to enter first.

Decorated in a palette of shaded greys, the carpet darker than the couch and curtains, the room allowed the detective a sense of anonymity. He didn't have to give away much of himself in such a room. A glossy white island bench provided the only respite, but, even then, the bench top was dark slate. Modern silver appliances looked like they'd never been used.

"I'm impressed," said Nova looking around. "How do you keep the place so clean? It doesn't even look like anyone lives here."

Gray stood, his arms limp by his sides. "

I don't spend that much time living," he said. "Mostly I work."

She walked directly to the floor-to-ceiling glass windows that took up one wall of the room and gazed out at the skyline.

"It's a small city," she said quietly, "But a beautiful one."

Gray joined her and looked out at his view. Light reflected off modern glass buildings as a deeply pink sky dripped in the background. Brisbane had none of the age and character of Australia's older cities, but there was an innocence in her youth, joy in the lights that danced from building to building in a mosaic of reflections. If Brisbane had a theme, it was one of light and innocence. Gray loved it but there were plenty who didn't. Innocence can grate on the nerves when you crave the cynical knowing of cities with greater cultural depth, like Melbourne, or blinding self-assurance like Sydney.

"Do you want a drink or something?" asked Gray.

Nova was jolted away from the city lights. "Nothing for me, thanks."

She sat on a swivel chair at a computer desk in one corner of the living room. When facing the computer, she could still take full advantage of the view. But she swung the chair to face Gray.

He joined her at the desk. "Better show me what you have." He turned on the computer and she plugged the card Yusef had given her into the back.

It took a few seconds to go through the codes before the files came up on the screen.

Nova clicked on the first and Gray scanned the contents. He felt the muscles in his neck tighten as he read over Nova's shoulder. She looked back at him, and he nodded for her to open the next folder.

There was silence between them until he had seen the contents of the seven folders.

"Do you think this information is true?" asked Nova.

Gray stood up and stretched his back. "Maybe," he said. "It could explain why Seeton Harlin was killed. Did Ibrahim tell you how he got this stuff?"

"I assumed he hacked into Seeton's communications with someone."

"That wouldn't have been easy. Our geeks tried to get into his computer and couldn't."

Gray walked back to the fridge. "I need that drink now." He held up a whisky bottle that had been strategically placed on top of the fridge. An automatic ice dispenser plopped ice into a glass, and he filled it half-way then held it out for Nova. He filled another for himself.

"We'll have to take this to Thompson and the others." Gray took a long swig of the drink. "They may already have it. But if they do, that begs the question: why didn't they share it with us?"

"It seems to have been heavily encrypted," said Nova. "Maybe Ibrahim is a step ahead of them. He certainly has the motivation."

"And the skills. He has an innocuous job here in Brisbane but apparently, he was employed in cyber-security in his own country."

With a glass of whisky in hand, Nova reclined in the swivel chair. It was the only piece of furniture that seemed suitable for sitting at eight-thirty in the evening in her coworker's apartment.

"Oh! I almost forgot," Nova swivelled to face Gray. "Yusef said Lividia Harlin is in contact with an entity called Spectre."

Gray looked at her for a moment before laughing. "Like James Bond?"

Nova smiled. "Don't shoot the messenger," she said. "The communications are encrypted so it's something they don't want anyone to see."

Gray nodded thoughtfully. "We'll pass the username on to Shaw," he said.

"Save a copy of the card on your computer. We need to cross-check these lists with the information Thompson's mob gave us."

Nova swiftly made the copies, drank the last of the whisky and stood.

"I'm starving," she said. "I need to get home."

Gray rested his elbows on the kitchen island as the last notes of a fading sky threw a shadow across the room. For a moment he could only see Nova in silhouette. Then the automatic lighting kicked in and he was startled by the coldness of it.

"I don't have much here, but we can order something, if you like," he said.

Nova smiled. "No," she said. "I'm beat. I can get an uber home."

Gray straightened up and zipped his coat. "No, you can't. I'll take you home. You did the right thing bringing this to me immediately. It could change the investigation. Or it might be nothing," he added quietly.

When they were in the car, Gray felt her eyes on him. He resisted for a while, then turned to look at her.

"What?"

Her face was soft in the dim light of the car. Neon lights from the nightclubs flashed pink and green highlights over her hair. "You live alone?"

He turned back to the traffic ahead. It could be hell driving through the Valley at this time of night. City workers were heading north after a long day at work, diners were coming out to eat and drink at the many popular bars and restaurants, and fitness fanatics were making their way to various gyms in attire that seemed to be applied to the body rather than covering it. Gray skidded to a halt, narrowly avoiding a couple of young women in leotards swapping phones and laughing hysterically at what they were seeing on the screen.

"It's alright, if you don't want to talk," she said turning her head back. Gray glanced in the side mirror to make sure the women had made it safely to the curb.

"It's not that. I just… I just don't talk about it."

They were silent for a couple of blocks.

"Christine," he said, at last.

Nova searched his face for more information.

"Her name was Christine. She died from a sudden aneurism about a year ago."

"My God! I'm sorry." Nova was staring at him now, eyes wide.

"There was nothing I could have done. It's just that I wasn't there. That's the hard part."

"Were you away?'

"Ha!" He turned a corner a little too quickly and had to adjust the car to get back into the correct lane. "I wasn't away," he said. "I was working. She called me at about eleven o'clock in the evening and said she had a screaming headache and was going to go to emergency."

He hesitated. "Is it that bad? That's the last thing I said to her. Is it that bad? She was my fiancé, and she was bloody dying." He shook his head. "Anyway, I got a call from the hospital about an hour later to say she'd died. She died in a cubicle in emergency waiting to see a doctor. Alone in a bloody cubicle." He shook his head again. "I should've been with her."

Gray parked in front of the florist, while Nova sat still, her face looking directly ahead.

"I should've raced home and taken her to the hospital," he went on. "She took a bloody Uber! I should've driven her to the hospital and sat with her. She shouldn't have died alone in a cluttered cubicle in a chaotic emergency room."

"Yes," said Nova slowly. "I agree. You should've been with your fiancé."

She opened the car door. "Thanks for the ride."

Nova climbed out and hesitated. "See you tomorrow," she said and left him.

Gray put his head on the wheel.

CHAPTER NINETEEN

BREAKING: Dr Nova Corbin joins Brisbane Homicide team to solve the city's first AI killing. Is this the new face of law enforcement? Or just a desperate ploy? This morning, as city officials met in closed session to address the rising panic over last week's tragic demonstration, Homicide quietly called in the expertise of Dr Nova Corbin, the globally recognised anthropologist of artificial intelligence who's been making waves, and a few enemies, ever since she claimed that "AI is not a technical thing. It is a cultural thing." Corbin's appointment has ignited a firestorm of speculation, both online and off. Is she the answer to Brisbane's new AI problem? Or has the city handed the investigation to a controversial outsider with an axe to grind?

Today on Newsnet's "Expert Eye," we dig deeper into who Dr Corbin really is, why her ideas challenge everything about AI's future in Australia, and what the rest of us can expect as intelligent machines slip further into the fabric of everyday life.

For the uninitiated, Dr Corbin cut her teeth at the Australian National University and rose quickly through the academic ranks, publishing a string of hotly debated papers on how societies shape, mythologise, and ultimately absorb disruptive technologies. She is currently an Associate Professor in the Anthropology Department of the University of Queensland. Corbin refuses to play by the old rules, publicly berating both Silicon Valley and Canberra for their binary thinking about machines and people.

When asked by NewsNet reporters for comment, Dr Corbin's response was succinct: "I'll speak when I have something to say. Until then, the only thing worth watching is the data." Homicide has not released details of her role in the investigation, but sources close to the department describe Corbin as "the only one in the country qualified to tackle the killer drone problem from a human angle."

But what does it mean to "tackle the killer drone problem from a human angle"? To answer that, we reached out to Dr Hans Mueller, a German-born AI researcher and former student of Dr Corbin's, who has spent the last decade working on algorithmic bias in justice systems. Mueller, currently at UQ's School of Digital Ethics, credits his former supervisor with "teaching me that every machine has a lineage, a logic, and a personality, whether we like it or not." Even so, he admits that Corbin's worldview can be "intimidating, especially to people who've never questioned whether a computer can be racist, or whether your self-driving car could inherit your grandfather's bad habits."

We asked our readers to submit their questions for Dr Mueller, who agreed to respond to the top three.

Our first question comes from Rene of Darra: "I've heard Nova Corbin talk about the bias inherent in our 'intelligent' machines. I want to know how a machine can be 'bias.' Isn't it just maths?"

Mueller: "Excellent question. Let's take a simple example. Suppose a court uses an 'objective' algorithm to predict which criminals are likely to reoffend. If the historical data used to train that algorithm includes more examples of Aboriginal Australians being incarcerated compared to white Australians, the algorithm will learn that being Aboriginal is correlated with reoffending, even if that's just a reflection of systemic bias in policing or the courts. The result? We automate and amplify existing prejudice under the guise of neutrality. The real danger is that unless we confront these patterns, we end up turning our own history into destiny, but with extra speed and efficiency."

Next up, Harrison from Rockhampton asks: "When Corbin talks about artificial intelligence, is she saying these machines have a brain? Is that actually possible?"

Mueller: "Corbin and her followers would say it's a category error to think about AI in terms of brains at all. The computer-as-brain metaphor is popular because it's familiar, but it falls apart under scrutiny. A language model can generate sentences that look meaningful, but it doesn't have beliefs, intentions, or even a sense of self. It's just pattern-matching at a vast scale, like an unimaginably fast parrot that's memorized every book in the library but has never held a conversation. The leap from clever imitation to true understanding is still, in my opinion, science fiction. But people keep making that leap, and that's what worries her."

Finally, Jemma from Brisbane wants to know: "Why do we talk about 'intelligent machines' as if they are human, like they're going to have feelings? Does Corbin think machines have feelings?"

Mueller: "Great point, Jemma. We do talk about these machines as if they are people. Humans have a psychological tendency to anthropomorphise inanimate objects. We see shapes of faces in clouds; we see a man in the shadows of the moon. We think of our AI assistants as friends. You know, back in the Afghanistan war in the earliest days of Artificial Intelligence, soldiers thought of the drones they used as soldiers. When they were destroyed in combat, they held funerals for them. It's human nature to make people out of objects. But it doesn't mean the objects are anything like people. Dr Corbin doesn't think machines have feelings.

Host: That's all we have time for friends. We'll continue following this story as it unfolds. This is NewsNet.com reporting. Stay safe and stay tuned.

CHAPTER TWENTY

S tanding in the middle of the desolate car park, Lividia felt both exposed and emboldened. Large warehouses dotted the expanse, some with walls that sagged, some covered in faded graffiti. But she fixated on the concrete building that loomed at the centre. The construction was crude, rough and undecorated, with dull light emanating from a row of air ventilation louvres just below the roofline, apparently the only form of window. The stark utilitarian structure seemed the kind of place where weapons could be concealed.

Moonlight glinted coldly from the corrugated iron roof, casting harsh reflections across the gravel. She stayed rooted in place, trembling slightly as a light breeze passed over her, sending chills up her spine. She felt the weight of her decision press down with almost physical force. A palpable sense of foreboding overcame her as she steeled herself for what lay ahead. She knew with certainty that once she entered this building, she would never be the same person again.

But she hadn't been the same since her brother's death. Anything was better than the person wracked with grief and frustration that currently inhabited her body. She would do this for Seeton. She would finish what he started.

It made sense when Spectre explained it. The problem was one of identity. The refugees had already changed the 'feel' of the city. What was needed was a successful revolt – a complete change of government direction. Spectre said that Australians needed to take back control of their destiny. But first, they needed to be brought to their senses. The drone attacks were already stirring up fear and hate on both sides. When the fear became deep enough, institutions would struggle, and people would look for new leaders, they would demand change. "The future belongs to those of us prepared to get our hands dirty," was Spectre's rallying cry.

Lividia glanced at her mobile screen. A tiny red balloon hovered over a point on the map. This was it. This was definitely the address Spectre had sent her.

She walked around the perimeter of the building, passing a wide roll-a-door that locked down one end, obviously intended for delivery of equipment. She knocked on the only other door she could see, a narrow side entrance. It felt like a long time that she waited, every moment elongated by nervous energy. Fear, anticipation, excitement all combined to make her feel nauseous.

Finally, the door opened and a girl looking much the same age as her peered around it.

"I'm Lividia," she told the girl, who stepped to one side and allowed Lividia to enter.

"I'm Freya." The girl threw out her hand. She was small, with a short black bob cradling her ears and a tiny fringe accentuating her high forehead. Her eyes were large and as dark as her hair.

The building had been gutted on the inside creating an expansive space, with high ceilings and rows of flickering fluorescent lights. On one side of the room, there was an assembly line of steel tables. Four people worked at different stations along the line. Lividia couldn't distinguish their ages or gender under the protective gear. They wore facemasks and safety goggles as they moved deftly about the machinery.

Large crates stacked high against the walls appeared to be filled with various parts: propellers, cameras, and other indistinguishable hardware. An array of screens mounted on the walls displayed real time data about production.

Freya moved to a large computer in one corner. She explained that she engineered and monitored the codes that would tweak navigation algorithms and targeting systems to dictate the drones' autonomous actions.

"This will be your job also," she said. "I can't work twenty-four hours a day, so you'll work twelve and I'll work twelve. To be honest with you, I'm glad Spectre found you. It's a really complex job and I'm struggling a little. There's only for a few days to go now."

Lividia stared at the screens. The sophistication and scope of the operation was overwhelming. She'd wanted to see how the killer drone had been made, but she had no idea there was a warehouse at the back of Bowen Hills where dozens of them were under construction.

She looked across the space to the centre of the warehouse where an area was marked off with bright yellow tape.

"That's the designated testing area," said the girl. "This is where we test the finished drones."

"Sit. I'll show you what we do. Spectre tells me you have superior skills in robotics. "There are so many ways this could go wrong. I'm excited to have someone to bounce ideas off."

Lividia sat in the chair offered to her. "This is so much more than I expected," she said looking around. "How long have you been working here?"

Freya shrugged milky white shoulders. "I don't know, maybe a couple of months on and off. The trial phase is almost over now, though. That's why I need help. We're moving into the combat phase."

"Combat?" asked Lividia.

"That's just what we're calling it. There really isn't any combat because the authorities have no response to what we're doing." She smiled as though they were talking about a computer game.

"From the amount of equipment, I can see here, we're talking about more than operationalising a single drone here and there." Lividia gazed at the wall of parts.

Freya nodded. "Hmm," she said. "There's one more trial to go. Then the big attack.

"Everyone's excited about it. Spectre gives us free reign to use our skills and imagination. That's how we've come this far so quickly. I was only a mid-level computer science student when Spectre recruited me. I've come years ahead in two months."

Freya gazed hard into Lividia's eyes and hesitated.

"The world is fucked. You know that, right?" she said, watching Lividia carefully.

"Yes," said Lividia simply. "It is."

"Well, it's all gone too far for anything to happen from elections or peaceful protests, or whatever. We need to punch the fuckers in the government right in the gut, to get their attention. We have to tear down the institutions, if we want to build them back up, the right way." Freya let her eyes slide away from Lividia's face. Her tone returned to that of a chatty girl who might have been a cheerleader.

"Anyway," she said. "It's awesome to have you on board, Lividia. We're going to have to smash it over the next few days to have everything ready. There's no way I could manage something so big by myself. But with you, I know this is going to be next level."

Lividia bathed in the girl's energy. As she gazed around the warehouse, she knew she would never have dreamed she'd have access to so much state-of-the-art equipment. It seemed apparent that, for someone, money was no object.

"Who pays for all this stuff?" she asked.

Freya shrugged again. "Spectre has backers." Her eyes lit up. "You know that politician, Leonie Nolan? She was here the other day." Freya turned back to her keyboard. "I think she's one of his backers. She has loads of money."

CHAPTER TWENTY-ONE

DAY FIVE

The next morning, the sun's rays beat down oppressively on the cement pavements, the glass buildings, and the citizens making their way to work in light suits and linen dresses. The attractive man on NewsNet.com warned the city of a heatwave that would bring temperatures higher than they'd experienced since temperatures had been recorded. This had become an annual refrain in late summer over the past decade, as every year temperatures rose almost a degree higher than the record from the year before.

"Stay indoors," advised the man with a broad grin that exposed perfect white teeth. Sage advice if you had an air-conditioned indoors to stay in. The elderly and the poor typically spent their days in shopping centres and libraries around the city at this time of year. Those unable to make their way to these public spaces kept the ambulance service busy rushing them to hospital to be treated for dehydration. Many simply died, saving the state the expense of a long hospital stay.

Reluctantly, Gray decided not to jog this morning, opting instead for a leisurely breakfast at Chez Nous. As he was savouring the last mouthful of French toast, Nova appeared in the shop's lengthy queue for coffee. She placed her order then joined him.

"Hot enough for you?" she said.

Gray smiled. "Ready to share your find with the others?"

"It's not my find. Yusef unlocked the encryption. I'm grateful he chose to share it with us, though."

"Me too," said Gray. "But there'll be others less pleased."

Nova squinted. "Why?"

Gray swallowed the last of his coffee and stood up as Nova's name was called by the barista. She picked up her coffee and together, her and Gray pushed through the crowd to leave the shop.

"The Federal Police will want control over this information," he said. "There'll be a skirmish, mark my words. They'll want to control the data and the narrative from here on in."

The sun caught them off guard as they stepped onto the street. Nova put on her sunglasses and Gray held his hand up to shade his eyes.

Once safely in the confines of the Homicide Unit, Gray assembled Glenda King and Rishi Chandra along with himself and Nova in his office. As the door to his office closed, muffling the sounds from outside, Gray's eyes fixed on his team members. They looked worn from the chaos of the previous days, and Chandra and King exchanged curious glances. Gray knew they'd be anticipating new information, but they could never have imagined the extent of what he was about to share.

He held up the computer card Yusef Ibrahim had given them, a small, yet potentially powerful piece of evidence that might change everything.

"This could be the break we've been waiting for," said Gray. He held the card aloft like a beacon.

"What's on it?" asked Rishi Chandra.

King's keen eyes narrowed. "How'd we get our hands on it?" she said.

Gray paused. On the one hand he didn't want too many people knowing that Yusef Ibrahim had provided them with the computer card. But on the other, he needed the help of his team to investigate the long list of names it included. He knew Glenda King would remain suspicious if he didn't share the source of the information. And she wouldn't let go until he did.

"Yusef Ibrahim," he said. "He's been working on Harlin's encryptions. He gave it to Nova last night."

"Nova?" King made no attempt to hide the disdain in her voice. She turned to face the anthropologist directly. "Why you?"

Nova Corbin met her gaze but didn't respond.

"We don't know why he gave it to Dr Corbin," said Gray, watching the women with some amusement.

King folded her arms across her chest and sat back in her chair, a look on her face implying 'this should be good.'

Chandra's face was open and eager as always.

As Gray outlined the gist of the intelligence contained on the card, both their jaws tensed.

"Holy shit," said Glenda, her grey eyes wide with disbelief.

"Indeed," replied Grey.

Rishi Chandra sat up straight. "So, the drone attack could be linked to these terrorist groups after all?"

Gray shook his head. "All we know so far is that Seeton Harlin was collecting intel on operatives and associates of Hezbollah, Hamas, Fatah, The Islamic State and other affiliates, both here and abroad. That provides a potential motive for the Harlin murder. Someone may have resented being on the list. But there's no evidence yet that the attack on Mohammed Hussain was linked to Seeton's activities. In fact, there's no evidence that the two murders are connected in any way."

Chandra tapped his pen quietly.

King watched Nova Corbin out of the corner of her eye. If the anthropologist noticed, she gave no sign of it.

Gray went on. "We're going to have to present this evidence to the Federal Police, who'll no doubt pass it on to ASIO. They may have already accessed it, but even so, they're going to be pissed we have it. So, strap in."

Gray clicked into Zoom, and the face of a man about his own age appeared on the screen.

"Richardson," he greeted the man warmly.

"Mate!" cried the face on the screen. "It's good to hear from you." Having trained at the academy together twenty-years earlier, Gray and Richardson had once been close. But Glen Richardson switched to the Federal Police after a couple of years on the force in Queensland and eventually, they lost touch.

"What can I do for you?" asked Richardson.

"We have something we think you need to see," Gray replied. He held up the computer card, ensuring it was in full view. Then he plugged it into his computer. "I'll bring it up for you. It should appear on your screen... about... now."

Gray clicked on the function key to share the screen with his friend and watched carefully for his reaction. Within seconds, the federal policeman's eyebrows shot up, and his eyes grew wide with astonishment. He sat upright, then leant in closer to the screen.

Gray clicked through file after file, showing him examples of the contents. A moment of stunned silence followed.

"Where did you get this?" he whispered.

Gray let the question hang for a moment, basking quietly in the satisfaction of his delivery. "It was left for me, anonymously," he answered, sitting back with an air of practiced calm. The team stood resolute behind him while Nova and the young detectives watched the exchange with intense focus. Gray could feel them stiffen at his vague reply but knew they wouldn't give the game away.

Richardson remained fixated on the files, then he shifted in his seat and pulled his tie tight.

"Jesus," he said. "Who the hell's been collecting and curating all this intelligence?"

Gray glanced sideways at his team. "The young man who was killed at the protest the other day."

"You're kidding! The one-punch killer victim?"

"Not kidding. This information was intercepted as it was being sent to a third party from Seeton's computer."

"Who's the third party?" Richardson wanted to know.

"Don't know yet."

Another tense silence.

"You need to hand this over to us," said Richardson. His face had become deadly serious. "We'll take it from here. Delete any copies you have on your computer. Until we analyse it, we don't want multiple copies circulating. Someone will be there within the hour to pick up the card."

"I haven't downloaded it onto my computer," said Gray truthfully. He didn't mention that his colleague Nova Corbin had it on hers.

Richardson picked up on something in his voice. He knew Gray too well. "This is information that relates to national security," said Richardson carefully. "You don't need the trouble that comes with this type of intel. Trust me."

Gray looked directly into his old friend's eyes for a moment.

"Understood," he said. But he'd hesitated too long, and he knew his friend had registered it.

They both signed off with an abrupt click, leaving Gray staring at the lifeless monitor for a few seconds. Turning to face his team he was met with a mixture of apprehension and anticipation. Nova's eyes remained steadily on Gray, questioning.

"They'll verify what's on the card and trace it for provenance," he said, his voice calm. "I expect they'll bring Thompson and Shaw into the loop. And share it with ASIO."

Nova kept her gaze locked on Gray. "And what do we do with the copy on my laptop?" she asked, her words cutting through the silence like a sharp knife through cheesecake.

Gray met her stare, unflinching.

"What about the copy on my laptop?" she repeated, challenging him to respond.

"Yes, about that..." Gray replied. "Pull it up. We treat the people documented on the card as potential suspects in the murder of Seeton Harlin."

Nova's expression shifted to one of cautious determination. She raised her eyebrows, her lips drawing into a tight line as she processed Gray's instructions. With a resigned nod, she did as he said, her fingers swiftly bringing the data to life on her screen.

"The Feds won't be happy if they find out we're running our own analysis," Nova warned, loading the files.

He didn't need to voice his thoughts; his silence spoke volumes. Let the Federal Police be unhappy. What mattered was the investigation, his investigation. "What the Federal Police don't know won't hurt them," he said out loud.

Chandra closed his tablet. "That's that, then," he said, and started to walk away but King stood firm. Chandra stopped and returned to his partner's side.

"Can we speak to you, sir?" King said. "Privately." She shot a sideways glance at Nova who looked up from her screen just in time to see it.

"I'll wait outside," offered Nova.

Gray gestured for her to stay where she was. "We'll go out," he said. He shuffled his two junior officers out of the office and shut the door.

He faced Glenda's cool regard. "What's going on?"

Chandra looked at King as though he wanted to know the same thing.

Glenda King pressed her lips together before beginning. "Sir, I just can't help wondering why Yusef Ibrahim would bring the intel to Nova Corbin rather than hand it in to the Police. I get he was trying to clear his name, but why give it to Corbin? Why not give it to you, directly?"

Gray's brow furrowed.

Chandra watched his partner closely.

"What are you getting at?" asked Gray.

King stood her ground. "If you haven't spoken to Yusef yourself, how do we even know the card came from him?"

Gray's head jerked back, and his eyebrows shot upward. "What? Why would she lie?"

"That's just it, sir. We don't know. Why don't Chandra and I talk to Yusef. Confirm the source of the information. All we have is a card with data, how do we even know it came from Seeton Harlin's computer? Yusef could have compiled that information himself."

Chandra's eyes returned to the Detective Inspector as the senior officer pondered the proposition for a moment. He was beginning to wish he hadn't revealed the source of the card. He knew Nova Corbin was telling the truth. Her story had been detailed and credible. Regardless of who compiled the data he was convinced Nova Corbin was telling the truth about how it came into her hands. Gray felt he had developed a sixth sense for knowing when people were lying to him over his twenty odd years in policing and he trusted his judgement.

"No," he said, at last. "I don't want Yusef spooked. He could be very useful to us over the next few days. He went to a great deal of trouble to bring the card to Dr Corbin. I think he's afraid, and I don't think he trusts us."

King opened her mouth to speak but closed it again when Gray went on.

"For now, we keep Yusef's involvement between the four of us," he said.

"Yes, sir," said King and Chandra in unison.

They kept their heads down, but Gray could see King was still suspicious.

"Keep the card with you and give it to the Federal Police when they arrive," Gray told Chandra. "Continue with the interviews from the list Cyber Security provided yesterday in relation to the drone attack. We'll use Nova's laptop to try and narrow down potential suspects for the Harlin killing."

Chandra tucked his tablet neatly under his arm and he and King made a move to leave.

"Oh, I almost forgot to ask," began Gray, "What did you learn about Lividia Harlin?"

Chandra opened his tablet to a spreadsheet. "Like we've already said, Lividia is an Honours student in the Robotics Science Unit at the Queensland University of Technology," he read. "She's extremely bright according to her lecturers but introverted."

King jumped in, "Classmates confirmed that, sir. They called her a loner. Apparently, she doesn't have any friends. In fact, her classmates didn't even know she had a brother, let alone that he was the young man killed at the protest. When we told them, they said his death explained why she was absent from lab sessions this week."

Chandra took over, swiping to the next page of his spreadsheet. "Lividia has a single savings account with a balance of sixty-four dollars. She appears to live on credit. There's a credit card in her name and the balance is paid in full monthly. Presumably by her parents. She has no part-time job or income. Seeton was in a similar position, financially.'

Gray nodded slowly as they shared the information they'd gathered with him.

"Did anyone mention an entity called Spectre?"

Chanda and King laughed. "The old James Bond movie, sir?" asked Chandra.

Gray shook his head. "No leads there, then," he said, turning to return to his office where Nova was concentrating hard on her screen. She seemed unconcerned by what the junior officers might have wanted to tell their boss privately.

Ten minutes later Gray received a text from Chandra to say the Federal Police had picked up the card.

Gray read the text and took a deep breath. He tapped out the number for the Chief Superintendent. It was early in the day, yet Charfield's voice already had a slight edge of fatigue when he answered. Gray described the information they'd uncovered and the federal response to it with words that were clipped and business-like. It frustrated him that even though his team had sourced the intelligence, he suspected the Federal Police would try to shut them out of that part of the investigation.

Charfield listened. "You handed the intel over?" he asked.

"I've complied with Federal Police instructions," said Gray.

"Did we keep a copy?" asked the Superintendent.

"They don't want copies floating around," said Gray, non-committedly.

Charfield paused. "Do we have a copy or not?" he repeated.

Gray hesitated, knowing he was already in dangerous territory with the Federal Police. He ran a hand through his hair.

"Yes," he said.

"Good man," said Charfield. "Keep it within your team."

"Of course," said Gray, with a sigh of relief. "We'll keep the focus on our investigation into the death of Seeton Harlin."

"They're going to be fucking pissed, but this intel could yield results," said Charfield.

"I want you to keep working on it, Gray. We've got dead bodies, and if you think this could link them..."

"Understood," said Gray, knowing that Charfield was right. Without the Superintendent's support he may not have been game to hold on to the information. This way, he had his bosses' blessing to not only keep a copy of the computer card, but to investigate it in relation to Seeton's murder and the killer drone attack.

"Charfield says to keep working on the data in relation to the murder of Seeton Harlin," he told Nova. "We'll let the Federal Police deal with any further implications from the intelligence."

She raised her eyebrows, but nodded, a small smile tugging at the corners of her mouth.

"Can you share the contents of Yusef's card with me in a secure file?" he asked.

"Done," said Nova.

"We're looking for anything that might relate to the murder of Seeton Harlin," he said. "I think Seeton was killed by someone who was waiting for an opportunity to do so and took it."

"The existence of these files on his computer is sufficient motive for murder," said Nova. "He's collected highly damaging information about individuals and provides detailed accounts of clandestine activities here in Brisbane. This opens a world of possibilities in terms of a motive for killing him."

"I agree," said Gray. "I think Ibrahim has given us the 'why' for Seeton's murder. Now we need to work out 'who'."

"There are so many potential suspects on this list. I'm not sure how to narrow it down," Nova said, leaning back in her chair. "And I don't see how the information here links to the drone attack on Mohammed Hussain," Nova shook her head slowly.

Gray glanced at his phone and up at the clock on his wall. They differed by seven minutes. It was getting closer to time to put the hands right.

"This list will have to wait," he said. "We arranged to speak with the Imam this morning. If anyone has heard anything in the Muslim community, it will be him."

CHAPTER TWENTY-TWO

Gray leant across from the driver's seat to open the door of his beloved car for Corbin. One leg in tight jeans and ankle boot slid in after the other. Then a briefcase and laptop landed on the bench seat between them.

Nova brushed her hair back from her forehead. "It's so warm," she said. "You haven't got a hair tie in the car, I suppose?"

The grimace on Gray's face said he did not.

He darted out in front of the traffic and pressed hard on the accelerator while Nova gripped the door handle tightly. He was eager to speak with the Imam and return to Seeton's files, but even so, Gray always drove as though on the way to an emergency.

"Perhaps you should use a police car with a siren," suggested Nova, glancing sideways at him.

He peered into the rearview mirror checking for an opportunity to swerve across two lanes to turn left.

"I have a siren," he said. "It's on the back seat."

Nova checked and he was telling the truth. An old-fashioned blue light lay on the back seat looking innocuous, but ready to jump into action should the need arise.

"I don't want to announce a police approach," he said. "This is a friendly community visit to the Imam."

Nova checked her watch.

"The men who belong to the mosque will have been at prayers. They should be finishing about now."

Gray slowed his Toyota Crown short of the spot where Hussain had been struck by the killer drone. Police tape still marked out the area. He pulled the Crown right and double parked beside a white AV while Nova shot him an anxious glance.

"What?" he said. "It's a smart car. It should be smart enough to get out if it needs to."

She rolled her eyes, then stared up at the mosque, a simple, but functional white brick building featuring a small dome at the centre, painted in soft green. The dome was flanked by a single slender white minaret rising modestly above the building. The minaret had a subtle crescent moon at its peak.

"The Peace Mosque," said Nova looking up at a sign over the narrow, arched doorway. She saw the puzzled expression on Gray's face.

"Masjid Al-Salam. The Peace Mosque."

"Ironic," he said, climbing out of the car.

A small, paved courtyard bordered by potted olive trees and benches enhanced the front entrance. Nova and Gray sat on one of the benches to remove their shoes before Nova retrieved a pale peach scarf from her bag and threw it over head. Gray noticed how attractively her face was framed by the scarf. He blushed slightly as the Imam appeared.

"Sheikh Khalil," said a man in his late fifties, his hand held out in greeting. His face generated calmness and patience, with tiny lines around his eyes from smiling. A trim white beard contrasted against his dark skin. Dark, thick eyebrows added intensity to deep brown eyes. His hair was partly covered by a white cotton kufi, intricately patterned with small geometric designs. A plain white thobe with subtle embroidery on the cuffs and collar reached down to his ankles, lightweight for the Brisbane weather. Over the thobe, he wore an earth-coloured vest with deep pockets for his prayer beads and a small well-worn Quran.

He smiled warmly at Nova. "Please let me show you around." He put his head down and clasped his hands behind his back as he led them into the main prayer hall. High ceilings allowed the small dome to cast a soft, natural light into the room. The floors were covered with prayer rugs; each marked with simple lines indicating the direction of Mecca. A few modest lamps provided additional light. The wall facing Mecca had a small alcove painted in soft blue. This was flanked by simple calligraphy of Quranic verses written in black ink. An intricately carved timber platform elevated by three steps stood to the right of the alcove.

"The Minbar," said Khalil.

"Pulpit," whispered Nova close to Gray's ear.

At the back of the prayer hall, a plain wooden partition with a thin lace curtain separated the women's prayer area. Gray supposed it was a movable divider so the mosque could accommodate everyone within a limited space.

The Imam pointed out a multipurpose room adjacent to the prayer hall which he explained was used for community gatherings, classes and meetings. Gray stood at the door and saw that it had a few shelves stocked with donated books in Arabic and English, a small library of Islamic texts and some educational materials for children. The room also appeared to serve as a temporary storage space for food and clothing donations.

"This was Hussain's space," said Khalil. "He collected donations and distributed them from here. He was tireless in his work for this community."

"His death must be a great loss," said Nova gently.

The Imam turned to her with dark eyes. "The mosque is much more than a place of worship," he said. "It is a sanctuary and a gathering place. It provides stability, connection and hope for those trying to build their lives here."

The Imam went on, "Indeed, Mohammed was organising a festival this Saturday, in the park across the road. It is to be a celebration for our community, but also an opportunity for the citizens of Brisbane to meet us and learn about our culture. There'll be traditional foods and dancing. Entertainments for the children. Many influencers have kindly agreed to advertise the event, and, of course, we will be placing event posts on the social media."

"Are you still planning to go ahead with the event?" asked Gray surprised.

"Of course. The community needs this event more than ever. The people of Brisbane must understand we are grateful for our opportunity to live peacefully in this place, and we hope we can demonstrate our gratitude through sharing some of our customs. We have been through decades of devastating war, Detective Inspector. Do you think one drone is going to bring us to our knees?"

"Do you know of anyone who would have wanted to harm Mohammed?" Gray asked. The Imam stopped to turn toward Gray. "No one," he said. "Mohammed was a good man. Everyone in this community loved and respected him."

"What about outside the community?" asked Gray.

Kahlil's thick brows knotted. He shook his head slightly. "Mohammed didn't really have contact with many people outside our own community," he said. "He visited the refugee job centre most days. But no one spoke of any trouble there."

Gray watched the Imam carefully as he asked his next question. "Do you have any reason to believe Mohammed was caught up in terrorist activities?"

The Imam's eyes narrowed momentarily. "Of course, we are all suspected terrorists," he said quietly.

Gray held his gaze without apology.

Kahlil's gaze softened and a wrinkle appeared at the corner of his eyes. "Let me assure you, Detective Inspector," he began in a measured tone, "Mohammed Hussain is the last man you would suspect of extremist behaviour."

Gray maintained eye contact for a moment longer, then said good-bye, while Nova smiled and thanked the Imam for his help.

As they walked away, Gray heard the Imam's soft steps as he walked back into the mosque.

CHAPTER TWENTY-THREE

On the way back to the office, Gray and Nova turned into a drive-through and ordered coffee through an automated dispenser. Gray wound down the window in readiness to receive the coffee and warm air rushed at his face from outside. He felt the tingle of sweat pooling under his arms, and he tugged at his shirt. Nova was sifting through her briefcase, still in search of a hair tie.

While waiting for their coffee, Gray checked his phone. He'd left it on silent to avoid distractions, convincing himself that he needed this break from incessant updates and demands. As he held the device, debating whether to turn the ringer back on, he noticed two missed calls that made him pause. Both were from his deceased fiancé's sister, Suzie. He stared at the screen, with a mixture of disbelief and uncertainty. His thumb hovered, about to return the call, but he hesitated, torn between curiosity and dread.

His heart was pounding. What could she possibly want? He hadn't spoken to Suzie since everything fell apart, since Christine's funeral, an event that had ripped through him with an intensity that almost broke him. The silence that followed him home was even worse. He'd been on emotional autopilot since he recovered from the soul-destroying grief that followed her death. The only emotion he registered lately, in relation to Christine and Alix was shame. Gray felt a rush of anxiety as he debated in his mind whether to call Suzie back.

Nova glanced at him from the passenger seat. Having magically produced a stray hair tie from the bottom of her briefcase she was securing her hair.

As Gray gripped the steering wheel, he replayed his last conversation with Suzie, the clipped words, the awkward parting. What could have changed in all this time? Was there something new to haunt him, or was it merely an attempt at reaching out, bridging the emotional chasm that had widened since Christine's death?

He tried to steady himself, but Suzie came with memories he'd just as soon forget. He remembered the way she looked at him, first with sympathy, then with the kind of pity that bordered on resentment. Disappointment lingered in her eyes, a reflection of what she must have thought of him, absent, unreliable, drowning in work when he should have been with her sister. And maybe she was right. Maybe he deserved that judgment, the whispered accusations, the awkward silence that filled the room like a physical presence. He sat there, gripping the wheel overwhelmed by the sense of guilt that was never far from the surface. Not only for not being there for Christine, but for not sticking by Alix either.

The notification light on his phone blinked persistently, refusing to let him push it to the back of his mind. He inhaled deeply, considering what to do next. If he ignored the calls, he knew they would only gnaw at him, just like every other unresolved part of his past. If he returned them, he risked reopening wounds that were slow to heal, drawing himself back into a chapter he was desperate to close.

While nova sat watching him, the phone pinged again. Suzie.

Gray caught Nova's eye, one eyebrow raised, and he answered.

"I'm in the car," he said. "I'll call back in two minutes."

A robotic arm passed two cups of coffee through a window and Gray handed them to Nova while he drove a few metres to the car park.

Nova still didn't ask, but she was watching him. Why were women always watching him?

"It's Christine's sister Suzie," he said in a tone that suggested Nova had been pressing him for an explanation.

Nova sipped her coffee.

"She and her husband took in Alix when Christine died. I haven't spoken to them in twelve months. I can't imagine why she's calling now."

Nova jerked her head back at the first touch of the coffee to her lips. "That's too hot," she said. "Did you ask for milk?"

Gray glanced over at the lid. "There's milk in it," he said.

Nova looked at the sharpie marks on the lid. "Is that what that says?" she muttered.

She decided to wait before trying the drink again. "Why haven't you spoken with them? I thought you said you and Alix were close."

Gray pulled into an empty space. "I don't know why."

He opened the car door, "This shouldn't take long," he said, as he climbed out. He stood about twenty metres away and returned Suzie's call.

"Hello, nice to hear from you," he said, unsure how else to begin when she answered the call on the first ring.

"Thank God!" she said. He heard the relief in her voice. "I need to talk to you about Alix."

Gray's heart pumped faster. "What about Alix?"

There was silence on the other end for a moment. "She's missing." Her voice was thin.

"Missing?" Gray repeated. "How long?"

"She didn't come home last night. We thought she was staying with a friend, that's why we didn't worry. But I ran into the friend's mother this morning and she said Alix didn't stay with them last night. They hadn't seen her."

"Have you tried calling her?" Gray was pacing now, in small circles in the car park.

"Of course, I've tried calling her. Her phone is going directly to message bank. I've left several messages."

Gray's blood pressure was rising rapidly. Alix was only sixteen. A missing sixteen-year-old girl could mean anything from a jaunt to a music festival with friends to dead in a ditch somewhere. He had to get his emotions under control. He had to keep a separation here between his professional and personal life. But all the grief and shame of Christine's death came pouring down over him. And now her daughter was missing. Was he going to fail her again? He took a deep breath. "Is this an official call?" he asked. "Do you want me to file a missing person's report?"

"God Mitchell, I don't know," said Suzie. "I'm calling because you and Alix were close. God knows you haven't bothered to contact her since her mother died, that's cut her to the bone. But since you're a police officer I thought you might know what I should do to find her."

The pain in Gray's chest felt as though it would crush him. It was true, he'd let his relationship with Alix go when her mother died.

"I didn't want to intrude," he said.

"Bloody hell, Mitchell, what do you imagine it's been like for the girl, losing her mother suddenly, and then you as well?"

Gray walked back toward the car, his head throbbing. He needed to clear his mind, to follow procedures, but the pain was destroying him.

"I'll be at your place in fifteen minutes," he said.

As he climbed into the car Nova looked at him expectantly. "Is everything all right?"

Gray gripped the wheel. "No," he said. "I'll drop you back at the station then I have to take care of something."

They drove silently for a few minutes, but Nova couldn't stop herself from asking. "What's happened?"

Gray's jaw was set. He realised he was in the wrong lane to take the next turn and swung in front of a car to the sound of a blaring horn.

Nova continued to stare at him.

"Christine's daughter Alix has gone missing," he said. "She's only sixteen."

"I'm sorry," whispered Nova.

"Why didn't you stay in contact with Alix?" Nova asked, her brown eyes boring into him.

He shifted uneasily in his seat. Tears pricked his eyes. "I don't..." He gripped the wheel tighter. "I was disappointed in myself. I told myself she wouldn't want to see me after what happened to her mum. I told myself she was better getting on with her life without me. She wasn't my daughter or anything. She had family. I told myself they wouldn't want me hanging around. But with all the things I told myself, I guess I just didn't want the emotional attachment. I was in so much pain after Christine's death. I couldn't handle it. I was a coward. That's the truth of it."

He kept his eyes on the road because he couldn't bear the look he might see on Nova's face.

"Do you want me to come with you?"

Gray shook his head. "You stay on the case, contact Yusef, see if he's come up with anything yet. I'll follow this up."

He dropped Nova off outside the Police Headquarters in Roma Street and continued to Red Hill. Suzie and her husband Robert lived in a renovated worker's cottage that looked small from the front but had been built on at the back taking advantage of the sloping block to create a spacious four-bedroom house. They'd taken Alix in after her mother's death without hesitation, even though they had not wanted any children of their own. Gray had assumed the three of them were happy.

At the front of the house, a veranda reached out almost to the sidewalk. Glossy white colonial trims contrasted beautifully against blue walls. On either side of the door, hanging baskets overflowed with vibrant geraniums, the scent of which filled the air. Gray felt the wooden floor-boards creak under the weight of his feet as he raised his fist to knock on the door.

Suzie appeared almost immediately wearing a dressing gown, her eyes weary and lined, her face unmistakably older than he remembered, even though it had only been a year since they had last seen each other. She looked as though she hadn't slept. Streaks of grey crept through her hair, now cut shorter than before, and she was wearing no make-up. It struck Gray that in all the years he was with Christine, he'd never seen Suzie so undone. She had always been a proud, polished woman, the kind who remained immaculately composed even in the most stressful of times. Now, her appearance told a different story. He read grief and worry in the slump of her shoulders, shadows beneath her eyes. He felt another pang of guilt.

Gray hesitated before following Suzie into the house, feeling suddenly like an intruder in a life he'd left behind. The furniture was just as he remembered, tasteful, expensive, chic. But the atmosphere seemed different now, heavier. He wondered if Suzie blamed him, if she saw him as the first domino in the chain, falling and knocking her sister out and now maybe her niece. He followed the smell of coffee. Suzie was making two cups on a sophisticated machine without asking if he wanted one.

He scanned the open plan kitchen area, warm, homey, but a little too perfect, like it had been decorated for a Country Homes magazine spread rather than a family. Gray sat on a high stool at the bar, trying to appear calm and professional, as if this were any other case, he was working and not a direct line back to all the things he'd lost. Suzie's back was to him as she poured the coffee.

"When did you last see her?" asked Gray deciding his best chance at surviving this visit with his emotions intact was to maintain a professional approach.

"Yesterday. She left for school as usual and said she'd be staying with Molly overnight. Her and Molly sleep over at one another's places most weekends, so I didn't worry at all. She took a few clothes in an overnight bag to school with her. Then I ran into Molly's mother this morning just by chance, and she said they hadn't seen Alix."

Suzie sat opposite him with her coffee. The other cup was left on the bench beside the machine. Gray assumed it was for him, but he didn't want it.

"Have you spoken to Molly?"

"She says Alix hasn't said anything to her about going anywhere. She assumed she went home after school."

Gray maintained his composure. "Does she have her phone with her?"

Suzie sat up straight on the bar stool, clutching the coffee cup with both hands as if to stop them from shaking. Her grey eyes were wide with hope. "Of course she does, I told you I tried calling her," she said, "She never goes anywhere without her phone."

"I can have it tracked, if you want," Gray said. "I'd need your permission as her guardian to do it – but it'll be the quickest way of finding her."

"Yes! Track the phone! How long will that take?" Suzie was almost leaping from the kitchen stool.

"Not long." Gray retrieved his electronic tablet and started tapping. "You can sign this electronic form, and I'll set the wheels in motion." He held the tablet out to Suzie, and she signed with a trembling finger.

While they waited for the request to go through to the telecommunications network, Gray struggled with how to frame his next question.

"Suzie," he said firmly, "Is there anything you're not telling me?"

"Like what?" she croaked, the sound hardly audible.

"Like, was there any trouble at home? Teenagers can be difficult, did you two have an argument?"

"No," she cried. "Alix was so quiet and compliant I wondered what all the fuss around teenagers was about. She never complained."

"What about Robert?"

There was an intake of breath. "What about Robert?" Her voice had become stronger.

"Nothing. I'm just asking if Alix got along with Robert as well?"

"What are you suggesting?"

"I'm not suggesting anything, Suzie. This is not time to get defensive. You need to tell me everything if you want me to find Alix."

"There's nothing to tell," Suzie said. "Robert and Alix got along fine." She hesitated for a few moments. "He thought she was odd, that's all," she added.

"What do you mean odd?"

Suzie's tone rang of desperation now. "I don't know. God, Mitchell just find her, will you?"

Gray nodded. "Ok. I promise I'll find Alix." He placed his tablet back in its leather pouch and tucked it under his arm. There he was making promises again, promises he may not be able to keep. He looked up at Suzie.

"Right now, I have to get back to the station," he said gently. "But I'll let you know as soon as information on the location of the phone comes through, ok?"

He headed back down the hall the way he had come and stepped out onto the veranda. Suzie stood at the door watching him as he climbed into his car and left. He could see her in his rearview mirror.

Grey was cutting the corner of Makerston Street and almost back at the police station when his phone pinged again. He checked the screen to see google maps showing an image of Brisbane with a red light pulsing somewhere around Eight Mile Plains. He called Nova. "I'm out the front of headquarters," he said. "Hurry. "I'm double parked." While he waited for Nova, he called Suzie to tell her he'd found Alix's phone and presumably she was with it. He was going to pick her up.

It was less than two minutes before he saw Nova stride from the building her briefcase swung over her shoulder. She jumped in and Gray took off toward the Victoria Bridge.

"What the hell's going on?" she said.

Gray's lips were tight. "I had Alix's phone traced. We're going to the destination now. I'm hoping your presence might help smooth out any..."

"Any what? Emotions?" She glared at him.

Gray's knuckles were white on the steering wheel, his facial muscles clenched tight.

He didn't answer.

Nova watched him out of the corner of her eye. "I get that you feel like you let Christine down," she said.

Gray shifted his grip on the wheel and clenched his jaw as he sped through a red light.

"There's no point feeling sorry for yourself, you know," she said. "It's a waste of energy."

"I'm not sorry for myself." The words sounded too loud in Gray's ear. "I'm ashamed," he added quietly.

"Same thing," clipped Nova.

Gray continued as though she hadn't spoken. "The truth is, I've never been good with responsibility. Not when it comes to personal relationships."

Nova stayed silent.

"My father was the most responsible man I know," Gray went on. "My mother passed when I was twelve. He didn't miss a beat. Took care of me while building a career for himself in the force. He was there for every sports event, for every graduation ceremony. Even when I graduated from the Police Academy, he was there with a catheter attached to his bloody wheelchair. He died from cancer three weeks later."

"So, you think you can't possibly live up to his example?"

Gray slowed down a little as they crossed a bridge, the bump of the struts jolting them across in a steady rhythm.

"I can't," Gray said matter-of-factly.

"Bullshit," Nova responded.

Gray tucked in his chin and tightened his grip on the wheel.

"You're trying to live up to an ideal in your head, an ideal that a twelve-year-old kid came up with." Nova sniffed.

"I've had one serious relationship in my life, and I blew it," Gray's voice was an octave too high.

"Everything is not about you," said Nova.

Shocked, Gray turned to look at her.

"Watch the road," she said, pointing toward the windscreen. "Your fiancé died, and you weren't around. You probably weren't present through most of the time you had together. Then you abandoned Alix because it was too painful for you to be there for her. You're right. Those were the acts of a selfish prick."

Gray was stunned.

"But they don't define the rest of your life. Get over yourself and put it right."

Gray couldn't speak for a few moments. His face was burning. He knew the red flush that always gave away his emotions when he was trying not to have any was creeping up his neck.

Nova watched the river speed by in the opposite direction as they veered west.

Gray chewed over the suggestion that he 'put it right' for the remainder of the drive. Would Alix give him another chance? Did he even deserve that? The girl will have healed. She was probably over the hurt by now. Did he have any right to risk causing her pain again by suddenly turning up and wanting to be part of her life? A voice in his head, which had annoyingly taken on the cadence of Nova's voice told him he was making excuses yet again. If he was honest, he didn't know if he was ready to give up feeling sorry for himself.

When they arrived at the address they'd been given, Gray noticed how run down the house and yard looked. The grass was knee high, and weeds had choked what once might have been a nice garden. Paint peeled off the wooden boards of the house.

They picked their way across the front yard to the bottom of the staircase. One of the lower steps had rotted through on one side and Gray and Nova slipped sideways passed the gap. They reached the top of the stairs to find the door ajar. Gray knocked twice on the open door, then they entered. Young people were strewn about everywhere, like a giant had flung them across furniture and floorboards. A group of five were painting signs on the floor, getting paint on the carpet, two in the kitchen ate cereal from plastic bowls, and several voices could be heard from the bedrooms. While Gray was trying to get his bearings, a girl came out of the shower in shorts and a singlet, drying her long hair with a towel. She stopped and stared at him.

"What are you doing here?" she said.

God, she looked like Christine!

"Looking for you," said Gray.

The girl wound the towel onto her hair and placed her hands on her hips. "They didn't call the Police on me, did they?"

Gray's tone was even. "Your Aunt and Uncle are worried about you."

The girl laughed and threw herself onto a settee. Stuffing burst through the vinyl.

"Is there somewhere quieter we can talk?" asked Gray.

"I saw a coffee shop a little way back," said Nova. "Maybe we could have coffee?"

Alix narrowed her eyes as she scanned Nova. "Who's she?" asked the teenager.

"This is Nova. Nova this is Alix."

Nova smiled.

"Is she another policewoman? Or worse, a bloody social worker," Alix scoffed.

"Neither" said Nova. "I'm an anthropologist."

Alix laughed again. "What am I? A lost tribe or something."

But she stood up and headed for the door weaving her hair into a colourful scrunchie as she did. Gray and Nova followed her.

They were quiet while they drove the few blocks to the coffee shop. Gray watched Alix through the rear vision mirror as she stared out of the window. She smelled of fresh apricots, presumably it was her shampoo.

"She's masking our sweaty odour," Nova smiled.

Gray screeched to a halt in the car park in front of the café.

"I see your driving hasn't changed," Alix quipped.

Nova shot her an amused glance.

Crossing the parking lot, they left the Crown behind and approached the coffee shop, with its exterior crowded by a wild tangle of tropical plants. Inside was an assortment of oddly mismatched wooden tables and chairs that seemed to have been rescued from a forgotten corner of the twentieth century. An Expresso machine whirred amidst the smell of fresh coffee.

Gray, Nova and Alix squeezed into a spot near the window. Gray looked at Alix taking in the familiar blue eyes and defiant expression.

"It's good to see you," he said as they settled in and placed their orders.

Alix met his gaze, accusation in her eyes. "Hmm," she replied. "I didn't think you were bothered."

Gray blinked, taken aback by the bluntness of her response.

"It's alright," she said, her tone more resigned than indifferent. "Why would you be. You were mum's partner. No reason to bother with me once she was gone." A note of vulnerability underlay the words, the air of someone who had given up on being understood.

Gray hesitated, searching for words that had eluded him for the past year. He glanced at Nova, silently appealing for help. Her raised eyebrows indicated there was none coming.

He took a measured breath. "I'm sorry, I didn't keep in touch," he said, at last admitting the truth. "I won't insult your intelligence with excuses. I just didn't know how." His voice bore the weight of regret, raw and unguarded.

Alix lifted blue eyes and looked at him from beneath long lashes. "I guess I didn't know how either," she said quietly.

A waiter interrupted the moment, delivering two coffees and a chai latte to the table. Alix took a sip, emerging with a frothy moustache that she swept away with an unconcerned swipe of the back of her hand.

"How's it been, living with Suzie and Rob?" Gray asked, conscious of how bereft and lost he'd felt losing his own mother in his early teens.

Alix threw her head back and groaned.

"Insufferable," she said.

Gray looked shocked. "Suzie's nice, isn't she?"

"Suzie's ok," she said with a dismissive shrug.

Gray tried a different tack. "What about Rob, then?" he pressed, his eyes searching hers.

Her expression was incredulous at first, then she recoiled with distaste. "God! It's nothing like that!" she said horrified. "What's wrong with you policemen? You see crims everywhere!"

She screwed up her face as if she'd tasted something bitter. "He's just a moron. He makes racist comments all the time and he watches right-wing news. He believes everything he sees on TV. He even gets on those rubbish internet sites that rant about the refugee crisis." She made quotation marks in the air with her fingers when she said, 'refugee crisis.'

"Like the refugees wanted to be bombed and shat on and sent away from their own country." Her words tumbled out in a rapid stream, fuelled by the righteous indignation of feeling constantly misunderstood.

Gray relaxed. "So, you don't agree with his politics."

"Of course I don't. I told you. He's a moron." Her voice left no room for doubt.

"Have you told Suzie about it?" he asked, wondering how much tension there was inside the home.

Alix's eyes met his with a fierce intensity. "Suzie just wants everyone to get along. I can't stay silent when he's talking shit. Bad things happen when good people stay silent," Alix said emphatically. She stopped to sip her latte, her stance unwavering.

"But you do have to live in his house until you can afford a place of your own," said Gray.

Alix shook her head, making her ponytail swing dramatically with the motion. "No. I don't," she said. "I can stay at the protest house. I'll be just fine there for now."

"Is that what they call that dump we just picked you up from?" he said, scepticism thinly veiled.

Alix placed her forearms flat on the table between them, leaning in with fiery determination. Her blue eyes were sharp as glass, and her cheeks flushed with defiant energy. "It might be a dump," she said. "But at least it's full of people with a capacity for critical thinking. At least it's full of people who have compassion and empathy." She glared at Gray, daring him to argue with her, her intensity unwavering.

"Sure, and cockroaches and rats too, I reckon," he said calmly.

"I don't care," she shot back, her lips pouting.

Gray watched her, his features softening into a mixture of frustration and concern. "You sound like a petulant toddler," he said. "How'll you pay rent and pay for food?"

She scrunched her nose, dismissing him with a tone that implied he was the one being naïve. "I can apply for a Centrelink allowance. We can pool our money and expenses." She rolled her eyes, as if the solution was glaringly obvious.

"That's not legal," said Gray, his voice edged with authority. "You'll have to declare all those people living together receiving benefits."

"Are you going to dob me in?" she asked?

"I might." Gray met her intense gaze, refusing to back down, but feeling the tension rise between them.

They stared one another down while the air crackled with the silent clash of wills.

Gray surrendered first, letting out a slow exhalation. He didn't want to lecture the girl, didn't want to be another authority figure trying to cage her spirit, but there were things she needed to learn if she was going to survive in this world.

"Look, I get it," he began, choosing his words carefully. "You're a smart kid and your mum and I always included you in our discussions about world affairs. You don't feel comfortable living with someone who has such divergent views from yours. I probably wouldn't either. But sometimes we have to bite our tongues and put up with it, for the short term."

By the look on the teenager's face, it seemed she was preparing for a new outburst, but Nova stepped in.

"Maybe you can help us with this case we're working on," she suggested.

Both Alix and Gray turned to look at her in surprise.

"Excuse me?" said Gray.

Nova continued undeterred. "Do you know anything about someone with the username Spectre?"

Alix stopped pouting and looked thoughtful. "I don't know much, but Carter does. He's back at the house. He knows all about Spectre."

"Do you think Carter would talk to us?" asked Nova.

Alix shrugged and drank the last of her chai. "He might," she said. "He doesn't like the police much, but he might talk to you."

"You're right," Gray told Nova. "We haven't followed up on this connection between Lividia Harlin and Spectre. This might be the ideal opportunity to do that."

"The name has the ring of youth to it, if you ask me," Nova said. "If you need to find out about a young person, ask young people."

"Good thinking," said Gray.

Alix had been watching them, her eyes darting back and forth. "Spectre is young," she said. "Even I know that much."

Ten minutes later they were sitting in a cramped office space at the Protest House. The kids had partitioned off one end of the veranda with an old wardrobe and created the makeshift office. A desktop whirred amidst a pile of tangled cables and mobile phones. Carter sat on an ergonomic gaming chair, the master of his space. Though eighteen at most, he was charismatic with a square jaw, piercing eyes and an asymmetrical haircut, shaved to his head on one side and flopping down over his right eye on the other.

Alix had gone in first and asked if he was prepared to speak with her 'stepfather' and his friend about Spectre. The sound of the word 'stepfather' coming out of her mouth made Gray's heart miss a beat. After he abandoned her in her grief, she was still using that term to introduce him.

"So, you want to know about Spectre?" Carter said in a voice deeper than expected for his age, once they had been allowed into his domain.

Gray was uncomfortable, his knees tucked up tight against his body in the small space. Nova seemed perfectly at ease.

"What do you know about them?" she said.

Carter flicked the hair from his eyes. "There's an organisation called Spectre, and it's led by a man who also calls himself Spectre. He recruits kids on-line and grooms them. He's only interested in young people. He argues that anyone over 25 is already irrelevant."

Carter watched their faces closely. "In that, he might have a point."

Gray's lips twitched, "Harsh," he said.

Carter sat back in his ergonomic gaming chair. "Well, it's a fuck up, isn't it?" he began. "The world. It will be up to the young to fix things. But that's where Spectre and I part ways. Spectre believes each Nation State needs to take care of its own. He thinks the first step is to get the refugees out of Australia through stirring up so much fear and hate the government will have to change tack. We suspect that Spectre has wealthy backers from political parties that support a return to the White Australia policies of a century ago. People like Leonie Nolan."

Gray took a moment to process the audacity of these young people. Nova, on the other hand, asked calmly, "And what about you Carter, what do you believe?"

Carter raised his eyebrows and spoke with the confidence of a man twice his age. "I believe the horse has already bolted. War ravaged deserts can't sustain large populations, there are too many people in countries that are too small to feed them, the climate is shrinking sustainable land masses - there's no practical choice but to learn to live together in a globalised world. We need to appreciate diversity and all play to our cultural strengths."

"Admirable," said Nova. "But..."

Gray feared a lengthy philosophical debate was coming and cut in, "Do you know the identity of this Spectre individual?"

"No," said Carter. "Hardly anyone knows who he is. We only know he's young because of his ideology about it being down to the young to save the world."

Gray chose his next words carefully. On the surface, the protest house appeared to be a place where an alternative ideology to the anti-refugee movement was growing, but did that mean he could trust this kid? "We have half the cyber-security specialists in the country searching the dark web. Why isn't there a red flag on this Spectre?"

"That's the trouble," said Carter. "You people go big. You're looking among known terror cells, international organisations. You couldn't imagine a group of young people could be quietly threatening peace from their garages and basements."

Gray blew air through his lips. "You don't think Spectre could be behind the drone attack, do you?"

Carter shrugged. "Why not?"

"I'm asking if you have any direct knowledge of his involvement," said Gray.

"I do not," Carter shook his head. "I'm just saying I wouldn't be surprised if he did. His rhetoric on-line is volatile enough. But most of his communications 'in-house' are encrypted. It's a small group when you get down to the actual members of the organisation."

A question came to Gray with such urgency it slipped out before he had time to think it through.

"Did you know Seeton Harlin?"

Carter's eyes narrowed. "I knew him," he said.

Gray waited for more. The younger man hesitated. "Seeton was collecting information on terrorist groups operating in Australia."

"We know," said Gray. "Was he working with Spectre?"

Carter looked like he might be considering that possibility. Then he shrugged his shoulders.

"Who knows? I really didn't know Seeton that well. Saw him a couple of times at rallies against the refugees. He certainly seemed to share the same views as Spectre. He could have known him. Most young people in Brisbane know of Spectre, at least. He's a bit of an enigma."

He turned back to his desktop. "I hope I've helped," he said flicking back his hair. He was already tapping at the keyboard. Interesting that he still had one of the older models with actual keys.

Feeling dismissed, Gray and Nova squeezed their way past the wardrobe partition and out onto the veranda where Alix sat cross-legged on the floor, absorbed in scrolling on her tablet. She looked up as they approached, scrutinizing their expressions with a curious tilt of her head. "Get what you wanted?" she asked.

Gray nodded slowly, "Yeah," he replied. "You know I'm going to have to take you home," he said.

Alix glanced at the overnight bag beside her. "I thought you would," she said resignedly, a hint of defiance lurking beneath her acceptance. Her fingers tapped idly on the screen she was holding. She picked up the bag and held it up as if in surrender. "If I don't come with you now, you'll send a cop car to pick me up, won't you?"

"Yep," said Gray, with a grin that was both amused and resigned. He admired her tenacity but felt a surge of protectiveness as well.

Alix slung her bag over one shoulder and made her way through the cluttered apartment. She paused for a moment, looking around. She turned back to Gray and Nova determination etched in her young features. "I'm not going to stop working with the protesters here," she said, as if daring him to oppose her decision.

Gray chuckled softly. "Wouldn't want you to," he replied, letting her know he respected her convictions.

Nova watched the exchange, intrigued.

Alix nodded as she continued her exit.

"I suppose I'll just have to stay in my room the whole time when I'm at home," she said. Her voice carried a mixture of frustration and acceptance, as though she were bracing herself for an inevitable battle. "Just to avoid confrontation with my uncle."

Gray watched her thoughtfully, his empathy deepening as he noted the weary resignation in her movements. He followed her down the stairs and out of the building. "I promise I'll come over and save you on the weekends," he said sincerely, extending a hand to help her into the car.

She paused, looking at him with a mixture of hope and scepticism.

"Now that we've reconnected, I don't want to lose touch again."

The girl hesitated, her defences lowering momentarily. She smiled at him, looking like an unsure sixteen-year-old, her previous bravado giving way to vulnerability. It was clear she didn't know whether to believe him entirely. Gray made a silent vow to himself, determined not to let her down, not this time. He wouldn't allow his past detachment to define their relationship.

"I've missed this old car," Alix said as they climbed into the Crown.

CHAPTER TWENTY-FOUR

Alix was dropped off to a very relieved Suzie and less than twenty minutes later, Gray and Nova were back at the office. They had only just arrived when Chandra came crashing in, his face flushed and his cardigan askew.

"There's breaking news," he said, out of breath. Gray quickly tapped into NewsNet.com.

At first the screen showed a chaotic scene that was difficult to make out. A red strip ran along the bottom of the screen. "Killer drone attack in Circular Quay."

In the foreground, terrified people, some in business suits and some in jeans and t-shirts ran along the harbourside in both directions and out onto the street stopping traffic. As they watched, an ambulance pushed through to the centre of the crowd, siren blazing. The ambulance was followed by a cavalcade of police cars.

Gray counted at least six of them park in an arc around a body on the pavement.

In the background the blue of Sydney's harbour sparkled, and the green and yellow ferries bobbed helplessly.

Gray's muscles tensed as he grabbed hold of the desk. This was a brazen attack made in a crowded space. Here it was streaming across the country in real time. It would already have been picked up by every influencer and amateur blogger in the nation, and soon the world. Circular Quay was probably the second most iconic spot in Australia, after the view of the Opera house flanked by the Harbour Bridge.

"Holy shit!" said Glenda.

"The victim...is he Arabic?" asked Nova.

They peered at the screen. A body bag was picked up and transferred into the back of the ambulance.

"A Palestinian refugee has been attacked by a killer drone..." the words travelled across the bottom of the screen. "Police fear the killing was an act of terrorism...."

"Oh My God!" said Nova, leaning back in her chair and holding her hands to her head.

"Our drone attack hit the airwaves fast," said Gray, "but this is such a crowded space. People must be terrified!"

"We can't find any motive for targeting Mohammed," said Chandra. "I wonder if this victim has links to Hamas, Hezbollah or Al-Qaida." He rolled his eyes.

"What if this is domestic," said Nova. "It's more likely to be the work of a right-wing extremist group like the National Socialist Order or someone off Terrorgram."

"But Seeton only collected data on terrorist activity from the Palestinian side," said Chandra. "If he had anything on white supremacists, it wasn't on the card."

"Why would the perpetrator bother going interstate?" said Gray, thinking aloud.

"Maybe to spark fear at the national level?" suggested Chandra.

King was chewing the end of her pen, horror in her eyes. "Spreading the attacks across state borders does give the impression of power," she said. "It brings to mind a large organisation with wide ranging reach."

Gray tried to imagine a large organisation spread across the nation co-ordinating these attacks. The National Socialist Order had around fifty thousand members in Australia, but presumably the cybersecurity experts found nothing in their searches to hint at their involvement in the drone attacks. If an organisation such as the National Socialist Order were involved, they'd claim responsibility. Otherwise, what would be the point?

Niggling doubts wouldn't leave him. It just didn't sit right.

Gray looked to Nova for her thoughts, but the expression on her face troubled him even further. Her jaw was clenched tight.

He wanted to demand she share her thoughts with him immediately, but something stopped him. He had to admit to himself he was afraid of what she might say.

He paced around the room instead, unable to calm the muscles that burned in his calves. His usual way of dealing with frustration or fear was to run. He could have run until his chest exploded, but it was time to think. He forced himself to sit back down in front of the screen where the grim face of the Prime Minister was issuing a statement of condemnation for the attack.

"Attacks that stir up hatred and terror such as these attacks in Sydney this morning, and in Brisbane two days ago, have no place in Australia. Those responsible for these attacks will face the full force of the law and my government will provide all necessary support for this effort."

"It's all very well," said Nova as she watched the screen. "But what are these people going to do? Stay indoors until we catch whoever's behind this?"

Gray shook his head. "I would," he said, and switched off the news bulletin.

Speaking with a calm authority he didn't feel, Gray said, "The NSW authorities will have their hands full for a few hours. We continue with the investigation here as planned, until we hear otherwise."

He turned to Glenda King and Rishi Chandra. "Get back to the interviews," he said. "If there's a lead, we need to know about it, fast."

"You, in here with me," he said to Nova.

She glared at him.

"Please?" he added.

She followed him into the office they shared temporarily.

"Spill it," he said.

"I'm worried that these two attacks are trials for something bigger," said Nova.

"What - 'something bigger?'"

"Sophisticated robots like we are seeing here can cost less than a smartphone." She said "Ok. But what makes you think the two events we've already seen are a trial for something bigger?"

"They have to be," said Nova. "What's the point of killing off the refugees one person at a time? If you want to make a statement, you would surely want a mass attack."

What she said made sense to Gray, though it sickened him.

She went on, "What scares me most about these drones is the potential for swarm intelligence."

Gray blew air through his lips and pinched his nose. "What's that?" he asked, scarcely wanting to know.

Nova looked earnest. "Groups of drones can work together, like a school of fish, or a flock of birds. They share information and co-ordinate their activities. If one drone detects a problem, the information will be shared around, as well as a solution. If some drones are lost, others automatically take over and complete the mission. They make split second decisions that prevent us from jamming the frequencies they're operating on.

They take counter measures faster than any human operator can react. They would be almost impossible to stop."

Gray was silent for a few minutes. "Let's not get ahead of ourselves," he said. "I'm finding it difficult enough to cope with what we already know, without speculating."

"I need to see the drones," said Nova, her face as grave as he'd seen it.

Gray's mind began racing through the conversations of the last couple of days trying to remember any reference to the drones having been located.

"No one's found the drones," he said. "At least no one's admitting to it. The experts are scanning the...'whatever' in cyberspace," Gray waved one hand over his head, "to try and ascertain how they were controlled or the flight path. But they haven't found any portion of the drones."

"Then I need to study the surveillance footage," she said. "Every angle. Whatever we have in relation to both drones."

"Ok," said Gray. "That we can do."

Twenty minutes later, Nova was still sitting in front of a wide screen watching the surveillance footage from the morning's incident in Sydney. Her face was centimetres from the screen and her whole body was tense. Gray stood behind her for a few minutes watching, then Nova looked up startled. A look of panic in her eyes chilled Gray.

"Are they targeting individuals? Or are they targeting ethnicity?" she breathed.

"Ethnicity... What?"

"We already know these drones are operating on artificial intelligence to kill. I don't think they're being programmed to kill certain individuals. I think they're being programmed to identify ethnicity."

Gray leaned into the screen over her shoulder. "What makes you think that?"

"This is CCTV footage from Sydney's North Quay," she said. "It's exceptionally well covered." She pointed a perfectly varnished nail at the screen. "Look," she said.

A tiny drone, small enough to fit into the palm of a hand, whizzed between people in the crowd, then it hovered for a split second before a man who was standing a little apart from others. There was a small explosion, and he went down. Something could be seen at the edge of the shot indicating the drone was already heading back to where it came from.

"It was the same at the mosque. The drone could have hit any one of the men heading toward the stairs, but the victim was a little behind after speaking with his children. It wasn't random, it was opportunistic. The easy prey falling behind the pack."

Gray's face went pale. "Fuck!" he cried. "Is that even possible?

Nova looked into his eyes and saw her own fear reflected there. "It's theoretically possible," she said. "You could adapt a recreational drone into a killer drone. You'd have to do a camera upgrade. It would need a high resolution capable of capturing detailed facial features. There'd need to be cloud based facial recognition software and a machine learning model database of labelled images from various ethnic groups to train the program to accurately identify one ethnicity. That would be the most technically complex part of the task. But we know basic facial recognition capability is common, the elevator at your apartment uses it." Nova stared deeply into Gray's eyes.

"There would need to be powerful processors on board, to handle real time data processing and analysis," she went on. "It would cost some money, but not a King's ransom."

Gray felt physically ill. This case had him so far out of his depth he was expecting to drown at any moment.

Nova shook her head and looked back at the screen. "You need to warn Charfield. If this kind of technology is being used," she turned her eyes to the detective, "it's a game changer, Gray."

The Chief Superintendent had his head down over a mess of paperwork when Gray arrived at his door. Charfield raised his eyes from the document he was signing and Gray walked in and sat himself heavily in the chair.

"I have some information," he began, then checked himself. "Well, not information exactly, it's a theory..."

"Spit it out," said Charfield irritably. Gray opened his mouth to speak but Charfield held up his hand for him to wait, pressing a button on his intercom, "Come in here a minute will you," he said. Assistant Commissioner Bryant strode in and stood, his shoulders pressed back against the wall, so he was looking down at Gray who shuffled uncomfortably.

Expectations were high.

"Dr Corbin has reviewed the surveillance for both incidents," he began, "and she is of the opinion that the drones are not only acting independently when they strike, they are likely programmed with some kind of ethnicity recognition."

Chief Superintendent Charfield and Assistant Commissioner Bryant stared at him with blank faces. "Let me get this straight," said Charfield, "you're saying the killer drones are not programmed to kill individuals – they're programmed to strike random targets of a specific ethnicity?"

"Correct," said Gray, shifting again in his seat. He felt their gaze like a laser to his head. "What makes her think so?" asked Charfield.

Bryant turned to face the window. He stood there staring out while Gray relayed Nova's thought processes.

"Is that even possible?" asked the Superintendent.

Gray nodded. "Apparently."

Charfield pressed his face against his chest until his chins were squeezed like an accordion. "Who knows about Corbin's theory?"

"Only us, sir. You two, Corbin and myself."

"We have to contain this as long as we can. If Corbin can think it, so can the other experts we have working on this. They'll get there and it will come out. Until then, we don't want the conspiracy theorists running rampant. No one is to know. You continue the investigation as if it were any other murder enquiry. The NSW Police are doing the same with their incident. The Federal Police and ASIO are pursuing the data found in Seeton Harlin's file.

Charfield shook his head causing his chins to wobble as he let out a sound that fell somewhere between a sigh and a groan. "This has got to be about the different factions within the refugees themselves," he said. "The Harlin data provides evidence of activity here in Brisbane relating to the Islamic State," he turned watery eyes on Gray. "They encourage this kind of thing."

Gray opened his mouth to object, but the Superintendent was in full voice by now. "The Lebanese have been here for a generation, they're not taking kindly to the influx of newcomers from Gaza, either. We've got Palestinians with loyalty to Fatah and others with loyalty to Hamas. There are Sunni and Shiites wanting to kill one another. Palestinians who still support Hamas and others who hate them for igniting the war that lost them their homeland. It's a bloody mess. It's no wonder we've got mayhem on the streets."

"I still don't understand why they'd be attacking their own countrymen, here in Brisbane." Gray's voice was again, an octave higher than he would have liked, but he couldn't believe what he was hearing.

Charfield shook his head. "It's about creating fear," he said. "Acute and catastrophic displays of violence stir up fear in a big way. They've achieved that, for sure."

Gray felt a prickling sensation at the base of his neck. "In that case," he said. "It may as easily be domestic terrorism, the work of some right-wing Nationalist group wanting to stir up hatred. The National Socialist Order, for example, are clear about their agenda to bring about a race war to facilitate the downfall of our institutions. The 'mayhem' in the streets, after all, has mostly been the result of white Australians protesting." The words hung in the air held by an underlying tension in the room.

Charfield stared at him, his rheumy eyes wide.

"But at the same time," Gray went on, "it might be about a small group of individuals wanting revenge for the killing of Seeton Harlin."

Charfield lifted his chin and blew air through ample lips. "This is the work of more than one bloody redneck who doesn't like Palestinians," he said. "This is organised."

"Regardless," Bryant cut in, turning around to face Gray, "Public sentiment is already simmering with anti-refugee rhetoric."

Bryant's phone pinged and he looked down, immediately silencing it, and placing it in his coat pocket. But not before Gray glimpsed Leonie Nolan's name on the caller identification.

Gray glanced at the Assistant Commissioner moments before he stood to leave the office. There was something in Bryant's eyes that made Gray's skin crawl.

CHAPTER TWENTY-FIVE

Gray rejoined Nova in their shared office. The room was small and cramped with two of them in it. Still, he was unexpectedly happy to have her there. It felt good to have someone to share his thoughts with, someone he wasn't directly responsible for. He'd become used to ducking and weaving between superiors who expected the impossible from him and underlings who needed his direction to achieve the impossible. Nova wasn't part of the system she sat outside it. And her insights in this case were invaluable.

"Explain to me what you're thinking," he said. "I want to understand."

Nova slumped into the chair and placed her elbows on the desk. He pulled his own chair around to her side and leaned in closely. When she turned her face to him, they were only inches apart. As she spoke, her breath gently tickled his skin.

"There's more to come," she said, her face pale.

Gray held her gaze for a moment, "How long till the next attack, do you think?"

A frown settled between perfectly formed brows. "A couple of days, no more. And the attacks will escalate, I'm certain of it. They're testing equipment, fuelling public outrage, they're preparing for something big."

"Do you think Seeton's death is part of it?"

Corbin nodded. "Probably. In some ways it doesn't matter which side dies, as long as the hate continues to grow. If white supremacists are involved, they would have expected Seeton's death to be placed squarely at Ibrahim's door. But, as it turns out, the confusion has only served their purpose more effectively."

Gray felt a lump form in his throat. Three men killed just to stir up hatred. It didn't seem possible. "Surely, we haven't come to this, as a society," he said. "Three decades of unmitigated hate speech on-line and here we are."

Nova shook her head. "People have always gathered in hate groups. We didn't need the internet or social media to generate hate."

Gray knew she was right.

"The holocaust didn't start with the gas chambers," Nova added. "There was a whole campaign of dehumanisation of a minority that set the stage first. Hate speech prepares ordinary people to become enablers of genocide. Don't get me wrong, social media is an effective way to spread hate. But people have always found ways. Hitler's Ministry of Propaganda, for example."

Gray took a long, deep breath. "We continue on as with any other homicide," he said more to himself than to Nova. He didn't know of any other way to proceed.

He looked up to see Rishi Chandra at the door wielding a tablet as though it were a sword.

"We've started the interviews with people Harlin outed as involved with nefarious organisations," he said. "So far, alibis check out for the morning of the protest. But we'll keep at it." He held the tablet aloft. "I have a spreadsheet," he said. "So, we can follow up with anyone if we need to."

Gray smiled. "Good," he said. "I knew you'd have a spreadsheet."

Chandra puffed out his narrow chest.

Gray nodded, still smiling. Sarcasm was lost on the young officer, and Gray admired him for it.

"Be careful," Gray warned. "We remain focussed on potential involvement with the Harlin killing. The Federal Police are investigating the drone attack."

"Of course, sir," said Chandra. His mop of thick brown hair had fallen over his face.

Gray knew the authorities would be poring over Seeton's files. The Federal Police, ASIO teams. It would take weeks to locate and interview all the people listed.

They'd be looking to link individuals with terror cells, identify potential plots and risks. The death of Seeton Harlin would fall far from their minds. If they identified his killer, it would be, at best, a welcome side effect of the investigation.

Gray felt certain Nova was correct in her assessment that there was something big brewing. And there was nothing in the intel from Seeton's computer to suggest the kind of attack that had taken place at the mosque in Brisbane or at Circular Quay. The drone attacks were something else, organised, yet somehow, small, naive...

Gray felt the sweat gathering on his forehead and tried wiping it away with the back of his hand. He stood up and turned away from the computer, loosening his shoulders and shaking his hands. Every cell in his body was straining to move forward, to do something, to take action. He was on edge, his muscles tight and coiled like a spring. Maybe I should go for a run, he said to himself.

He turned back toward Nova, who was staring past her screen, rather than into it.

"I've been there," she said.

"Sorry?" said Gray unsure where, exactly, she meant.

"Gaza. When I was little, Nine or ten, I think. I was there in 2000 and 2001."

"Really?" Gray's eyebrows shot up. "How?"

Nova glanced out of the window at the open-plan office beyond. "My parents were both archaeologists," she said. "They were working for the University of Edinburgh at the time and operating as consultants on the Gaza Research Project."

"Wow," cried Gray. "You travelled with your parents."

"Yes. They had unusual ideas about parenting. They treated me as a small adult. I went everywhere with them. I didn't have any friends my own age. But I did go to some exciting places." She looked at Gray. He glanced sideways to catch her smile.

"What were they digging up in Gaza?"

Nova laughed. "Nothing that would shake your world," she said. "There were some pots found by a team in 1996. My parents and their team went back to carry out an investigation of the site, date the pots and provide some context."

"I didn't know there was archaeology in the Gaza strip."

Nova's eyes opened wide. "Oh yes, there are many sites of significance. This site was at al-Moghraga. The word means 'swampy ground' because it is more low lying than most of the sites in the region. It's in the vicinity of the Wadi-Gaza. The region is at the Palestinian terminus of the 'Ways of Horus', a trade and military route between Egypt and the Asian landmass. It was an important bronze age settlement."

"What was it like when you were there?" asked Gray.

"Dessert and rocks," said Nova looking at him again. "My parents planned to be there for at least three years. They were very excited about it. But the Palestinian Intifada in 2000 meant the dig was stopped. They had to leave the site with the work unfinished. It's a shame."

"Intifada, that's the uprising, right?"

Nova nodded. "Suicide bombings, Israeli airstrikes, the whole cycle of attack and retaliation that led us to where we are today."

Gray was trying to imagine this woman as a six-year-old girl sitting in the sand in Gaza while her parents dug up pots.

"It's a beautiful place, the devastation of war aside. Most of the refugees would gladly go back if they could. The land means everything to them."

Gray watched her as she recalled an idealised Gaza strip, through the eyes of a privileged little girl. But he understood what she was saying. Most of the refugees had not run away from their land, they had been forced from it. They weren't here by choice.

A message flashed up on Gray's screen. Chief Inspector Robert Curry of the Federal Police, Sydney office, wanted to speak with him via zoom. Gray sat back down at his desk and pressed the function key. The face of a man in his early sixties, comfortable in his own authority appeared on the screen. Introductions were made concisely and efficiently. Gray had never met Chief Inspector Robert Curry. He tried to get the measure of him, but the man's face gave away nothing. Gray was comfortable with that. He had his own lifetime of experience in not showing his emotions.

"This is an official call, Gray," said the Inspector, as though it could have been mistaken for anything else.

"We need to know where the computer card came from," he said.

Right to the point, then.

"I'm sorry," Gray replied. "I can't help you with that. It was left for me anonymously."

The Inspector paused. It was clear to Gray that he didn't believe him.

Let him go to hell.

"The card provides information that came from your victim, Seeton Harlin's computer. Encrypted information that our own specialists have been unable to decipher."

"Yes, I'm aware," said Gray.

The Inspector paused again. Hawk eyes watched Gray steadily until he felt like prey in an open field. But Mitchell Gray showed no outward sign of emotion, he could play that game as well.

"Questions of origin aside," the Inspector went on, "We'll be managing the case of the killer drones from here on in. As a matter of national security. Of course, your team will continue to lead the investigation into the Harlin killing. But intelligence in relation to the drone attacks you will pass on to me personally."

"Understood," said Gray.

"The attacks are being investigated within the context of national security and fall outside your auspice," Inspector Curry added for emphasis.

"Understood," said Gray.

"I mean it," he went on. "We don't need a band of 'tryhards' from Queensland blundering all over a National Security case."

Well, that went too far.

Gray intended to respond but he choked as the words started to form.

"Nice talking to you," said Curry, and signed out of the meeting.

He was gone before Gray replied, "And you."

Nova was sitting behind the computer listening to the exchange.

"They're wasting time," she said. "Whoever is responsible for the drones that killed Mohammed, and the Sydney victim is making more. I'm certain of it."

Gray watched her for a moment. "What I don't understand is why the perpetrators would use such an innovative device to kill one man at a time, alerting the world to the existence of the weaponry in the process, and without claiming responsibility."

"Surely, they'd bide their time and make the strike count."

"I want to know this - what's the end game?" said Gray.

The germ of an idea had begun to sprout in his mind. He'd been mulling it over since their conversation with Carter earlier in the day. He picked up his phone and tapped. "Carter?" he said.

Nova looked up from her laptop.

"I have a proposition for you. I want you to approach Spectre on-line. Create a new persona for yourself, if you like. See if you can find out what they're up."

Nova shook her head wildly. "This could be really dangerous," she hissed through clenched teeth.

Gray ignored her.

"We can pay you for your time. Like a consultant." He directed a smug glance toward Nova.

Nova was about to object strongly when her own phone rang. The screen read 'unknown caller.'

CHAPTER TWENTY-SIX

Nova answered and whispered to Gray. "It's Yusef, he says he has more information."

Gray peered over his computer screen at her. "Has he decoded the encrypted files?" he asked.

Nova started to repeat the question, but Yusef must have stopped her because her voice broke off. "He wants to meet," she said.

Gray raised an eyebrow. "Where?"

"The petrol station, like last time."

"Tell him we'll be there in ten minutes," Gray grabbed his keys from the desk and headed for the door with Nova close behind him. Before they reached the car, Gray's mobile pinged.

He looked at the screen to see a message from Shaw at the Cybersecurity Centre.

Chatter around the group called Spectre identified. Mostly encrypted. Will keep working on it. Also following the group on open-source communications. Will cross-check names on Seeton's list for links to this group.

Gray pressed 'ok' as he and Nova climbed into the car and settled in the cool leather. He started the engine. "Shaw's team are monitoring Spectre," he said.

"The more I think about it, the more it makes sense," Nova said. "Especially in light of Lividia's connection with them."

"Hmm," Gray's lips were stretched tight. "Spectre, encrypted messages...it's hard to take it seriously." But his face was deadly serious.

They saw the busy service station Yusef had set for the meeting to their left. It was just after school pick-up time and Commercial Road was crammed with mums in large four-wheel drives heading for the shops on their way home from picking up kids. The scorching sun had heated the bitumen to the point where it bubbled and stuck to the tyres like treacle. A thunderous sky had descended unnoticed so that it pressed down on the city like the lid on a pressure cooker. Everyone on the road was in a bad mood.

Nova recognised Yusef in the same hoodie he'd worn the first time they met. "There he is," she said pointing.

"How's he wearing that 'get-up' in this heat?" Gray asked.

The car slowed down until it almost stopped, "jump in," said Nova pushing the back door open. She wriggled back into her seat and re-fastened her safety belt while Yusef climbed in.

They'd agreed they'd take him back to Gray's apartment so they could speak freely. As they drove, Gray wondered for a moment whether they were taking a risk involving Yusef in the investigation. What if he was working against them? He pushed the idea aside. Yusef was simply trying to clear his name. He'd already proven himself to be a step ahead of the authorities. Whatever his motives, he was useful. Gray stared into the rearview mirror at the man in the tracksuit and hoodie pulled up over a baseball cap. Given the stifling heat, Gray wondered if he wasn't attracting attention in the outfit, rather than blending in.

Then he noticed the silver chain around Yusef's neck with two curious rings attached to it. They stood out against the black fabric of his tracksuit.

"What are those," he asked into the mirror. Yusef's hand went immediately to the tiny rings. He rubbed his fingers around the outside of each ring and Gray noticed they had numbers engraved on them. Yusef met Gray's eyes in the mirror.

"They are nothing," he said, almost breathless. He turned away to look out of the window. But a moment later, he turned back to catch Gray still watching him.

"I used to catch birds," Yusef said at last. "When I was a boy. It was my job to capture migrating birds and place tiny rings around their legs so their migration could be documented by the Environmental Centre." He looked down at the two rings he twisted between his thumb and forefinger. "These two birds, I let go, without ringing them. They carry the souls of my parents."

Gray shifted his eyes away from the mirror and exchanged glances with Nova. She shook her head so slightly Yusef would not have seen it. But Gray saw and didn't ask any more questions. He couldn't begin to imagine what Yusef's life was like prior to the war, prior to coming to Australia. They travelled the remainder of the way in silence.

Gray pulled into the driveway of his apartment block and slipped the Crown under the raised gate. It crashed down behind them providing the impression of security if not the substance. He and Nova hustled Yusef up the elevator while he kept his face down, hidden beneath the stifling hood.

Once established in the air-conditioning of Gray's s apartment, Yusef took another computer card from his pocket and slipped it into the portal on Nova's laptop.

"Wait," she cried, "Is that clean?"

Yusef ignored her.

"I've been tracking Lividia Harlin's on-line communications," he said. "It hasn't been easy. She and her brother have sophisticated encryption programs. Getting access to the lists from Seeton's computer was child's play compared to the security strategies Lividia's using now. But at the end of the day, I was able to do it."

Gray and Nova looked over his shoulder as the screen flashed and flickered on the laptop.

Gray desperately wanted him to tell them what he'd found out.

"You see, here," he said pointing to the screen. "As I told you, Lividia's in contact with this group called Spectre. She's been in communication for several hours per day every day since Seeton's death. I'm still working on the code so I can't read all the communications yet. But I investigated Spectre. There isn't many of them, but they have a significant presence on-line and much of their communication is not encrypted at all."

Yusef leaned back, his eyes darting between Gray and Nova. "They're very careful about their identities, and as I say there's not many of them. I'd guess no more than thirty or forty. But from what I can gather, they're a right-wing nationalist group that's been gaining traction online. All young, from what I can see, university students, some even younger. They push a lot of anti-immigrant rhetoric, especially targeting refugees. Their posts are full of conspiracy theories about how refugees are invading and replacing true Australians. And Lividia's been in constant contact with them since Seeton's death. I really think they may be behind the killer drone attacks."

Gray's brow furrowed. "This might make sense. There's something...naïve about this whole scenario. But...could a group of kids be responsible for building and executing killer drones?"

Nova faced him. "A group of young people would exactly fit the profile for the drone attacks." Her brow furrowed. "But I thought we were told to leave that investigation alone."

"We can't help it if we find something out while investigating Lividia Harlin, can we?" Gray's crooked grin was mirrored by the twinkle of his eyes.

"If we think this Spectre is a contender for the drone attacks, we need to tell Curry," Nova pointed out.

"And we will," Gray assured her. "As soon as we've interviewed Lividia."

He caught a sideways glance from the anthropologist.

"What? We don't have anything to say, yet. We need to know what Lividia and this Spectre are communicating about. First, Yusef needs to decrypt those files; second, we talk to Lividia. Once we know what her relationship with Spectre is about, we'll have the right questions."

"I'll get back to the safe house and continue working on the encryptions then," said Yusef.

"If we create a shared file on the cloud we can work on it together," Nova suggested. A few deft strokes of the keys and she had created the file and secured it.

Gray grabbed his keys. "I'll give you a lift home."

"No," said Yusef. "I can get the train. Within seconds, he was out of the apartment and gone.

CHAPTER TWENTY-SEVEN

ividia Harlin sat at Seeton's computer watching a live action feed of Circular Quay. Her eyes were red from lack of sleep, but she was used to working through the night. She preferred it. She'd left the warehouse in Bowen Hills at 6:00 a.m. and was home before her parents awoke at 7:00 a.m. Since then, she hadn't moved from her spot in the basement. The room formed a cave of shadow and silence around her. She hadn't bothered to switch on the lights, or open the blinds, preferring instead the feint blue glow of the monitor.

On the feed, a river of workers flowed steadily towards the terminals at Circular Quay. Business suits. Hi-Vis. The mundane details of their lives merged into one current. She let her gaze drift over the crowd, detached.

Then it happened. A single man in the crowd staggered forward, and his body crumpled. Around him people stopped, then surged back. Some screamed and ran. Some looked around in terror for a perpetrator.

Lividia leaned in, her breath catching in her throat. Her eyes locked on the screen, searching for... there. Just a moment, a flicker of motion above the heads of the onlookers. A small, dark shape zipped past, so fast it could have been mistaken for a bird or a speck of debris caught on the wind. But it wasn't. Her pulse quickened. She felt the weight of her body as though her limbs had grown heavier. She tried to steady her breath, but the air felt thick in her lungs.

Was this what she wanted?

She thought she would feel a sense of satisfaction. Pride. Anything. But she was numb. She ran the footage again from the beginning with the eye of a technician. The process had gone smoothly, the drone behaved exactly as she'd programmed it. This is what she loved the most about robotics. Machines were predictable. Up to a point, at least. There was always the possibility that artificial intelligence would come up with a unique interpretation of commands. Coding required surgical level precision.

Nonetheless, it was done, and she was satisfied. Authorities would now be casting a wide net in pursuit of the source of the "killer bots." Spectre had been wise to spread the trials across state borders. It had taken only ten hours for one of the kids to drive the prepared drone to Sydney and deliver it to one of Spectre's followers there. The drone had been programmed and ready to go, and there were no last-minute glitches.

Tonight, she would continue her work on the swarm.

CHAPTER TWENTY-EIGHT

NewsNet.com A Second Killer Drone Attack! Is Australian Identity really under attack?

BREAKING: The heart of Sydney pulsed with terror and confusion this morning when a killer drone left a man dead at Circular Quay just before midday. Eyewitnesses describe a scene "like a war zone," with pedestrians hitting the pavement as the device hovered in, evaded security, and unleashed a projectile into the crowd. Within seconds, the target lay motionless, blood pooling on the sandstone, while the drone buzzed off into the cityscape, destination unknown. Police responding to the incident immediately placed the entire CBD under lockdown, while the Prime Minister's office called it an act of unspeakable violence against the Australian way of life.

This marks the second such attack this week, and the parallels with the Brisbane event, a nearly identical drone, a dead man of Middle Eastern descent, and a crowded location have stoked fears that a coordinated campaign is underway. With two high-profile assassinations in major cities, public anxiety is nearing breaking point.

Parliament, already riven by debate over the resettlement of recent Palestinian refugees, has erupted into open blame. Member of Parliament Leonie Nolan, whose hardline stance on immigration has made her both a lightning rod and a rising star, seized the morning's tragedy to bolster her familiar refrain: "Terrorism has been brought to our shores by the Palestinian refugees. If we continue to tolerate Islam, our democracy will be lost."

On a special morning edition of "Breakfast with Banter," Nolan sat in-studio, hands clasped and jaw set, fielding questions from viewers across the country. "This is a test of our national character," she declared, her voice a blend of outrage and resolve. "Either we stand up for Australia, or we give away our children's future to foreign interests and foreign faiths."

The segment opened its lines: Message us your questions now, on 0407-009-010 IDENTITY, and the text scroll lit up with an avalanche of grievances, confessions, and demands for action.

Campbell from Inala: "We need to stop being the dumping ground for the world's problems. Why are we trading our peaceful country for this kind of violence?"

Leonie Nolan MP: "You sound angry, Campbell. And you should be. We need to collectively decide what kind of country we want to live in, in the future. Migrants who come to this country must have a desire to embrace our culture, our laws and our flag. The Palestinian refugees clearly do not have this desire. They pursue a way of life that is, quite frankly, in opposition to our own."

Jo from Ipswich: "We have an enclave of refugees here in our city. The government has built mosques for them. The children go to 'special schools.' Our local businesses are all staffed by Muslims. I can't even order my fish and chips without speaking bloody Arabic."

Leonie Nolan MP: "That's what we're all seeing, Jo. We have to understand that Islam is not just a religion. The religion and the law are the same thing. There's no separation. Slowly, but surely, we'll see our Christian values, ethics and customs being replaced."

Jim from Cleveland: "We've got mosques springing up everywhere. What can we do?"

Leonie Nolan MP: "There's an organisation called 'Stop the Mosques'. Get in touch. They help residents resist planning applications for mosques. Remember, mosques are where terrorists form plots."

The host, never one to dampen the flames, leaned in, eyes wide with earnestness. "Leonie, isn't it true that terror cells have used faith institutions as cover before? Isn't it time for what you've called 'uncompromising vigilance'?"

Nolan, eyes glinting, nodded. "Absolutely. And we're seeing the results now. For too long, we've let political correctness dictate policy, and our enemies have used that kindness as a weapon."

Another set of texts pinged on screen:

Tommy from Bundaberg: "My old man fought in Korea. He'd be rolling in his grave to see this. Why let in people who hate us?"

Leonie Nolan MP: "That's the question we all need to ask. This isn't about race, religion, or background. It's about allegiance. If you come here, you're expected to commit to Australia. If not, there's no place for you."

A grandmother from Wagga Wagga wrote: "Our grandson started school last week. He's the only English-speaking kid in the class. What does that say about where we're heading?"

Leonie Nolan MP: "It says we've lost our grip on what made this country great. We need to take it back, one classroom at a time."

Beyond the rhetoric, Federal Police have released a statement urging calm, but social feeds churn with speculation and #IdentityUnderSiege has been trending all morning.

Meanwhile, city streets are filled with nervous commuters, some openly praying, others scanning the skies above for the whine of tiny rotors. A halal bakery in Parramatta has been torched this morning; and police in Brisbane have reported a significant rise in hate crimes in the days since the attack in that city.

In Parliament, the Opposition called for restraint and unity, but few expected the mood to shift any time soon. Nolan, emboldened by her surging poll numbers, announced plans for a "National Values Summit," inviting only those "willing to put Australia first."

As protests erupted outside mosques throughout New South Wales and Queensland, counter-protestors gathered on the steps of the National Gallery, brandishing homemade banners painted with Arabic phrases and Palestinian flags. A scuffle broke out before police cordoned off the perimeter.

Nolan's final word, broadcast on all major networks: "If the government won't safeguard our communities, we will. This is the line in the sand. Are you with us?"

A public poll hosted on NewsNet's homepage showed 71% support for an immediate immigration freeze. Comment sections overflowed with a mix of fear, bravado, and veiled threats.

CHAPTER TWENTY-NINE

DAY SIX

Gray sat in the car with Nova, watching for any sign that someone might be home at the Harlin House. A hint of damp earth hung in the air from light rain overnight and it was already steaming up. Gray thanked his luck for the tall canopy of trees that shaded the car.

He watched the stark façade of the house looming at the end of the driveway, windows shut tight, and blinds drawn. No sign of life, just an unsettling stillness. The building had an institutional feel, a place where life was tightly controlled, not lived.

"Lividia could be in over her head," said Gray as he watched. "She's only seventeen, and there's so much anger." He wiped his face, as if to wipe away doubt. He knew the potential reach of men like Spectre, how they drew in the young. Perhaps Lividia didn't realize how much danger she was in.

Nova nodded, her eyes fixed on the house, reflecting their shared anxiety. "You think she's in danger?" she asked. "Or just lashing out to a sympathetic ear?"

"Both," said Gray.

He remembered Lividia's look of defiance mixed with fear, her eyes burning with the same grief and anger he'd seen in Alix at her mother's funeral.

He wasn't sure Lividia had any direct involvement in the recent attacks, but he suspected there was a good chance she knew something about them. At the very least, Spectre would be discussing the attacks online, perhaps even cheering the perpetrators on. It wasn't inconceivable that the group had orchestrated the incidents themselves, pulling strings from behind the scenes and using the chaos to further their agenda. Gray's mind raced through the possibilities knowing how quickly things could spiral out of control. Lividia was vulnerable, angry. She could have become involved in something she didn't understand. He hoped he and Nova would be able to draw some information out of her, for her own sake as well as the sake of others.

"Things are about to get worse for her," he said. "We need to hear what she knows."

Nova was silent, lost in her own thoughts.

"She might be neglected by her parents, but she still lives in the sheltered world of the wealthy. She's not used to people getting hurt." Nova closed her laptop and slipped it into her bag. "She's naïve." She paused before adding, "And full of righteous outrage."

Gray thought about that. "I know one thing," he said. "She doesn't trust us."

He could picture the inside of the house, its stark white walls mirroring the emptiness Lividia seemed to radiate. Her inability to trust, he knew, ran deeper than distrust of the police. It grew from the emotional distance her parents had sustained throughout her life. If you didn't learn trust from your parents, where would you learn it?

This thought led Gray to wonder whether Lividia's parents were home. It might be difficult for her to speak freely in front of them; their presence would almost certainly keep her guarded, at least in respect to her conversations with Spectre. As she was only seventeen, Gray knew he'd have to walk a fine line between 'talking' to her and 'interrogating' her without an adult present, a delicate balance that could mean the difference between gaining vital information and having her shut down completely. But it was essential they learn more about her knowledge of Spectre's activities.

Everything was still and quiet outside the house. Her parents might well be overseas again.

"It's hard to tell what's going on," said Gray. He opened the car door. "Let's do this," he said climbing out.

The two of them walked up the drive, and Gray reached for the doorbell, looking directly at the surveillance camera fixed above the entrance. "Think they have us on a do-not-answer list?" Gray asked.

"They won't ignore us, if they're in," Nova answered. "They'll want to know what we know."

They stood waiting.

The door stayed shut, the camera blinking in little red flashes. Nova shifted her weight from one foot to the other, but she looked more composed than Gray felt. The air was still and heavy with anticipation. He was about to ring again when the hydraulics kicked in and the door opened.

"Here we go," he said.

Lividia filled the doorway, her black clothes clinging haphazardly to her frame, and her hair, messy and unkempt, falling over eyes, bloodshot and rimmed with exhaustion. Her face was drained, like she hadn't slept for days. She seemed lost and disoriented.

"What do you want?" Her voice cut through the awkward silence. Without waiting for a response, she turned her back on them, a dismissive wave of her hand indicating she expected them to follow.

"We have some questions for you." Gray spoke with deliberate calmness. "Can we come in?"

Lividia was already halfway down the stark hallway. "Do what you want," she said, her voice flat and indifferent. She didn't glance back as she disappeared into the heart of the house.

Gray remembered a place of minimalism and order, that now echoed loneliness and neglect. Dirty bowls and piles of discarded take-out containers cluttered surfaces that were once immaculate. The house felt as though the life had been sucked out of it. Lividia moved through the spaces with detachment, her presence like a haunting.

She yanked open the refrigerator allowing a burst of light to cast an eerie glow on her hollow features. The stark illumination highlighted the pallor of her skin and the sunken quality of her eyes. She seemed almost translucent, like she might fade away at any moment. From where he stood, Gray saw bare shelves, containing only a limp, half-forgotten bunch of celery, an open carton of milk, and several cans of coke.

Lividia grabbed a can of soda and perched herself on the kitchen island, swinging her legs. She looked impossibly young, a teenage girl embroiled in something far beyond her years.

"What do you want with me this time?" she said, her voice tight, and charged with defiance.

Nova's eyes softened as she engaged the young woman. "How have you been doing?" she asked.

Lividia turned her head to meet Nova's gaze. "How'd you think?" she spat.

"Are your parents' home?" asked Gray looking around for signs of life.

Lividia rolled her eyes. "Of course they're not home," she said. "They're in Hong Kong"

Gray's brow furrowed in concern.

Lividia made a scoffing sound as she opened the can and took a long drink.

"Buying trip, or something. Some business. Whatever," said the teenager.

"I would have thought they'd stick around, at least until after Seeton's funeral next week," said Gray.

Lividia rolled her eyes. "I'm sure they'll be back for the funeral. They won't want to miss the attention."

"Didn't they leave you any food?" asked Nova.

Lividia shrugged her shoulders. "I have credit. I order UberEATS."

Nova shook her head. "We were hoping you could help us with information about an organisation we've heard about."

Gray watched the girl closely, while Nova went on without taking a breath. "Have you heard of a group called Spectre?"

Lividia's face reddened slightly despite her attempt to maintain composure.

"I may have heard of them on-line," she said. "Why do you want to know about them?"

"We think they may have been involved in Seeton's death," said Nova.

Gray's eyebrows shot up. That wasn't true.

Lividia's face reddened to a deep fuchsia. "Spectre had nothing to do with Seeton's death," she hissed. "You people are idiots."

"Enlighten us, then," said Gray.

Lividia's lips pursed.

"What can you tell us about Spectre?" asked Nova gently.

"They're just a group of people around Seeton's age, who think the influx of refugees has caused havoc in Brisbane. They think it's wrong that there's been no justice for Seeton's killing. They're the only ones who've been bothered about me since his death."

Gray was about to suggest that wasn't true. But looking around the empty house he thought it could, in fact, be true. How could the girl's parents leave her alone so soon after the death of her brother?

"Aren't your parents worried about the effect Seeton's loss has had on you?" He couldn't help himself asking.

"Sure, they are," said Lividia. "They've arranged for me to see a therapist three times a week." She made a hollow sound. "I haven't been though."

Gray felt his throat tighten. What kind of parents…? He reminded himself not to judge, but the lump in his throat remained, just the same.

"Do you know how many people are involved in Spectre?" asked Nova.

Lividia fiddled with the ring pull from her can. She was grinding her teeth as her eyes rested stubbornly on the aluminium circle she pushed on and off her fingers.

Gray caught Nova's eyes and with a subtle shake of his head communicated with her to wait. Experience told him the girl would speak if they left the door open for her to do so.

"I only talk to one person," she said at last. "He calls himself Spectre, he's obviously the leader of the group. He talks about justice and action."

"What kind of action?" asked Gray.

Lividia looked up at him, her face a wall of defiance.

"I don't know," she said. "Protests, I suppose."

Gray and Nova stared long and hard.

Lividia's jaw tightened.

"Tell us about your parents," said Gray.

Lividia breathed out noisily. "God," she cried. "Why do you keep talking about them? They're totally wound up in themselves, and their business, all right? They've never been interested in Seeton and me. They didn't even know him. Not who he was, really."

"So, you and Seeton must have been close all your lives?" suggested Nova.

Lividia's jaw relaxed a little and she chewed her lip.

"Surely, you want to help us find out who killed him?" she said.

Lividia threw her head back and groaned. "You people are so fucking stupid!" she shouted. "Spectre didn't kill Seeton. The Spectre group are the only people who cared about him."

Her face was contorted with rage and tears were forming under her eyes.

"We suspect that an organisation such as Spectre might be behind the recent drone attacks," said Gray watching the girl closely for micro-changes in her body language.

She glared back at Gray, her eyes cold. "If they are, I don't know about it," she said.

Gray held her gaze a moment longer, then, without further warning, she jumped from the Island.

"Get. Out. Of. My. House," she seethed.

Gray put up his hands in surrender. "Ok," he said. "We didn't mean to upset you. We're going." He turned Nova toward the entry hall, and they left calmly. They heard the door slam behind them.

Gray and Nova were relieved to be back in the car and driving toward the city.

"What do you think?" asked Nova.

"I think she knows more than she's saying." said Gray. "We need those messages back and forth between Lividia and Spectre decoded if we want to interrogate her properly. For all we know they've been discussing the latest Hollywood movie."

"In encrypted files?"

Gray shifted in his seat and placed his hands on the top of the steering wheel. "Who knows what teenagers will do," he said.

At that moment, Nova had a message come through from Yusef. "Haven't got anything from communications between Lividia and Spectre yet. But intercepted message between Spectre and an unknown third party. Trials effective. Capacity to fill large order immediately?

CHAPTER THIRTY

As he was turning into the car park under Police Headquarters, Gray directed his mobile assistant to book a small conference room on the second floor and to notify King and Chandra to meet him and Corbin there. It was at least two degrees cooler in the underground car park than it had been outside, so he was happy to step out of the car and head upstairs into the air-conditioned building. As Nova walked ahead of him, he noticed her dark blonde locks hanging limp on her shoulders. He tried to consolidate his thoughts before he reached the conference room and had to share them.

Exactly what had he learned pertaining to the Harlin murder? He knew Harlin was collecting intelligence on foreign terror groups. Could he also have been investigating domestic terror organisations? Did Seeton Harlin know about Spectre? Could he have been working with Spectre? The organisation's leader had been quick to connect with Lividia after her brother's death. Seeton's sister might be continuing her brother's work with the organisation. There was no separating the Harlin case from the drone attacks in his mind. Were the drone attacks revenge for the murder of Seeton? Or was there something even more sinister going on? There had now been two men killed by the drones and he was convinced Nova was correct in her assessment that more was coming.

It occurred to Gray that he needed to update Shaw and Thompson and find out what they'd picked up. He decided to get them on a conference call to join the meeting with King and Chandra. After the meeting, he'd call the Chief... and Curry from the Federal Police. Maybe he wouldn't call Curry.

King and Chandra were already in the meeting room when Gray and Nova arrived. Thanks to the efficiency of his mobile assistant, Shaw and Thompson's faces were looking out from a split screen on the table in front of Chandra. "Thank-you for making yourselves available at short notice," said Gray as he settled in at the opposite side of the table. He quickly explained the circumstances of his meeting with Carter.

"The lad confirmed the group known by the name Spectre, are led by an individual also calling himself Spectre. Carter didn't have a location for the entity, but he agreed to make contact and find out what he could."

Glenda King's eyebrows shot up. "Is that wise?" she said. "This Spectre could be dangerous."

Nova's left eyebrow was also raised. "That's what I said," she quipped.

"He's a smart lad," Gray assured them. "He won't put himself in danger. The thing is he knows how to contact them, how to speak their language." Gray went on. "In other news, Yusef has the ream of messages back and forth between Lividia and Spectre, beginning the night of Seeton's death. Apart from the initial greetings, the messages are encrypted, but Yusef is working on them."

"We're onto them, as well," said Shaw, quietly, but with commitment. "It sounds like this Spectre might be the link we've been looking for."

"Finally," Gray said, "Nova's assessment is that the two drone attacks have been a trial for something bigger, like a swarm attack. This may be borne out by messages Yusef has been able to decode between Spectre and a third party. The communications refer to successful trials and the ability to fill a supply order quickly."

"Supply of what?" asked Thompson.

"We don't know," replied Gray.

"Are we thinking it could be about preparations for a swarm attack?" Thompson went on.

"That's what Yusef thinks," said Gray.

There was silence for a moment while the others took in the information.

What do we know about Carter?" Shaw asked, blinking at Gray's chest.

"It appears he's heading a group of teenagers living together in a suburban house, where they organize protests in opposition to the anti-refugee movement. Essentially, they support refugees and advocate for a multicultural society where everyone contributes according to their abilities."

"Hmm," said Thompson. "This broadens the possibilities for the Harlin killing."

"I know," said Gray. "It's clear that Lividia Harlin is involved with Spectre, as well."

"Do you think she was working with her brother and Spectre all along?" asked Shaw.

Gray and Nova exchanged glances. "No," said Gray. "She doesn't appear to have begun communications with Spectre until after Seeton's death. Nova and I think Spectre may have been grooming her for involvement in developing the drones, though. She's a gifted robotics student."

"We need to decode the communications between Lividia Harlin and Spectre," said Thompson, "as soon as possible."

"Agreed," said Gray. He chose not to point out that Yusef was already a good deal closer to success in that regard than Shaw's team. "If we can identify and locate Spectre we'll crack both cases and hopefully prevent a massive drone attack."

Gray studied the faces staring back at him on the screen. They both seemed so young. Thompsons carefully groomed boyish features were matched by a level of confidence that came naturally to those who were good looking and aware of it. Shaw, on the other hand, appeared older than his years to look at, but his reticence and awkward manner took off a decade.

"Is there any way to locate Spectre from the IP address he's using?" Gray asked.

Shaw groaned. "He's bouncing off satellites worldwide. We're trying, but it's taking too long."

Rishi Chandra and Glenda King had been listening to the exchange without comment thus far.

When it was clear the cyber security experts had covered their own questions, King asked, "What do you want us to do?"

"Concentrate on Lividia," said Gray. "She's our only direct link to Spectre. Follow her socials, she might let something small slip, on open communications. And keep eyes on her physically. She might lead us to him."

After that call ended, Gray tried the Chief Superintendent.

"You're on speaker," Charfield said when he answered. "Bryant's here."

Gray rolled his eyes then told them what he and Nova had found out. When he finished, he asked about the Federal Police. "Curry told me to inform him directly, if we came across new information," he said.

There was silence for a few moments on the other end of the line.

"Should I call Curry?" Gray asked.

"I'll call," said Charfield and Gray allowed himself a sigh of relief. He didn't want to deal with that prickly bastard again.

While he was still on the call, Nova received a text from Yusef.

She read it aloud. Files accessed. Can't give detail via text.

Gray quickly relayed the text to his superiors. "We'll go to the safe house to see him," he said, then signed off.

He took a deep breath. "If Yusef doesn't think it's safe to use text, I'm not calling him back," said Gray. "Who knows what those kids can do with communication devices. We'll have to go to the safe house and talk to him. Old school."

Within minutes they were back downstairs in the car park and climbing back into the Toyota Crown. Gray pulled directly into the traffic on Makerston Street, accelerating as he did so. Two cars changed lanes hurriedly to avoid him.

The coffee shop, the Chez Nous was on the right as he made a screeching left turn into Roma Street. Out of the corner of his eye, Gray caught Nova grit her teeth and grasp at the door panel. They passed the Fire Station, then swept right, rocking Nova in the other direction so that she almost landed on Gray's lap. He sensed her holding on for dear life as they passed Suncorp stadium, then merged onto the M3.

Gray watched the rearview mirror closely. He'd seen a red AV pull out behind them as they left the police station. It was still following two cars back.

"I think we might have a tail," he muttered.

Nova glanced at the wing mirror, "It's probably just normal traffic," she said. But her reassurance fell flat. He couldn't shake the feeling that they were being followed.

He had options. He could turn off at Herston Road and risk getting stuck in hospital traffic that could trap them for an hour or take the inner-city bypass and enter the airport link tunnel where they could also be trapped together with their tail. Either way, he wasn't going to lose the red AV. He decided to stay on his planned route. It was probably nothing. All his senses were suddenly at the edge of his skin.

Entering the tunnel, the AV drew directly behind them. The car's driver had taken over the wheel and was matching their every move. Gray panicked. He and Nova exchanged glances. "Shit!" he said aloud.

"It's probably the police," said Nova, "chasing you for dangerous driving."

Gray watched the rearview mirror instead of the road in front of him. "Then why haven't they stopped us?" he said quietly.

They exited the tunnel at Airport Drive and sped alongside the creek until turning. Gray floored the accelerator and swerved between cars throwing Nova back against the seat. "Sorry," he said, but he didn't slow down.

He manoeuvred through traffic along the flat expanse of Nudgee Road. Then he saw something in the wing mirror. Was it a drone? It flew directly towards them.

"Holy shit!" Nova had seen it too.

Without hesitation, he veered off the road into the Nudgee Beach Hotel parking lot.

"Out!" he screamed frantically, launching himself from the car. His body tumbled across the rough pavement until he collided with the curb, the impact sending shockwaves of pain through his shoulder blade. Nova leapt from the vehicle seconds before the device made contact with the car.

Gray lifted his head in time to see a blinding flash engulf one side of his beloved Toyota Crown and hear a deafening, thunderous boom that left his ears ringing. A wave of heat radiated outwards and slapped him in the face, while the smell of burning metal and rubber overwhelmed him. He licked his dry lips. It felt like licking a battery.

"Your car!" cried Nova, her voice tinged with shock and disbelief. They huddled together, leaning on one another for physical support, watching. Gray's heart sank, as the passenger door of his cherished, irreplaceable car fell away from the tangled metal and landed on the ground with a thud.

Someone had stabbed him in the chest. He loved that car.

But there was no time to dwell on it.

Gray grabbed Nova's hand and jumped to his feet. "Run!" he cried. They ran up the steep slope of the Australian Catholic University grounds behind the pub. Gray's breath came hard, burning his chest and throat as he exhaled. But still, the earth blurred beneath his feet as he charged forward, not daring to glance back. His grip on Nova's wrist was relentless. She stumbled up the slope a stride behind him.

Finally, they disappeared into the campus's labyrinth of towering buildings. Breathless and gasping for air, they collapsed against a cool, brick wall, their bodies quivering with adrenaline and raw fear.

For a long time neither of them spoke. Then, as soon as the gripping pain in his chest subsided and he was able to breathe again, Gray said, "Are you injured?"

"No," said Nova, still catching her breath. "But I'm so sorry about your car."

Gray rested his head against the wall and rolled his shoulders to return oxygen flow to his bruised muscles. He felt like he'd been run over by a truck.

"It's only a car," he said with a crooked grin.

She made a small sound like a laugh that was starved of air.

"Since when?" she said. "You love that car."

"Hmm," he said. "Maybe it can be fixed."

She leant forward and looked him in the eye. "You're joking, aren't you? The whole passenger side was blown out."

Gray watched her eyes. Dark brown rims circled her pupils and blended into warm hazel. When had he become so interested in eyes?

"You weren't damaged," he said. "That's the important thing."

She smiled. "You're a protector, Gray," she said. "I know you can't help it, but I don't need protecting."

They stayed cloistered by the buildings for an hour, peering closely for anyone who might be searching for them. They saw no one. It was University break and there were no students about and very few lecturers.

When Gray was confident no one was pursuing them, he summoned an Uber, and they waited. The minutes stretched on, but half an hour later the Uber pulled up in front of the cloisters. If the driver thought anything about their appearance, smeared with dirt and grass stains and smelling of burnt gasoline, he didn't say anything. He waited politely for Gray and Nova to climb in and started the car. It only took minutes to reach Yusef's safe house, but Gray scanned the streets all the way for any sign of pursuit. There was none.

An unsettling sight greeted them when they turned into the street of the safe house. An unmarked police vehicle was idling on the curb directly in front of Yusef's home. Gray recognized it. There was only a dozen or so in the fleet and they were all basically the same model and colour. A couple were newer versions, but essentially no different.

On seeing the unmarked police vehicle, Gray instructed the Uber driver to halt just around the corner, under the cover of leafy trees. He and Nova slipped out of the car. They crept into the front yard of the nearest house and navigated their way around to the backyard, careful to remain unseen. From this concealed vantage point, they could observe both the driveway and the front steps of the safe house. The dark, unmarked car sat across the driveway; its windows tinted to obscure its occupants.

Their wait was brief. Soon, they saw Yusef being escorted out by two imposing figures, with broad shoulders. Gray recognized them as members of Tarrant's 'Special Operations Unit.'

"They must be moving him to a new location," whispered Gray.

"So, the attack on us was meant to delay us so they could move him?" asked Nova.

Gray's face was grim. "I think the attack was meant to do more than delay us," he said. "But having been unsuccessful in stopping us altogether, someone was left with no choice but to move Yusef."

Nova's eyes grew as wide as saucers. "Bloody hell! Who knew we were coming here?"

"No one," Gray answered. "We told the whole team about Carter, but the only people we told about Yusef decoding the encryptions were Charfield and Bryant. Clearly, someone didn't want us reaching Yusef."

"But who? And what do you think they're up to?" asked Nova as they watched Yusef being driven past them along the street and around the corner.

"I'm not certain, but I would bet my life Bryant has something to do with it. I've never trusted that man. I've seen Leonie Nolan leaving his office, and he silenced a call from her when I was with him."

"That's not much," said Nova. "What do you think he could be up to?"

"I don't know," said Gray. "They've separated Yusef from us, and they'll have taken his phone," said Gray. "I'm not sure how we'll contact him."

"Can't you find his new safe house from someone at the station?"

Gray considered it. "No. Tarrant, the Sergeant in charge of 'Special Operations' is a good cop. I'd trust him with my life. But if Bryant has given the order not to reveal the location of the new safe house to anyone, Tarrant will take it to his grave."

They retraced their steps back onto the narrow footpath and climbed a handful of creaky, wooden steps up to the front door. The door was firmly locked, the handle cold and unyielding. Skirting around the side of the house, they picked their way through the tangled backyard until they were at the back stairs. The house sat high on wooden posts that were crumbling in patches from a past infestation of termites. They found a small, slightly ajar window to the right, but too far for them to reach from the top stair. Gray guessed, from his experience with these post-World War II houses, it led into a bathroom.

Nova, nimble and determined, shimmied up a rusted drainpipe instead, and deftly squeezed through the window's narrow opening. Once inside, she unlatched the front door, allowing Gray to enter. He cast a cautious glance toward the neighbouring houses and across the quiet street. The neighbourhood was cloaked in silence. Once inside, they were greeted by a pile of dormant black towers, no longer blinking with life, and an array of large, dark screens. Nova quickly scanned the cluttered desk, her eyes searching for something amiss. The server was missing. "They've taken his computer," she said with a tone of urgency.

Gray thumped his fist against the gap on the desk where the server case had been. "We need to know the information he decoded," he muttered. He flopped onto a battered couch and wiped his face with his hands.

Losing his car felt like a minor inconvenience compared to the looming catastrophe, a potential mass attack of killer drones could unleash unless they uncovered the details and thwarted it. Yet, his mind was in a tangle. The memory of Leonie Nolan leaving Bryant's office nagged at him. Sure, it was routine for the Assistant Commissioner to meet with Members of Parliament, something he did frequently. But this memory left Gray with an uneasy feeling he couldn't shake off. And he'd seen Nolan's number on Bryant's phone. He was clearly trying to hide it.

Nova joined him on the couch. "Don't worry," she said. "I can access Yusef's work."

Gray lifted his face to look at her. "How?"

"We set up a secure folder on the cloud," she said. "So, we could work together. Everything he did, will have been saved there. Unless he allows them access, the people who took him won't be able to get into the folder."

Gray stood up. "What do you need?" he said.

"I need to get to my place to access my computer," she said. "My laptop went up in flames with your precious car."

"I can't call for a police vehicle to pick us up. I don't know who to trust." He stood up, clutching the forgotten bruise to his side. "Another Uber, then," he said.

"It was a full hour before they arrived at the woolshed. Nova and Gray entered the apartment looking exactly like they had been in a car crash.

Gray took a longer look around. Artifacts from Nova's travels and work covered the walls and every available surface. He realized each item must hold a story, a memory, an experience that had shaped Nova. The clutter revealed a vibrant and chaotic life, filled with meaning and connection. Photographs of First Nations peoples, vintage technology, and abstract art pieces made the space feel alive with curiosity and passion. It provided him with a sharp contrast to his own sparse apartment. Here, the warmth was almost palpable, as tangible as the scent of musty wood and old feathers that wafted through the air. He understood that the room reflected Nova's personality, her history, her life, her values. Every corner told a part of her story, revealing an authenticity and openness he admired. No one could enter this space without learning all about her, without being touched by her essence. It became clear why she had been careful not to allow others into such an intimate world until now. Gray knew the significance of this gesture. He felt honoured she was letting him in.

"Get us something to drink," said Nova as she sat down and booted up the computer.

"Tea? Coffee?" asked Gray scanning the kitchen bench.

"There's whisky on top of the fridge," she said.

Gray hadn't realized how much he needed a drink until that moment.

The scent of whiskey filled the air as Gray poured two glasses over ice and placed one beside Nova. The cool, smooth taste of the whiskey soothed his nerves as he took a sip.

Nova's fingers worked quickly as she booted up the computer and tapped in a password. Within seconds they were looking at the latest entries made by Yusef. "Here it is," she said.

A list of encrypted files rolled down the screen gradually morphing into English text as they went.

Nova read from the screen aloud while Gray looked over her shoulder. "This is not just casual contact," she said. "From what I can piece together, Lividia became deeply involved with Spectre in the days since Seeton died. The timestamps show conversations lasting hours late into the night."

Gray exchanged a look with Nova. "So Lividia blames the Palestinian community for her brother's death, and she's been spending all her time with a group that hates refugees." He rubbed his shoulder and grimaced when reminded of the pain. "That's a dangerous combination."

"It gets worse," Nova continued, clicking through to another screen. "Look at these purchase records Yusef found cached on her system."

Gray leaned closer, scanning the list that appeared. His blood ran cold. "Drone parts," he murmured. "High-end processing chips, specialized cameras, facial recognition software packages..."

"Custom lithium batteries, miniature explosive components..."

"It looks like...there's a mass attack planned..."

"But what's the target?" asked Gray.

Nova clicked through several more screens. "That's what I've been trying to figure out. There's encrypted communication about some kind of operation, but nothing specific about targets or timing. She looked up at Gray, her eyes haunted. But there's something else. Look at this."

She pulled another window showing a series of code. "They've been building dozens of miniature drones, all programmed with the same facial recognition software, designed to identify and target people of Middle Eastern appearance."

Nova stared at the screen, her face ashen.

"My God. If they deploy these in a crowded area..."

"It would be a massacre," finished Gray, his voice hollow.

He took a long draft of whiskey and checked his phone for the messages that had piled up over his eventful day. A message from Carter had come through about an hour earlier.

Contact made with kid in Spectre's inner circle. Attack planned for Muslim Community Cultural Event. Location Spectre still unknown.

"The Muslim Community Cultural Event!" Nova almost shouted. "That's tomorrow!"

Gray started tapping on his phone.

"Who are you calling?"

"The Imam. He needs to cancel the event." Gray continued tapping on his phone with increasing urgency, his fingers barely keeping pace with his racing thoughts.

"Come on, come on," he muttered as the phone rang continuously without answer. After several attempts the Imam finally answered the call. Gray hurriedly explained the threat. At the end of the call, Gray's hand, still holding the phone fell to his side.

"He won't cancel," he said. "He says the community day is a goodwill event for the people of Brisbane, and he's refusing to cancel it. He says he has faith in Allah."

"Allah helps those who help themselves," said Nova.

"I don't think the Imam thinks the threat is real," said Gray.

Nova shook her head. "How can he doubt it after the first two attacks?"

Gray ran both hands down his face.

"I need to notify Charfield," he said. "Before we do anything else." Gray tapped his superior's name on the screen of his mobile and waited. A standard ringtone followed, then a message bank. Gray hit stop.

"We'll update Thompson and Shaw," then try again," he said.

"I'll get them on a conference call and tell them what's happened today. They may have more information themselves by now."

Seconds later, the boyish good looks of Thompson and the open geeky expression of Shaw filled the screen. They both appeared spellbound as Gray described the day he and Nova had been through, ending in the information Yusef had decoded from communications between Lividia and Spectre.

Dr Shaw remained silent until Gray finished his tale. "How did Yusef Ibrahim decode this information before the best coders working for the government could do it?" he then asked in his quiet voice.

Gray was aware he was stepping on toes by working with Yusef outside the system.

"Do you think he has some insider knowledge?" asked Thompson more forcefully.

Dr Shaw shook his head slowly and blew air through his lips. "I don't know," he said. "It seems odd."

"Whether we trust Yusef or not, we need to act on the information," said Thompson. For the first time, Gray saw tiny lines appear between his eyes, at the top of his nose. "We can't afford to ignore it, and we don't have time to wait for it to be verified. We both have teams working on the same communications, within hours we'll know one way or the other whether their translations agree with those of Yusef Ibrahim. Meanwhile, we need a plan to move forward."

Gray and Nova agreed.

"Why don't Gray and Dr Corbin meet me at Civil Aviation headquarters," Thompson suggested. "Can you get across here, Shaw? This is the best place to work from if we want to plan contingencies against an aerial attack."

Everyone nodded.

"Give us twenty minutes," said Gray.

"I still have to call Charfield and update him," he told Nova. "I'm sure he's already heard about the explosion on Nudgee Road. He may even know it was my car."

"Will he believe your theory about Bryant being behind your car being bombed?"

"I don't know." Gray took a few deep breaths. He looked deeply into Nova's eyes.

"What if Bryant is in his office, or he calls him in?" she said.

"I know that's a risk, but we're going to need back up. We don't even have a plan yet, for tomorrow."

Gray stared at the keyboard as he hesitated. "We won't be able to stop this by ourselves." He glanced up at Nova, almost pleading for an answer.

"Shouldn't you also call Curry and the Federal Police?" she suggested.

Gray shook his head. "Charfield directed me to inform him first of any developments. He said he would pass information on to the Feds."

Gray tapped on Charfield's name. The private line was transferred to his personal assistant. Gray hesitated. "Hi," he said at last, "Gray here, I need to speak with Charfield urgently."

"I'm sorry, Detective Inspector Gray, the Chief Superintendent has left for the day," said the ever pleasant, automated voice.

Gray tapped in the Super's private number for emergency contact. The call went back to the personal assistant.

"This is an urgent call," said Gray. "I must speak with the Superintendent immediately. Can you tell me where he is?"

"We appreciate that your circumstance is urgent," said the automated voice, "and we value your service, however the Superintendent is unavailable at this this time. Can I transfer your call to Assistant Commissioner Bryant's number?"

Gray was adamant and succinct. "No."

Where was the Super? There was no point arguing with an automated voice. It could circle round and round his request indefinitely without so much as a change in intonation. Meanwhile he would be smashing the phone against a wall in frustration.

There was nothing he could do but try again later. Perhaps it would be better to speak to him once they had a plan in any case.

CHAPTER THIRTY-ONE

Gray and Nova didn't need to travel far to reach the Aviation Authority Headquarters. They swept across Brisbane city and along Airport Drive, arriving in less than twenty minutes. Dr Shaw had already arrived and was sitting in the Situation Room with Thompson. Large screens filled one entire wall of the room. Gray and Nova had been escorted in by two uniformed security officers. They all settled down facing the screens, which were, so far, blank.

"Yusef downloaded the communications he decoded onto a cloud file that we share, so we have access to everything he uncovered prior to being moved from the safe house," said Gray.

"Yusef is ahead of our teams," said Shaw. "They're still trying to decode the encrypted files."

Shaw was irritable. Gray guessed he didn't appreciate Federal resources being outmanoeuvred by a seventeen-year-old student and a twenty-four-year-old refugee.

"So, what do we know, so far?" Thompson began.

"We know they're preparing a swarm of drones for a major attack on a public event," said Nova. "We have reason to believe the Muslim Cultural Festival at the City Botanic Gardens tomorrow might be the target.

Thompson's eyebrows shot up. "Jesus, as soon as that?"

"Where is Yusef now?" asked Shaw.

"That's it, we don't know," said Gray.

"After Gray's car was torched, Special Ops moved Yusef from the safe house," said Nova.

"They must have also taken his phone," added Gray. "Because we've been unable to contact him since."

Dr Shaw shook his head slowly. "Someone inside the force must be involved," he whispered. "No one knew Yusef had cracked the code, not even us."

"Exactly," said Gray. "I called Charfield and Bryant was on speaker, right before we left for the safe house."

"What does your Super say now?" asked Shaw.

"He's disappeared too," replied Gray.

Thompson sounded stunned. "What? How does the Chief Superintendent of Police disappear?"

"I don't know," said Gray. "But he's not contactable, that's for sure."

"So," began Shaw, frustration simmering in his voice, "We're several steps behind a bunch of kids looking to blow up picnickers in twelve hours."

Gray had nothing to say.

"We need direction from a higher pay grade than ours," Thompson pointed out.

Gray continued, "We believe a mass drone attack is planned for tomorrow morning at the City Botanic Gardens. The organisation responsible for the attack is called Spectre, as unlikely as that sounds, an organisation made up of radicalized young people, possibly being supported by right-wing politicians. We don't know where Spectre is based or where the drones are being made. But Lividia Harlin is involved at some level."

Thompson went on to add, "We know the drone that killed Mohammed Hussain was sent from somewhere in the central Brisbane area. The drones don't travel far because no one sees them prior to the attack. We think they fly directly upward, out of sight, they're only small so that isn't necessarily that high, then they descend when almost on top of the target."

Shaw picked up where Thompson left off. "The same was true in the Sydney case," he said. "The drone wasn't seen until the last moments before the attack. A drone that small, carrying a sophisticated processor and weaponry, would probably not have a long range."

"So, we're looking for a building near the inner-city area where the modification and programming of drones could take place," said Gray.

"I need to contact my superiors," said Shaw. "The four of us can't do this alone. We need to take action to secure the site of the attack."

"Agreed," said Gray. "I'll try Charfield, again."

"And I'll alert the Civil Aviation Authority with the updated intelligence," said Thompson.

There was no answer on any of the numbers connected to Superintendent Charfield. The next person in the line of command was Assistant Commissioner Bryant, but Gray suspected him of orchestrating the attack on his car and having Yusef moved. He would probably block any attempt they made to prevent the drone attack or safeguard the area.

He decided to call Kenneth Tarrant, in charge of Special Operations.

"Tarrant, it's Gray, here," he said when the commander answered the call.

"We have a situation." Gray described the circumstances as he understood them. Everything except his suspicions of Bryant. No need to air those, yet.

Tarrant listened without a word.

"I need to get in touch with Charfield," Gray said. "We need to act immediately on this."

"Charfield is in hospital," said Tarrant. "He had a heart attack on the way home from work. He's having open-heart surgery as we speak."

Gray sucked in air. "What? Oh my god! No wonder I couldn't contact him."

"You need to call Bryant," Tarrant said. "He's next in line. I'll keep the phone on me and wait to hear the plan. We're here to support you. But you need a cohesive plan, and an order from Bryant."

Gray tapped off the call. He couldn't call Bryant.

Shaw was finishing his call with his boss. "We have all the capability of this agency on alert," he said. "But we need more than technicians, we need boots on the ground.'

Gritting his teeth and staring hard at Nova, Gray sucked in his ego and decided to call Curry at the Federal Police. When the prickly bastard answered, Gray spilled everything he knew. He left out nothing, not even his suspicions of Bryant.

The call went on for some time, while Gray answered a myriad of questions. But, to Gray's surprise, the man didn't waste time reprimanding him for not keeping him updated. Gray was sure that would come later.

When he turned back to his tech friends and Nova, he was calmer. The Federal Police are taking over the operation as far as securing the botanical gardens is concerned," he said. "They'll have sharpshooters positioned on rooftops at strategic locations around the gardens with electromagnetic pulse rifles. They'll have with them officers with thermal imaging goggles to spot the drones before they are visible to the naked eye. They'll be in radio contact with you guys, here, and you'll provide an ongoing account as the drones become visible on your screens. They're also placing plain clothes officers within the crowd to assist with crowd control. There'll be temporary shelters installed over the next few hours that will look like art installations. The plain clothes cops can funnel people to safety within them."

While Gray had been busy, Nova brought up a map of Brisbane on her screen. She circled an area thirty flight minutes in diameter, allowing that they believed the drones fly up and back down again.

"They need space, look for an abandoned warehouse," said Gray.

Hundreds of red pins appeared on the map on her screen. "Changes in the way we work in the digital age have led to the shut-down of many large warehouses," she said. "There are empty warehouses all over the city."

"We know Lividia is involved," Gray said, pacing the room with restless energy. "We need to put a watch on her."

"Do you think she'll lead us to Spectre?" asked Shaw quietly.

Gray's jaw was set. "We've seen how determined she is. She's not going to lay low while this happens. She'll want to be in the middle of everything."

Nova leaned forward her eyes narrowed with concentration. "Do you think she'll actually go to the warehouse where Spectre operate?"

"Probably," Gray replied, resuming his pacing. "Kids like to hang out together. It would be difficult to run an operation this big with programmers all operating remotely." He paused. "At least a core group must meet somewhere working on the hardware."

"We have to assume Lividia's in deep," Nova said. "If Spectre trusts her with technical work, they'll want her close."

"Then we stick to Lividia like a shadow, let her lead us to the warehouse," Gray said in a decisive tone. "But she isn't the only one with a grudge. It's more than just her brother's death that's driving this."

Nova interjected. "We all saw the messages. Lividia and Spectre have been talking constantly since Seeton was killed. She doesn't just want revenge; she's making a statement."

Gray rubbed his chin thoughtfully. "She's angry and upset, she'll be distracted. That will work to our advantage."

Nova glanced at Shaw and Thompson and back to Gray. "And what if Spectre is using her just as much as she is using them?" she asked. "If Spectre thinks she is expendable, they might have her lead this attack, then leave her out in the cold."

Gray nodded. "Either way, we need to find this warehouse and Lividia is our best hope." He took a deep breath and called his most reliable officer. Rishi Chandra answered on the first ring.

"Where are you?" said Chandra surprised to hear his boss's voice. "No one has heard from you all day."

Gray ignored the question.

"Take King and find Lividia Harlin," he said. Keep a watch on her. I want to know where she is every minute." He didn't say more for fear of interference in the call. He didn't know what resources Bryant might have at his command to listen in on his communications with his team. He knew Rishi Chandra and Glenda King would trust him implicitly and follow his instructions to the letter.

Gray shook his head. "That's the best we can do about the origin of the swarm until we get more info." He exhaled slowly, trying not to let the feeling of helplessness settle in. Was it already too late? "What do we know about stopping the drones?"

Thompson crossed his arms. "There are two options: find the location where the drones are launching and shut them down before they leave or intercept them in flight."

Gray frowned, his frustration mounting. "We'd have to know the exact launch site, and once they're airborne, we can't shoot them all down. They're too small, too fast, and they don't become visible until the last second. We'd barely stop a few."

"Especially if they were to deploy them across multiple locations," Nova added, grimly. "There are too many variables."

Gray groaned. "Who said anything about deploying from multiple locations?" he cried.

Nova shrugged her shoulders. "It's a possibility," she said.

"What about these electromagnetic pulse guns?" he asked Shaw.

The younger man pursed his lips. "I suppose if they were able to create a large enough blast, they might disrupt the frequencies," he said. "But the AI running the drones will likely counter the effects."

Shaw chewed his lip thoughtfully. "Unless we crack into their coding system...figure out the frequency and jam the control signals." He shook his head vigorously. "But the frequencies change millions of times during the flight. It won't be easy, not with whatever encryption they're using."

"It's the only thing we've got," Nova said, determined. "We have to figure out a way to disable the drones. Anyone making a weapon like that is likely to include a 'kill switch'," she was speaking quietly as if to herself.

"What's that?" Gray jumped on what seemed to him like a possible ray of hope.

Nova looked up at him. "A kill switch, to shut the drones down if something goes wrong. Complicated weapons like that can easily go haywire, and start attacking unintended targets, even their programmers. So, you would expect there to be a 'kill switch'."

"Could we access the kill switch remotely?" asked Gray.

"Theoretically," replied Nova.

Gray ran a hand through his hair. "Yusef could help with that," he said.

"But we don't know where they took him," Nova said, a shadow crossing her face.

Townsend checked his watch. "It's late," he said.

CHAPTER THIRTY-TWO

Lividia stared at the door for a few minutes after it had closed on Gray and Nova. She was too anxious to go to the basement, and she was certainly too wound up to sleep. She waited twenty minutes to be sure they were well and truly out of the way then she left the house. Back at the warehouse she could feel useful. There was a stretcher to take a nap on when she was tired.

Eight hours later, Lividia sipped from her rainbow-colored water bottle, a constant companion as she navigated the challenges of the day. It had been a gruelling ordeal. Programming a swarm of bots was exponentially more intricate than handling a single drone, stretching her capabilities to their very edge. Freya had made strides, but Lividia bore the brunt of the coding burden. She was glad she'd come back in. Even Freya said she might not have been able to have everything ready on time if left on her own. Lividia meticulously checked and rechecked her work. The daunting complexity of the task kept her mind from pondering its ethical implications. Despite her firm belief in Spectre and a deep-seated desire to conquer such a sophisticated endeavour, a nagging doubt lingered at the back of her mind.

Nonetheless, she was proud as her shift drew to a close. She reflected on how far she'd come in such a brief span, far beyond what her peers in robotics could even envision. She appreciated Freya's collaboration; their skills complemented each other well. But Lividia knew she was the more skilled and innovative programmer. She wondered for a moment if it was truly her mission to complete her brother's work or if ambition was clouding her judgment. Was this more about proving what she could do?

Just as she was about to sign off, her weary eyes caught the flickering triangle Spectre used to announce their messages. It pulsed insistently on the screen, pulling her from her exhaustion.

"I'm impressed by your work, Lividia," the message read.

She felt her chest swell with pride, and a rush of validation washed over her.

"Thank you," she replied, her fingers trembling slightly as she typed. "That means a lot."

The response was almost immediate. "I want you and Freya both at the command centre tomorrow for the big event. Rest. I want you at your best to lead the operation. 7:00 a.m. tomorrow."

Lividia blinked at the words, hardly able to process them. Twelve hours. Lead the operation. LEAD! She glanced at the mass of tiny black drones, each small enough to sit in her hand spread across the warehouse floor in military like formations and her chest tightened. She would be in charge when the moment of truth arrived. In twelve hours, she would send the swarm out into the world to complete the mission on Seeton's behalf. She grinned to herself, excitement pushing through her bone-deep fatigue.

How was she going to relax? She'd only had about two hours sleep on the warehouse stretcher in the last twenty-four hours. She thrived on the adrenaline and focus that working at the warehouse provided and the next twelve hours without that buzz stretched like an eternity before her. But she needed to sleep. She needed to be on her game in the morning to lead the operation.

She shrugged on her jacket and packed her water bottle into her knapsack. The warehouse was eerily quiet in the evening light, a stark contrast to the frenzied activity of the day. She hesitated at first, reluctant to walk away, reluctant to leave behind the comforting hum of computers and the glow of screens.

She had to find a way to get through the night. She'd go back to her parent's empty house, sleep if she could, order food. It all seemed so pointless when compared to the importance of her work. The impact it would have on the world, not least of all on her own small city. The anticipation filled her mind, making time stretch and warp.

She stepped out from the harsh fluorescent lights into the soft glow of the summer evening. The sun still had a bite, even as it descended. The last rays of sunlight fell over the tops of the buildings, casting long shadows over the city. Her heart was still pounding with the thrill of Spectre's message, and she felt a fierce sense of belonging.

She mounted her scooter with a single fluid motion, kicking off with sudden energy and sped through the sprawling industrial area, the world blurring by in a rush of wind and fading light. She could hardly remember what her life had been like before she met Spectre.

CHAPTER THIRTY-THREE

DAY SEVEN

The morning sun cast a rosy glow over the landscape illuminating the trees and the face of Glenda King as she took a sip of her coffee. The unmarked police car waited across the road from the Harlin family home. Shadows danced across the car's sleek exterior while King watched the sprawling house.

Trees more than a hundred and fifty years old stretched above the driveway and the river sparkled in the early light, just visible through the leaves.

The feint scent of freshly brewed coffee lingered, mixed with the sharp tang of petrol from the service station behind them on the main road. Glenda wasn't a fan of service station coffee, but she savoured the last sip before setting the cup down. A slightly bitter taste lingered.

She looked across at Chandra who slept peacefully in the driver's seat, his cardigan slumped over his chest. A trickle of drool travelled from the corner of his mouth to his chin. It was time to wake him and take a nap herself, but she wasn't sleepy. Too much coffee.

At 6:00 am, Rishi Chandra stirred and sat up, blinking the sleep from his eyes and throwing his cardigan onto the back seat. "No movement?" he asked groggily.

Glenda shook her head.

"Are you ok while I do a coffee run?" he mumbled.

"Of course, none for me though, I won't sleep for a week as it is."

Chandra chuckled and scrambled sideways out of the car, stiff from having his long legs tucked up under his chin all night.

Just as he'd managed to persuade his muscles to work. A small figure emerged from the trees at the side of the Harlin house. Glenda sat forward and placed her hand on his arm.

"It's Lividia," said Glenda.

Chandra quickly pulled his legs back into the car and closed the door quietly. They both watched as Lividia jumped onto her electric scooter and headed down the road.

Chandra rubbed his eyes, wrestling to wakefulness, then yawned as he started the car. Glenda watched Lividia disappear down the street. "Let's go, Chandra," she urged, "She's getting away."

He ignited the engine, and they followed at a safe distance. On the main road, they hung back, careful to avoid detection. Lividia was several car lengths ahead, her knapsack slung casually over her shoulder as she rode. The early morning traffic was heavier than usual for that time on a Sunday morning. Crisp, trendy urbanites were on their way to the markets. Chandra and King tucked their car behind others, making sure never to pull too close to the scooter.

Chandra's eyes were droopy, but his hands were steady on the wheel. They had tracked Lividia from the moment she left the house, through the sprawling streets of the inner suburbs and into the city centre. Lividia crossed intersections a little too fast, the traffic lights working in her favour, but it served their purpose to stay well behind. As she weaved around the corner into the warehouse district, they struggled to keep her in sight.

"You need to keep up," Glenda said, her voice tense. She shoved her service station coffee cup into the holder and leaned forward.

"I don't think she suspects anything," said Chandra.

"Don't underestimate her. Just keep your distance." Glenda flicked a glance at the rearview mirror. Another car was trailing behind them. She couldn't tell if it was a coincidence, but she wasn't taking any chances. "Let this one pass," she said.

Chandra let the AV slip past them.

"We can't cut this close," protested Glenda as they caught up with the scooter. "If she realizes we're following her, we're done."

"Make up your mind," said Chandra. "We're either too close or too far away."

He wiped sleep from his eyes with one hand, while the other remained firmly gripping the steering wheel. "Gray owes me big-time for this," he said. It was the longest sentence he'd managed to string together since they switched shifts at dawn. He pulled back, allowing a bus to get between them and Lividia.

"He'll be quaking in his boots," said Glenda, dryly.

The city streets turned into smaller lanes winding through an industrial area, and Lividia slowed her pace. Glenda resisted the urge to bark at Chandra again, forcing herself to stay patient and alert. She assumed they were following Lividia in the hope of finding the source of the drones. If the surveillance was blown now, they'd lose their best chance to stop another attack. She picked up the phone, dialling Gray.

"We've got her," she said when he answered.

His voice was hoarse with exhaustion. "Does she know she's being tailed?" he asked.

"Not a clue. Chandra's driving. He drives like my grandpa." She shot him a sideways glance. Anyway, we're about half a block behind her."

The road narrowed, and the bus turned to the left, leaving the unmarked police car exposed. It was too soon to see if Lividia noticed.

"Pick it up," Glenda said, without covering the receiver.

"Stop nagging me," Chandra muttered.

"I heard that," said Gray.

They ducked behind a delivery van, hoping it would offer them some cover. This part of town was almost deserted, and aside from the occasional night shift worker or startled stray cat, there wasn't much to hide their presence.

"Keep us in the loop," said Gray. "It's life and death. Don't lose her."

Glenda nodded, then remembered he couldn't see her. "She's definitely headed to a warehouse," she said. "We're in Bowen Hills, turning into the street that runs between the two sides of the old Exhibition grounds. We'll call when she stops."

"Stay with her," Gray said. Then he hung up.

Eventually, Lividia swerved into a vacant car park, with a large concrete warehouse at the back, the only windows narrow and high, just under the corrugated iron roof.

"Perfect," said Glenda as Chandra pulled the car to a stop behind a high wall decorated with graffiti.

"I'm glad you approve," he said, reaching onto the back seat for his cardigan.

They were in the old Exhibition Grounds where the "Royal Shows" used to be held annually, bringing together the country and the city. There hadn't been a Royal Show for nearly a decade, but the place still smelled of cattle. Glenda tapped the co-ordinates into Gray's contact on the phone. Then they waited.

CHAPTER THIRTY-FOUR

At the Cyber Security Australia headquarters on Airport Drive, Gray, Nova, Thompson, and Shaw worked at a relentless pace, pushing through the night with hardly a break. They were exhausted but focused, determined to break into Spectre's network and stop the impending disaster. The hum of servers surrounded them, and the glow of monitors filled the sparsely furnished room with an eerie light.

Gray was on the phone with Curry ensuring the preparations that had been ongoing through the night were in place.

Nova was the first to notice a new entity enter the cloud. "Yusef!" she cried, turning her beaming face toward Gray. "He's managed to connect with us in the shared space."

"How?" asked Gray, leaning over her shoulder to watch the screen.

"He says he found an old phone with its leads in a drawer in the safe house. It had no SIM so he took one from the guard's phone when he left it unattended to go to the loo and fixed the old phone so it would work."

Gray was baffled. "What the hell?"

"He says he's not restrained he just can't leave the house. There are guards at the doors. He reckons, if he's quiet, they probably won't notice he's talking to us."

Nova glowed.

"Allah must be watching over us," she said. "Yusef will be able to help us crack this code and find the 'kill switch' if anyone can."

Yusef had accessed the shared cloud file and was feeding them critical data they desperately needed. The team now sifted through the layers of encrypted codes, each new find fuelling their determination. Even Shaw was on board with including Yusef in the team. He muttered in awe about how he could work so fast. They all knew time was not on their side. They had to hack into the systems Spectre was using to operate the drones within the next hour. Once the public started arriving at the event, everyone was in danger.

"Got something!" Thompson shouted, startling both Gray and Nova with the suddenness of his exclamation.

"Is it a way in?" Nova asked.

"Damn close," Thompson answered, a mix of frustration and excitement in his voice. Nova moved closer to where he sat, watching his screen intently as the possibility of a breakthrough loomed.

Gray felt a renewed sense of urgency. He was hunched over Nova one moment, gazing over her shoulder intently, then he was pacing the room the next.

He felt his phone vibrate and answered instantly.

"Lividia's at the warehouse!" he shouted. "If we move quickly, we might be able to catch her and the core group of programmers before the swarm's activated."

He tapped out another number. "We need the tactical team on the ground at this address," he barked into the phone. "We'll meet them there."

Nova looked up hesitant. "You stay," said Gray, "You're more valuable here. I'll meet up with Chandra and King. The tactical team should get there at about the same time we do."

Gray took the department car and drove to the warehouse in Bowen Hills at high speed, even for him. When he caught up with Chandra and King, he contacted Curry again to update him about the warehouse. This might be their only chance to stop the drones from leaving the ground. Once they were in the air, it could be too late.

They waited, nerves on edge, for the tactical team. Gray had sent the request through the proper channel at central communications, but as the minutes ticked by, he wondered if that had been wise. He was second-guessing every decision he'd made since this case began.

"Did you hear that?" asked Glenda, her head tilted to one side.

"Gray and Chandra were still and perched on the edge of their seats. Nothing, at first. Then a dull whir.

"That's it," cried Gray, as the whirring grew louder, and a cloud of drones rose through the roof of the warehouse. The sound intensified. The drones circled as a swarm then turned back toward the city, flying upward at a sharp angle as they did so.

Gray's heart pounded as he, Chandra, and King scrambled from the cramped confines of the car. They were already wearing their police vests, the thick Kevlar pressing against their ribs as they drew their guns and held them in front of them. Gray's sense of urgency felt like a fever in his veins. He scanned the exterior of the old warehouse, clocking the worn brick and shuttered windows just under the roof, everything finally real and tangible. The building stood quiet and imposing in the morning light, a stark contrast to the chaos inside his head.

"There's only one way in," Chandra said, his voice barely above a breath as he motioned for them to follow. "There's an automated door at one end, but it can only be opened from the inside. We go around the side."

They moved with deliberate precision, feet crunching on gravel as they approached. Gray felt the inevitability of it all, the culmination of all they had discovered hanging in the air like an electric charge. Chandra and King were instantly in position, crouched on either side of a steel door. Firearms steady, eyes sharp and unblinking. Gray took several steps back, gauging his distance to maximize the force of what he had to do next.

"One, two, three," he counted, each number a heartbeat. On three, Gray nodded to his team. Without hesitating, he lunged forward and kicked the door with the full force of his boot. Years of experience guided him to the precise spot, the weakest link in the chain, and he felt the rush of adrenaline as the door yielded.

The three of them charged into the warehouse, boots pounding against the concrete floors. The space was cavernous, echoing with the sounds of their intrusion, the harsh fluorescent lights casting stark shadows across the room. Moving quickly, they rounded a corner and saw the group they were after, a collection of half a dozen young men and women who had been huddled around an array of laptops and equipment. The youths were high fiving one another in celebration, but they stopped short at the sight of the intruders barrelling toward them. Faces that had been triumphant just moments before now looked utterly dumbfounded, as though some idiot adult had spoiled a computer game.

Gray looked up as a voice boomed through an amplifier and filled the room. "I'm afraid you're too late," the voice said, echoing against the steel beams above. Everyone froze, scanning the bare walls, trying to identify the direction of the proclamation. It reverberated around the warehouse, making it impossible to pinpoint and as they turned their heads, the voice rang out again.

"The drones are on their way. No one can stop them now." The words seemed to ricochet off every surface. "You're already too late. This is the future. This is tomorrow."

"Everyone stay where you are," shouted Gray. The young people froze, their hands slowly raised.

Gray pushed forward, his heart pounding. His voice rang out, creating an echo in the cavernous space.

"Spectre!"

The name reverberated, loud enough to drown out even the persistent hum of electronics. The workers stood still, staring wide-eyed in shock and confusion.

To the left of the warehouse, a narrow steel staircase led up to an office suspended in one corner of the building. The structure was rickety, a thin and precarious skeleton against the cold metal of the walls. Gray's gaze flicked to the motion of a shadow descending those stairs, cutting a stark figure against the backdrop of fluorescent lighting. A young man moved quickly, his black clothing blending seamlessly with the steel around him. His hair was strikingly white, and his eyes, like crystal, glinted with an unsettling clarity.

"Hands where I can see them!" Gray's voice rang with authority, cutting through the tension. "You're under arrest." His gun was levelled with precision, but Spectre appeared unfazed.

Spectre's laugh echoed through the warehouse, dismissive and light. "Put the guns down," he said, his voice a calm command. "Watch the show."

The young man gestured with a casual nod toward the screen, where the drones were shown soaring higher and higher, capturing images from within the clouds. The detectives cast a swift glance at the screen, aware of the advancing threat outside but unwilling to shift focus entirely from the danger before them.

"Come to me," he said to Lividia, holding out one long slim arm. Lividia ran to Spectre's side as Gray shouted, "No!"

Spectre placed a hand on the girl's shoulder, his touch authoritative. "I'd like you to meet my star programmer," he declared. Lividia's eyes met Gray's with defiance and pride.

"It wouldn't be an exaggeration to say she's responsible for the successful launch of today's attack." His arm slipped more tightly around her neck.

Gray advanced, his face locked in determination. Chandra and King were close behind, their movements in sync. They trained their weapons on the group of programmers huddled together to the right of Spectre. The programmers stood frozen to the stop, hands raised.

The air between Gray and Spectre was charged, thick with the imminent clash of wills.

"We're shutting you down and bringing you in," Gray stated, his voice edged with determination. He levelled his gun, unwavering. "There are three of us with guns, and we will shoot."

But Spectre appeared to have an unshakeable belief in the chaos he'd set into motion. He absorbed Gray's words with the cool detachment of someone who had already won.

His gaze flicked back to the screen, and he watched the drones as they began to descend from the clouds. The image on the screen zoomed in, revealing the unmistakable outline of their target.

Gray could see Glenda to his right from the corner of his eye. She was looking from the young man to the screen and back to the young man, gauging every flicker of response from him and his followers.

"There must be a way out of this," Gray heard her hiss to Chandra, who was a step behind her and out of Gray's sight.

The path of the drones was unmistakable now, the target horribly clear. On the screen was a grim picture of the drones heading straight for the City Botanical Gardens.

Spectre looked at the screen, then back to the police, a twinkle at the corner of his eyes.

"Do you really think you can stop something like this?"

Gray bit his lip. "The drones are far enough up that we still have time," he said quietly. "Where's the bloody tactical team?"

"No one coming to help?" said Spectre. His eyes a luminous blue, but also sharp and knowing. He turned toward the screens clearly mesmerized by his own work.

Gray made his move. He sprang into action, lunging forward, his weapon unwavering, locked onto Spectre's head like a hunter closing in on its prey.

But in one fluid motion, Spectre drew a gun that had been tucked into his belt beneath his jacket. The movement was lightning-fast, and he pressed the gun ruthlessly against Lividia's throat, his free arm wrapped tightly around her neck to hold her still.

"The girl's terrified eyes stared out at Gray.

"Don't," Spectre threatened, his voice sharp and cold. "It would be a waste to stifle such talent, he tipped his head toward Lividia, "but I will if I must."

Gray assessed the situation. Spectre had Lividia in a chokehold, using her as a living shield.

Not far off, the young programmers still stood rooted to the spot, with Glenda King and Rishi Chandra holding their guns steady and daring them to move. On the enormous screen, the drones persisted in their ominous flight, inching ever closer to their target.

"Let her go," Gray commanded, edging forward with his gun still fixed on Spectre. "You're only making this worse for yourself."

Spectre's icy blue eyes blazed with a dangerous zeal. "Worse?" he sneered, a twisted smile curling his lips. "This is just the beginning. Today, we take back our country."

Lividia quivered in Spectre's grasp, her eyes clouded with doubt. Gray saw the turmoil on her face. He registered the dawning realization that her own actions had brought her to this perilous juncture, that everything she had worked toward was culminating in this terrifying climax.

"Lividia," Nova called out gently. "This isn't what Seeton would have wanted."

"Let her go," Gray insisted, his gun still on Spectre. "This. Ends. Now!"

Under his breath, he cursed the tactical team, who should have been storming through the doors. "Where the fuck were they?"

Gray measured the distance, his instincts honed by years of high-stakes encounters. He could feel the shift in the room. He saw Lividia trembling, saw the fragile thread by which her life now hung. There was no time to waste.

"Don't do this," he urged as he inched closer, his voice a steady lifeline thrown into the void, decades of de-escalation kicking in. "It's not going to end the way you want." His words hung in the air, thick with desperation.

The screen flickered with images of the drones soaring across the clouds. There was a hum of anticipation, of inevitability, which buzzed like static around them. Gray watched as Lividia's chest heaved and she squinted against the tears. He knew she was trying to see past her fear, past the immediate panic and into a future that seemed to be rapidly slipping away. Her breath came in ragged gasps while Gray knew she was struggling to comprehend the enormity of what was happening, the betrayal she must be feeling, not only from Spectre, but by her own ideals.

Gray, determined to reach her, took another small steady step and then another. He watched as Spectre's manic energy intensified. Spectre's face contorted into a grimace while the colour in Lividia's face grew deeper until it was almost blue. Gray saw the tension in the muscles of his neck as his grip on her neck intensified. There was madness in his eyes, a cold disregard for life. Every second was precious, every word a chance to alter the outcome. Gray realized Lividia was at her breaking point, and Spectre knew it too.

A loud noise shattered the silence. Spectre's attention was directed momentarily to the back of the warehouse. Bursting through one of the narrow, grimy windows, a team of twelve federal police officers poured in with practiced precision. Their silhouettes cut sharply against the dim interior as they moved with swift, synchronized agility. With tactical gear gleaming in the low light, one after the other, they executed deft jumps to the warehouse floor.

"Everyone stay where you are!" ordered the team leader. Gray recognized his friend Richardson from the Federal Police.

In the midst of the new commotion, Gray acted with razor sharp decisiveness. Seeing Spectre distracted, he seized the opportunity. Gathering all his strength, he drove his shoulder forcefully into Spectre's torso. The sudden lurch caught Spectre off guard, causing him to stagger backward and momentarily loosen his hold on Lividia. The impact knocked the gun free from Spectre's grasp, sending it clattering across the concrete floor. Gray swiftly pulled Lividia into his arms, her form surprisingly light against his chest as he lifted her away from danger.

King swept across the floor to retrieve the gun Spectre had dropped.

Two officers lunged forward and wrenched Spectre to the floor. With one knee on his body, they twisted his hands behind his back. His defiant smirk faded as they secured his wrists in handcuffs, immobilizing him and removing his weapon before he could make any further move.

Spectre's voice remained taunting even as they captured him. "It's too late," he shouted. "The drones are already on their way. You think you've won, but you've changed nothing."

A girl with purple hair ran to the roll-a-door and pushed a button opening one end of the warehouse. The young coders all found their feet at once.

"Stop! Police!" cried an officer while sending a shot into the air for emphasis.

Most of the young people stopped in their tracks, but two rushed toward the opening and threw themselves into a slide to make it under the door before it was fully open. Two Federal officers leapt after them and tackled them mid-slide. The remaining coders stood still, hands in the air and accepted their handcuffs.

Lividia stumbled alongside Gray, her legs struggling to keep up with his urgent pace. He crouched low as they dashed toward the exit, shielding her with his body to protect her from any potential threat. Behind them, the scene was one of chaos and capture.

Outside the warehouse, Gray and Lividia reached the safety of a squad car. Gray released her, and she leaned against the vehicle, gasping for breath. The adrenaline still coursed through her, leaving her trembling and wide-eyed. Gray's own breath came in ragged gasps as he tried to process the rapid turn of events. Relief mingled with a simmering frustration. The tactical team hadn't arrived, jeopardizing the entire operation and nearly costing them everything. "Thank Allah I brought Curry in," he muttered between breaths. He winced at his invocation of a deity that wasn't his own.

He gazed at Lividia, his expression hardening as he understood the full extent of her involvement. Her eyes filled with a mix of fear and betrayal. And the dawning realization that she'd been a pawn.

Gray's frustration boiled over. He slammed a fist onto the hood of the car, rattling the metal with a resounding thud. Where the fuck were they? The words echoed in his mind, underscoring his boiling frustration. He turned to Lividia, unable to contain the anger that the delay had kindled within him.

Gray firmly pulled Lividia's hands behind her back and cuffed them. Then ran his hand through his hair. The drones were still on the way.

CHAPTER THIRTY-FIVE

Nova, Thompson and Shaw stared at the screen in horror. First, they saw a single drone emerge from the warehouse like a wasp from a nest, glossy, obsidian with tiny wings that blurred the air. Then ten more. Twenty. A hundred. These were not like birds, they were fractal, insect like, clawing at the human ancestral memory of plagues, of hornets and stinging beetles. They weren't quite organic but were certainly more than machine. Even from a distance, Nova felt the vibration, a feint trembling in her ears.

Nova's fingers blurred over keys. She'd never had to work like this, with her body rigid and her heart whiplashing between her ribs. Thompson and Shaw hovered over her sweating. As she was in contact with Yusef, and Yusef was the closest to cracking the code deep within the system that controlled the drones, they agreed to pool their energy, while Nova followed Yusef's instructions. Shaw had one hand unconsciously at his temple, as if bracing for the moment of no return.

On the other end of the video call on Nova's phone, Yusef's face was half in shadow. His glasses reflected lines of raw code, flickering as he ran simulation after simulation. "The swarm isn't completely coordinated," he muttered. "They've built a mesh-net but it's amateur. Can you see the node frequency?"

"It's spiking," Nova said, her tone between terror and analytical focus.

"We're out of time, Yusef," Nova typed, but her voice echoed louder, as if the air itself might listen before the swarm did. She didn't look up at Thompson or Shaw. "It's now or never," she typed, wincing at the cliché.

Yusef nodded. "I don't know if this will work," he said. "There's an error in the coding. It's a rookie error really, not something I would have expected from a team so skilled. I'm sending the piece of code I'm talking about to the cloud. Nova, you need to access it from your end."

A second window bloomed across the screen, strings of hexadecimal and alien glyphs, a cipher within a cipher. Nova could almost feel the breath of the coder who had seeded the kill command so deep in the system. She scrolled, parsed, double-checked the gaps. For all the urgency, her brain slowed the world to a crawl.

She felt the presence of Thompson's breath on her neck. "Can you do it?" he whispered.

"Yes," she snapped, more abruptly than she intended. "But I need to be left alone."

The words cut through Thompson's hovering. He stepped back and exchanged an anxious glance with Shaw. Nova felt a slice of guilt but ignored it.

"I see the patch," Nova called out, reading back the code to Yusef. "But there is a checksum. If we rewrite it, every bot will know."

Yusef nodded, a slow, deliberate movement. "You'll only get one cycle before the swarm reboots. You must act within the window. Inject the kill switch, then sever the uplink."

Nova exhaled once, shuddered and typed. The code moved like a virus, infiltrating the swarm's command structure, biting out the block and inserting a line of death.

***

People had already gathered at the City Botanical Gardens for an early breakfast, where the aroma of spices wafted through the air from the many food stalls selling traditional Palestinian delights. The atmosphere was vibrant and alive with a sense of festival, as coloured flags fluttered like vibrant petals in the gentle breeze. People donned traditional dress, and stalls displayed an array of intricate handicrafts. Popular Arabian music blared out across the park, its lively notes mingling with the laughter and chatter of the crowd.

The first to notice was a small boy seated atop his grandfather's shoulders, an untidy mop of black hair barely tamed by his keffiyeh. He pointed into the sky, his sticky fingers smudging the lenses of his grandfather's glasses as he squinted upward. At first the dark patch overhead resembled smoke from a distant grass fire. The boy, unsure, tugged at his grandfather's ear. "Look Baba," he whispered awe softening his voice. "What is it?"

The old man, reaching for his morning flat bread paused to follow the line of the boy's finger as he pointed into the sky. His eyes narrowed. He recognized the pattern: machines, disciplined and precise, forming a black halo above the city. The recognition struck him dumb for a moment, so that he stared open-mouthed.

Instantly, the music faded, and he was no longer in the lush gardens with his grandson. He was in the rocky desert of his homeland. He was in the street, the markets within earshot with the traders shouting, the tight alleys twisting East and West, the ditches and rubble, the remnants of shattered buildings that had once pulsed with life. Instead of his grandson, he was carrying his eldest daughter, his firstborn, his beautiful Abir. The deafening whir of the drones filled his ears and entered his head until there was no room for anything else. Knocked off his feet by the blast. His beautiful Abir lay twisted and burnt on the ground. Rubble everywhere. But it wasn't the vision of her body that kept him awake at night, it was the smell, the acrid odour of burning flesh, flesh of his flesh, his Abir.

As the drones descended, he fell to his knees.

A hot dry wind swept across the lawns.

He folded his body over his grandson and held him tight. The boy didn't fuss or complain, he clung to his grandfather and kept his head down.

Time stretched, each heartbeat filled with the relentless approach of the buzzing swarm. For a fleeting moment, the crowd seemed unified in silence. Until the boy, still clinging tight to his grandfather, began to scream.

The child's cry cut through the silence. Almost immediately, dozens were screaming. Panic became a living thing rushing like electricity through the crowd.

The old man, still hunched over his grandson, scrambled toward the riverbank. Vendors abandoned their stalls, knocked over tables and scattered fresh pitas in their haste to run.

The plain clothed police took charge, funnelling the panicking crowd toward the prepared shelters, as many as they could. In the distance, men on rooftops aimed their pulse rifles into the swarm, but their efforts were fruitless. The programmers had been smarter than that.

The cloud descended, lower and wider than before, casting a tangible shadow that swept across the gardens. The air filled with the cacophony of shrill alarms, clattering stalls, and the hollow, almost mocking drone of the machines. The old man struggled, almost on all fours, toward the riverbank, with a small boy clinging to his hair and beard like a frightened animal to its mother.

The old man scrambled down the cement wall onto the muddy rocks at the edge of the river and established for himself and the boy a nest there, pressed up against the wall, with the river to their back. He released the boy's grip and relieved himself of his weight for a moment.

"Hold your face to the wall," he said.

And the boy did.

The old man, his eyes only barely above the wall peered back across the park. Most people tried to flee across the road toward the safety of the apartment blocks. But the roads quickly became clogged with cars that had been attempting to enter the gardens, and cars that were now trying to leave. Terrified civilians found themselves trapped in congestion at the entrance gates, unable to move forward or retreat. Many couldn't help but turn their eyes skyward watching with mounting horror as the swarm of drones swept ominously over the city, heading directly for them. The old man cringed at their mistake.

The old man breathed in the mouldy smell of the riverbed.

"Keep your face to the wall," he told the boy.

The boy kept his face pressed to the wall.

Above the cloud pulsated with intent, now close enough for the leading edge of the drones to be distinguished as individual units. For a moment they hovered in formation as if waiting for a cue. Then, they surged forward. The hum of the machines built into a roar, and it became the only sound in the world.

And then, as if someone had flicked a switch, there was silence. People dared not move, afraid to disturb the silence.

From the heart of the sky, the swarm descended. Tiny objects, as small as your smartphone dropped like rocks from the sky. At first a few, then a torrent of them.

A few braver souls straightened from their hiding and followed the descent with wide, unblinking eyes. The first of the drones landed with a clatter, a scattering of beetle-like shells and spindly legs dotted the lawns. Some fell onto the steel roofs of the food vans with a crashing thud, others hit the pavement or became caught in the trees. There were cries of "shit!" as some bounced from people's heads and they ducked and cursed. But there were no explosions, no violence, only the accumulation of the strange artifacts on the ground.

The old man stood up shaking and blinked away tears of relief.

"It's safe now," he said. "You can take your face from the wall."

The boy looked up, his face covered in the green-grey sludge of the riverbed.

He stared, eyes huge at a drone that had landed only a meter away.

"It's over!" someone in the distance cried, their voice a cry of relief cutting through the tension.

CHAPTER THIRTY-SIX

Gray was still on edge when he returned to the station. The office was buzzing with news of the thwarted swarm attack and the arrest of Spectre. Officers were in a state of confusion about the events and why they had been left in the dark while the federal police were on the scene and came off as the heroes. They'd been swamped with terrified calls from the public and they'd had no idea how to respond. Gray was met with a million questions as soon as they saw him. But Gray was in no mood for explanations.

"Where the bloody hell was the Special Operations team?" he called into the room. A young constable at the communications desk stared up at him.

"The order was cancelled, sir," he said. "By the Assistant Commissioner."

Gray's eyebrows furrowed. "Tarrant didn't receive the order?"

"No, sir."

Gray felt a sudden rush to his face.

Tarrant, the Chief of Special Operations strode in. "I'm sorry, Gray," he said. "We received the call out, then seconds later Bryant cancelled it. I thought it was odd so I tried contacting him, but I couldn't get through. I kept the team on 'stand by' waiting for the go ahead, but it didn't come. The next thing I heard, the federal police had made the arrest at the warehouse in Bowen Hills, and it was all going down at the gardens."

Gray shook his head. "It all happened so fast. Thank God I told the feds what was happening. The result might have been different. Where's Bryant now?"

"No one knows where to find him. He's not answering any calls, and he hasn't been to his house since he left for work yesterday."

Gray shuddered. "Keep an eye out for him. The federal Police will be looking for him in connection with this mess. What's happening with the Chief Super?"

Tarrant's face twisted in a grimace. "He had a heart attack on his way home from work. He stopped the car when he felt ill apparently, then a bystander found him slumped against the steering wheel and called 911. He's in the Princess Alexandra Hospital now. Going to recover, they say, but he's had a rough night. They carried out an emergency by-pass."

Gray looked up to see Rishi Chandra leading Spectre into an interview room. Glenda King had a firm grip on Lividia's arm and was taking her into a room further down the corridor.

"An informant told me Leonie Nolan was funding Spectre," said Gray. "I can't be certain, but it makes sense."

"Someone had to be supplying him with resources," said Tarrant. "I suspect Bryant was 'close' to Leonie Nolan as well."

Gray lifted one brow. "I've wondered that, myself."

Gray nodded toward the door. "I better see what he's got to say for himself." He called out to his junior officer as he closed the door to the interview room behind him. "Chandra."

Rishi Chandra walked over to join Gray and Tarrant.

"Where's Nova?" asked Tarrant. "Doesn't she want to be in on this?"

"Nova's working with Civil Aviation and the Cyber Security mob. There's a lot of data to wade through in the background to this mess. At 1:00 she'll be live on NewsNet.com attempting to calm public panic over the killer drone threat," said Gray.

Tarrant nodded.

"Get King," Gray told Chandra. "You can both sit in on this." Chandra rushed off, and in a heartbeat both Chandra and King were by Gray's side.

When they entered the first interview room, Spectre looked up with pale eyes as cold as ice. They sat, turned on the recorder and said their names.

"Your full name?" said Gray, looking directly into the eyes that bore into him.

"We need your birth name," Gray repeated. "The name on your birth certificate. Presumably your mother didn't call you Spectre?"

Gray sighed when Spectre didn't answer. "Ok, as it happens, the police officers who arrested you retrieved a driver's license from your jacket. The name on the license is Glen Stewart."

Gray held the license up for Spectre to see. He pointed to the image on the card. "Here, right under the picture of you, it says, Glen Stewart."

Spectre twitched slightly and averted his eyes.

"We know you are behind the two drone attacks and the attempted carnage today," began Gray. "You were caught red-handed. We know you recruit vulnerable young people and manipulate them to help you. What we want to know, is who is backing you in this endeavour."

Arrogant defiance looked back at the detective inspector.

"You're going to jail for life, for this, Glen. Whether you share any information with us or not. Do you really want to go down alone?"

The icy eyes narrowed. "I want a deal," he said.

Gray and his junior officers exchanged glances, a slight tug at the corner of his lips indicated this was the response Gray wanted.

"Names and details," said Gray. "Your co-operation will be taken into account during sentencing."

That was all it took for Glen Stewart, the great man of ideology, to turn on his backers like a rat. Once he started talking, they couldn't stop him. Not that they wanted to.

"Who bank rolled your operation?" said Gray.

"Leonie Nolan," Glen said immediately. "I met her through my parents, went to a few rallies to hear her speak, then I started sleeping with her."

Out of the corner of his eye Gray saw Chandra and King smirk.

"Leonie Nolan is more than twice your age," said Gray, his tone a little too high.

Glen shrugged.

"Who came up with the idea to use killer drones to murder Muslims?"

Glen pursed his lips. "We sort of came to it together," he said. "But you misunderstand. The idea wasn't just to kill Muslims. We couldn't kill them all. The idea was much bigger than that. We were trying to create civil unrest; bring pressure to bear on the government to stop bringing refugees in."

"And you had no problem with the murder of innocent people?" Gray struggled to get his head around the cold arrogance.

"You persist in misunderstanding," said Glen. "This was never about murder. It was about revolution. To create real change, some people must be prepared to get their hands dirty." He leant forward across the table toward Gray. "Western civilization needs saving, and I will be the one to save it," he said quietly. Then he sat with his back straight and his chin high.

"Probably not from a jail cell," Gray muttered.

"Maybe not," said Glen. "But maybe, that's exactly the right place to be." He glared hard at the detective inspector.

Gray took a deep breath and continued. "So, you recruited tech savvy young people on-line to help you?"

"It was easier than you imagine."

"Apart from the programmers arrested at the warehouse at Bowen Hills, who else was directly involved?"

Glen didn't hesitate. "Leonie groomed someone high up in the police," he said. "Some old codger who sympathized with our cause. Still, he wouldn't have gotten involved with anything as practical as killer drones, on his own. She was sleeping with him, you see. He became besotted. Couldn't let it stop. He would have done anything to keep it going. There's that... and I told him I'd inform his wife."

Chandra and King shared a distinctive look that screamed, "Eew!"

"I only met him once. The night I blackmailed him. He was getting skittish. His name is Brian, or something like that.

"Bryant," offered Gray.

"That's it," said Spectre. "It was easy."

Gray fought down the bile rising in his throat. "Was Seeton Harlin working with you?" he asked.

Glen pulled himself back in the chair. "Seeton? No! He was the only bug in the system. In fact, without Seeton, you would never have stopped our mission."

Gray was getting a headache. He'd been awake all night in a state of acute tension, he was dehydrated, and he was over this low life with his delusions of grandeur. He considered sending Chandra or King to get water, but Glen Stewart was on a roll, and he didn't want to break it.

"How so?" he asked, knowing the only way to get the details of all those involved was to humour this madman's Ego.

"Seeton Harlin was one of those academic types who think they know everything," said Glen. "He managed to infiltrate the organisation. He was good, I'll give him that. He kept up the rhetoric everywhere he went. He didn't miss a beat, ask anyone and they'll say he was part of the anti-refugee movement. I only became suspicious when he started recruiting other students, inviting them to protest, trying to bring them onboard. It was overkill. Everyone in the organisation knew that only I did recruitment. It was the only way to keep the organisation contained. Anyway, I had him followed, and the evening before the rally, he met with this other kid, Carter, another jumped-up little prick that thought he could bring me down."

Glen stopped for a moment. The mention of Seeton Harlin was the first time he'd shown any emotion at all throughout the interview. He seemed to calm himself.

"I only went to the rally to watch him," he went on. "But an opportunity presented itself and I took it. I thought the bloody Palestinian would be charged and I'd be rid of the problem."

Gray sat up straight. "You're telling us you killed Seeton Harlin?" he said.

"Of course. I couldn't believe my luck when his head hit the cement. Proof that the Gods are on our side," Glen said smiling.

CHAPTER
THIRTY-SEVEN

Lividia sat with her hands in her lap as she looked around the blank walls of the interview room. Her parents were on their way back from Hong Kong. She dreaded seeing them, not because she was ashamed, she wasn't. If anything, she was numb. She'd decided that Spectre's betrayal meant nothing to her. Her real mission had been to finish Seeton's work. She felt close to him, convinced he would be proud of her work in developing the drones and in standing up for her beliefs.

When the detective and his young female offsider entered the room, she avoided eye contact. There was already a social worker sitting beside her. A lot of help she'd be. She would not be lectured by these idiots who knew nothing of her passion and commitment.

The detective turned on the recording device and introduced those present in the room, then he looked at her. She felt his gaze even as she refused to meet it.

"You waved your right to have legal counsel present," began the detective. "Is that still your position?"

Lividia didn't respond.

"Your parents may wish to engage legal counsel on your behalf. Are you prepared to answer some preliminary questions before they arrive?"

Lividia shrugged.

"For the recording," said Gray.

"Yes. Whatever."

"We're going to need you to describe your relationship with the man calling himself Spectre," said Gray. "Start at the beginning."

Lividia tossed her hair back off her shoulders. Every muscle in her face was set as though in stone.

"You know already," she said. "You've read the messages."

"We need you to describe the timeline for us," said Gray.

Lividia continued staring into her lap.

"For example, did you know of Spectre before you started communicating on-line?" asked Nova.

Lividia shook her head, almost imperceptibly.

"When did you learn about Spectre's involvement with the killer drones?" asked Gray.

Lividia looked past him toward the door. She would not yield to this crap. They knew what they knew. She was involved in creating and releasing the swarm that was meant to attack the cultural event. Why all the questions?

Nova leant forward over the table. "You're going to have to talk about this," she said.

"The sooner you get it over, the better. Otherwise, we, or people like us, will keep asking these same questions for hours and hours on end."

Lividia rolled her eyes.

"Let me tell your story then," said Gray. "You can stop me if I get it wrong."

He paused.

She knew he was waiting for her to respond. She didn't. She wouldn't give him the satisfaction.

"Ok," began Gray. "You were sad and lonely after Seeton's death, and angry that no one was being arrested for the crime. So, you got onto his computer to feel close to him."

Lividia stared blankly past him.

"You came upon Spectre's posts on BLAZE and began chatting to him privately on-line. He said the things that Seeton had been saying, and he understood your desperate need for justice. He sympathized."

There was no sign that Lividia was listening.

Gray went on. "Spectre found out about your skills in robotics and encryption and invited you to join his group to develop the drones that would kill Palestinian refugees and perhaps stir up sufficient fear and hate to change the government's policy on refugee intake."

Lividia sighed and looked up at the ceiling. If this idiot thought he knew what was going on in her mind, why did she even have to sit here?

"Explain this one thing for me," said Gray. "How did you feel when you saw the first two drones kill those men?"

Lividia's eyes turned to Gray for the first time.

"When I saw the first man die, I felt relieved," she said steadily. "When the second one died, I felt pride. That's when I knew I was involved in something worthwhile. I was proud to be extending Seeton's work. I felt like my brother, and I were working together."

She cast a smug self-satisfied grin. It felt crooked and uncomfortable, even to her.

Gray tapped his pen on the table for a moment.

"You see," he said, Seeton was working to bring Spectre down. He collected intelligence on a range of nefarious characters and organisations. He was playing a part. He took it too far, I'll grant you that. Everyone believed he was committed to the anti-refugee movement. But he wasn't."

The blood drained from Lividia's face.

"I don't believe you," she hissed. "No one knew Seeton better than me."

Gray took a deep breath. "In fact, it was Spectre who murdered Seeton when he found out what he was up to. He's confessed to it."

Lividia felt her head spin. A black shadow tugged at the edges of her vision, closing inward until she could see only a pin prick of light. That closed over as well, and she fell from the chair.

CHAPTER THIRTY-EIGHT

Glenda King was always the most punctual among them, so it was no surprise to Gray that her impatience crackled through the air of the corridor, electrifying the mood with a tension that was part nervous energy, part exasperation. "Hurry up. We're going to be late," she snapped, and it sounded to Gray like it was less a suggestion than a summons. King's hands seized the limp sleeves of Chandra's suit coat with practiced efficiency.

"You can hack into anti-refugee posts, but you can't dress yourself?" she added, pulling the sleeves down over his long brown arms with a forceful tenderness. Her tone was merciless, but the gesture itself, the deliberate, almost motherly smoothing of his lapel, spoke of fierce loyalty. "I can't believe you sometimes," King muttered, but beneath the irritation simmered a protective pride.

Chandra responded with a sheepish look, the colour rising on his cheeks as he cast a plaintive glance in Gray and Nova's direction, as if seeking rescue. "I don't wear suits," he said, his voice retreating into his collar.

"We know," said Glenda, not missing a beat. "You wear cardigans," she said, stepping back to evaluate her handiwork. She gave the tie a final, emphatic tug, ensuring that the Windsor knot sat flush against his throat. Next, she reached out and straightened the badge on his lapel.

Gray watched all of this with a small smile. The clumsy camaraderie among colleagues made him feel proud of his profession. It always came down to little rituals: making of coffee, swapping of jokes, mutual grooming before public displays. It was the small acts of care that held a group together when the world threatened to tear them apart.

He looked down at his own suit, which was immaculate. When it mattered, he could be meticulous. He looked across at Nova who looked smart and professional in a black pencil skirt and patterned silk blouse. She looked tired with fine lines clinging to the corners of her eyes.

King, gave Gray a brisk nod, acknowledging the chain of command, before grabbing her jacket from the coat stand and slinging it over one arm.

As they gathered at the apartment door, each fell momentarily silent. Gray glanced at Nova, who smoothed her skirt with a nervous hand, and for a heartbeat neither spoke.

Chandra looked from one to the other, inhaled sharply, tucked his chin, and squared his shoulders.

They exited in a single file, as though the narrow corridor demanded a ritual procession. They stepped into the elevator, King in the lead, Chandra behind her, Nova and Gray bringing up the rear.

Down on the street, the warm late-summer air made them perspire in their suits. The city was quiet for a weekday.

As they drew nearer to the chapel, they joined others whose formal dress was too much for the sultry day. Uniformed officers clustered in small groups. Gray spotted Richardson and nodded, his face again radiating gratitude that his team had arrived in time to save Lividia, and less importantly, himself. Each of Richardson's men nodded at Gray's approach, the silent acknowledgment of shared pain and responsibility. Even among the civilians, there was a sense of solemn unity, an understanding that something irrevocable had happened, and that it demanded witnesses.

Gray and Nova spotted Thompson and Shaw among the crowd gathering in front of the chapel. Thompson wore an expensive suit and pointed shoes polished to a mirror-like shine. Less eye-catching, Shaw was dressed in nicely ironed trousers and a smart shirt in dark green. He walked a pace behind Thompson and kept his head down as though trying to make himself invisible. They both shook hands with the tight group of Gray, Nova, King and Chandra and offered greetings appropriate to the sombre occasion. Each gesture was laden with silent acknowledgment of their collective struggle.

At the entrance to the chapel, Gray could see the backs of Mr and Mrs Harlin. Stiff and formal even in grief, Mr. Harlin stood straight, but Mrs. Harlin's body language indicated someone who had lost her resolve. Her frail frame bent under the weight of sorrow. Her head was bowed, and she was clutching a handkerchief, shoulders tremulous with silent sobs.

And then they saw her. Lividia Harlin. She was hand-cuffed, with two uniformed officers a step behind her, a shocking addition to the mourners. Gray had a partial view of her profile. Her skin was grey rather than white, her lips thin. She looked simultaneously defiant and in shock.

Inside the chapel, the smell of flowers was overwhelming. Benches were already full, and several rows of extra foldaway chairs had been added.

Gray took a seat in the front to the left, where a whole row of seats had been reserved. He was flanked by Nova and the other senior officers. There was an unspoken script for these things, and he followed it to the letter: Eyes forward, hands folded, jaw set in grim determination. But as the first hymn began and the auditorium filled with the low hum of voices, he allowed himself one glance over his shoulder where King and Chandra sat side by side, King's expression a mask of stoic defiance, Chandra's an open book of curiosity.

Gray felt a sense of pride in these people who had placed their trust in him and followed him through the turmoil. Together, they would see this last task through.

He took a deep breath and savoured the sense of relief that always followed a dangerous investigation. The tension had fallen from his body, and a deep exhaustion had replaced it. But it was good fatigue, the kind that came from a job well done.

They let silence fall between them, profound and almost reverent, as the Minister appeared at the altar.

Seeton wasn't at his memorial service. He'd already been cremated elsewhere. The Minister took a deep breath and began to speak, his voice resonating with sombre clarity. He talked about the value of human life, emphasizing how fragile and fleeting it could be. The importance of faith, he continued, could not be overstated.

The Minister's voice grew more impassioned as he spoke about how we, as humans, have more in common than the sum of our differences. He called on everyone to look beyond themselves and see the broader connections that bound them together. There was a subdued power in his words, a call to unity that felt almost radical in its simplicity. The crowd shifted in their seats, the weight of the message settling on them.

Gray turned around, his gaze sweeping across the people packed tightly into the chapel. Some bowed their heads, others stared straight ahead, their expressions a mix of reflection and unease. The Imam stood tall and dignified at the back, a figure of calm amidst the murmuring sea of attendees. Gray caught his eye and nodded slightly, an unspoken acknowledgment of their shared concerns and unvoiced fears. The Imam nodded back.

When the service was complete, Gray and his team filed out of the chapel with the rest of the congregation. The Imam was already gone.

He sensed a familiar figure step up beside him.

"Yousef," he said and held out a hand to greet him. "How are you feeling now that you have been fully exonerated?"

Yusef grinned from ear to ear.

"We couldn't have stopped the swarm attack without you," said Gray.

Yusef shook his head vigorously. "Dr Corbin and your team would have done the same thing without me," he said.

Nova turned her head at the sound of her name and smiled at Yusef.

"I'm sorry about your Superintendent," said Yusef, his face growing more serious. "It must have been a shock to the whole department."

Gray rubbed his hand over his chin. "I don't know whether it was stress or bad luck, but it certainly caught us off-guard. We were desperately trying to contact him while he was being rushed off to hospital in an ambulance, having a heart attack. Definitely bad timing, but it looks like he'll be back at work sooner than we thought. He's supposed to make a full recovery after surgery."

"Thanks to Allah," said Yusef, relief softening his features. "If anything happened to Chief Superintendent Charfield you'd be left with that beaky fellow in charge. What's his name?"

"Bryant?" said Gray with a sly smile. He suppressed a chuckle thinking of how Bryant would squawk if he knew they were having this conversation. "Actually, Spectre has been singing like a bird since his arrest. He's naming names left and right."

Yusef leaned in further out of interest.

"He's thrown in a Member of Parliament," Gray said, the implication hanging in the air between them. "Leonie Nolan. He claims she's been bankrolling him. Also, he's suggesting that Bryant is inappropriately involved with her, if you know what I mean."

Yusef looked stunned, his eyes widened as he absorbed the information.

"Nothing solid yet, but Bryant is under investigation. Nova and I believe he was responsible for sending the tail that blew out the side of my car."

"What about your car?" Yusef's question changed the subject.

Gray paused, a brief flicker of amusement passing across his face. "Maybe I can have it repaired," he replied. "The force can pay." His grin widened as he savoured this potential triumph.

Gray shook hands with Thompson and Shaw and Nova hugged them warmly before they left for the car park. Yusef also gave Nova a hug, then surprised Gray by hugging him as well. As he was walking away, Gray called out, "Do you need a lift?"

Yusef raised his hand to wave but kept walking.

Gray and Nova found themselves alone on the grass in front of the chapel.

"It's been good working with you, Detective Inspector," said Nova.

"And you," said Gray.

Nova tilted her head to one side. "What will you do now?"

He tugged at his chin. "Right now, I'm going to pick up Alix. We're going to see a movie."

"Not a James Bond classic, I hope?" said Nova cheekily.

Gray laughed.

"Do you think we'll work together again, Detective Inspector Mitchell Gray?"

Gray smiled. "I hope so," he said.

CHAPTER THIRTY-NINE

BREAKING NEWS: In the aftermath of Saturday's unprecedented drone attack on the cultural event at Brisbane's Botanical Gardens, disturbing new revelations continue to shock the city and the nation. The investigation into the incident, which left scores of attendees injured or traumatized, has uncovered damning evidence that prominent Brisbane MP, Leonie Nolan, was the principal financier behind the operation. Even more sensational is the newly public knowledge that Nolan was engaged in an extramarital affair with none other than Assistant Commissioner of Police, Jim Bryant, a high-ranking officer now accused of shielding the terrorist plot from detection within law enforcement.

The breadth and depth of the betrayal now unfolding has left local politicians reeling and public confidence in law enforcement at an all-time low.

While both Nolan and Bryant had long maintained spotless public records, Nolan for her tireless advocacy of border security reform and Bryant for his three decades of decorated police service, private messages recovered from a secure messaging app paint a far darker picture. The exchanges reveal not only plans to create panic at the event by targeting refugees but also detailed strategies for misdirecting internal investigations. According to police sources, "the level of collusion between elected officials and law enforcement was sophisticated and deliberate."

Yet perhaps most jarring was this morning's discovery at 4:37 am, runners along the Kangaroo Point riverbank found Jim Bryant's body at the base of the cliffs. Reports confirm suicide. The fallen officer leaves behind a wife and three young children.

Leonie Nolan remains at large as of this writing, her office declining all requests for comment.